SuperVisions

Michael Kovitz

and

Dr. Dorothy Mead

ISBN 978-0-2857148-0-9

eladi publications
eladi-publications.com

Contents

Dust to Dust

The taxi had not even left the airport before she leaned forward and told the driver she wanted to make a stop along the way.

"Of course I'll pay you to wait," she said. "I won't be long."

***

Jake was sitting quietly on the old stone bench near the grave of his boyhood friend when he noticed the taxi driving slowly up the road. No sooner had it stopped than the passenger stepped out, leaving the door open behind her. Jake could not help but watch as she walked briskly up the path in the direction of a well-manicured grave marked with a modest headstone. He would have turned back to his own solemn vigil were it not for the fact that when the woman took her first step onto the soft grass, the high heel of her red shoe plunged deep into the ground, breaking her stride and nearly tripping her. His attention now fully engaged, he watched with fascination as she righted herself, seemingly unfazed, and in one swift move stripped off her shoes and carried them with her to the grave…

***

Later that day, sitting in the chair that looked out over her garden, she took a sip of wine and examined the muddied shoe in her hand. A wry smile flitted across her face, and then she reached for the phone.

"Hello Anne," came the friendly voice of her mentor. "How was the conference?"

"I would say my presentation went very well, and what I saw of London was quite wonderful."

"Well congratulations then, it sounds like it was a success."

"I imagine so Margot, but…" she hesitated.

"Yes?"

"Well, it's almost embarrassing to say, on the last night of the conference, I slept with the director."

"Oh dear, yes I see. Old patterns certainly die hard."

"Indeed."

The Kitchen Table

The journal lay open on the old kitchen table between them. Her fury unbridled now, jaw fixed in defiance, her large hazel eyes shooting angry daggers at her mother, fingers clawing through the tangles of her long brown hair—she should have known, she should have known better. What had made her think the progress she had been making in therapy—the tiny insights and the techniques she had only recently learned—could stand up against the age-old fortress of her mother's denials, rebukes, and defenses?

Only a short time before she stood poised at the entrance of the old house, the home of her birth, waiting for her mother to unlock the heavy wooden door. She was Anita Burrows; she was an adult; she was confident and strong—she was no longer a victim like her poor brother. She was ready now, and she was eager to confront her mother and the demons that had haunted her since childhood. But within five minutes of feeling her mother's icy greeting at the door and smelling the familiar scents of the old house—heavy food and furniture polish—she forgot everything—her tools, her intent, her newfound self.

"Have you ever seen this before?" she accused her mother, pushing the little brown book closer to her.

"Never," Grace shot back. "How do you even know it's Ronny's?"

"Just read it. Just pick it up and read it," she demanded and watched her mother's eyes narrow as she scanned a page, then grow wide as she read further. She saw her mother's posture stiffen, her mouth open as if she was about to say something, then clamp shut as she all but dropped the journal back onto the table between them like she was ridding herself of something unclean.

Anita looked down at the journal; she felt her heart beating in her temples; she knew she was losing it. "I cannot believe you insisted that Ronny continue to be tutored by that sick degenerate," she heard herself shriek, and she beat her fists on the table, overturning her coffee cup—the spreading dark stain creeping along the table toward the precious journal. Anita grabbed it up and clasped it tightly against her chest as her mother feverishly tried to blot up the liquid with paper napkins from the yellow plastic holder on the table.

"Now look what you've done—for the love of Christ control yourself!" Grace yelled while reaching for another napkin. "Will you never learn to leave well enough alone?"

"Well enough alone? What the hell is that supposed to mean? Didn't you read this?" Anita shot back, waving the journal at her mother, who sat staunchly defiant, her face set in an expression of stalwart self-righteousness, her teeth clenched tight in denial behind pale loveless lips.

"I really had no idea it was happening," she said while averting her eyes from her daughter's fiery stare, "and frankly, I still don't know whether it was. He was only a boy; perhaps he was making it up."

"Making it up! You still can't admit it, can you? You read it! Here, read it again." Anita slammed the journal down on the table in front of her mother and, pointing to the words, read aloud, *'He is my mentor; he is my confessor... he is evil.'* How could you think he was making it all up?"

"He was only a boy," her mother repeated and stared back at Anita. In the intensity of that moment, Anita was able to see, clearly see perhaps for the first time, the truth behind the expression on her mother's face: the eyes that saw only what the mind wanted her to see and the mouth locked by lips that would admit to nothing save the mind's attempts to turn fault into accusation. It revealed all that was wrong and perverted about the Catholic Church—how the fertile ground of its hypocrisy could nurture and protect child molesters and abusers within its ranks.

Anita's anger and sense of betrayal were beyond all bounds; she was on her feet and pacing now—inflated with rage she felt ten feet tall—a ten-foot-tall twenty-two-year-old adult regressed to an eight-year-old child. Totally out of control, her hips crashed against the old wooden table, shoving it to within inches of where her mother sat bracing herself against her rampage.

"That is quite enough!" Grace shouted at her daughter, her voice loud and shrill with a mixture of fear and anger. But Anita did not hear a word of it; blinded by her own frenzy, she had been transformed into a giant wild creature writhing in hatred against everything in her sight. The perfectly stacked dishes behind the cabinet's glass doors, another symbol of her mother's control and repression, further stoked the raging fire within her, and when her wild stare rested momentarily on the carved cross that hung in shadows on the wall above the sink, she saw a malevolent darkness radiating from it—like death—mocking her anger and shrieking its damnation.

"Shit!" she screamed when she saw the dishtowels neatly folded on the countertop, remembering how her mother always folded the dirty side under so no one could see. "How long are you going to keep folding those damn towels so no one can see the dirt?" she yelled.

"Don't swear, and sit down!" her mother yelled back, attempting to regain some control over the situation while she continued to grip the old wooden table, but her admonishment went unheard against the roaring tempest her daughter had become. "Look at yourself," she continued to fight back. "Is this what you've been learning from that Godless psychology you practice? You would be better off going to church every day to beg forgiveness for your own sins."

Anita thought she was going crazy—serpents writhed inside her belly; she was a caged tiger. She imagined herself smashing plates, coffee cups, the furniture itself, and pulling that damn cross down off the wall. "Damn the Church and damn the hypocrisy!" she cried out loud.

"Anita! Calm yourself and listen to me. I do know the truth! Your brother got in with the wrong sort. He was experimenting with drugs. We know that now. There isn't a day goes by I don't pray for his soul…"

"Pray for *his* soul? Why in hell would you have to pray for *his* soul? As if he were to blame! And for God's sake don't talk to me about his soul. Do you think you can see his soul? Nobody can see his soul. Why don't you pray he just becomes invisible? Then nobody will see; nobody will remember. Just like your damn dishtowels!"

Grace looked over at the towels. She really had no idea what her daughter was talking about.

"He was just an innocent boy!" Anita continued to shriek while glaring at her mother with a fury that offered no escape. But her mother's defenses were set in denial—she would not give in.

"It appears I need to be praying for your soul too," she shot back. "Your brother was mixed up. No doubt the drugs made him believe things that weren't true. His suicide is a mortal sin, and I must pray to the good Lord to release him from the retribution…"

Anita never heard the end of her mother's sentence. She covered her ears and started screaming as loudly as she could, "Don't, don't, don't—don't tell me *he* is the one who sinned—who pushed him to it? Who? Oh, of course not the good Monsignor Aleksy, defender of the faith and servant of God, envoy of Jesus Christ Himself! Not that lecherous asshole!"

"Anita! That is more than enough!" proclaimed her mother as she rose imperiously from the table. "I will not tolerate such blasphemy. Take this infernal journal," she commanded while throwing it at her daughter, "take it and burn it and NEVER speak of this to me again."

Anita imagined herself grabbing the knife off the counter and plunging it into her mother's chest. Instead, she scooped up her brother's journal and bolted from the kitchen. She wanted to run and never stop.

As she turned the corner at the bottom of the stairs, she nearly toppled her father, who had just come through the front door. He looked down on her pale, tearstained face in alarm.

"Nita? What?" he said, though he knew without her saying anything that she and her mother had been fighting again.

Anita threw her arms around him and started sobbing. He gently embraced her.

"You had another argument, didn't you?" Her body wracked with sobs, but she managed to nod.

"It was about Ronny, Daddy. She's blaming the whole thing on him! I hate her! I hate Father Aleksy and his whole damn Church. Oh Daddy…"

Her father did what he had done so many times before— cradled her head in his hands and sweetly caressed the hair away from her face.

"Oh Daddy," she repeated and looked up into his eyes—those incredible eyes with their deep pain so beautifully arched with love. So incredible, they had always been like balm for her, soothing the pain of all her hurts and disappointments. And even now, in the throes of her deepest agony, she could feel the anger beginning to wash away, the heaving sobs subsiding. She felt dizzy, but quieter. He could always do this for her, but this time as she looked at his face she saw—she felt—something more, something different that deeply disturbed her, something in his eyes she had never seen before.

"What is it, Daddy? Tell me," she quietly implored. But he remained silent, stroking her face, tears beginning to well in his eyes. Anita felt herself going cold as the chill of fear possessed her.

"Daddy? Please…"

His heart was pounding. How could he tell his beloved daughter what he had just learned? Somehow, he would find a way to prepare her; but now was not the moment to add more pain to her already overflowing cup.

"Only that it hurts to see you so upset… and of course, it reminds me of Ronny," he replied, averting his eyes.

She searched his face for a clue, but whatever she had seen, or thought she had seen, was gone.

"Daddy, why won't she admit it—that Ronny was abused by Father Aleksy? She has to know he was and is just trying to hide it from everyone—like her damn dishtowels!"

Her father looked at her with a blank stare; then his eyes lit up—he hated those hypocrite towels too—and he started to shake with laughter. So did Anita, releasing what her tears could not.

Chill Winds

Paul Burrows was a quiet man, the kind of man people say keeps his own counsel. He met Grace Wolowski when he opened his account at the Savings and Loan after being rescued from a Viet Cong prison camp in late 1971. He was immediately attracted to the austere beauty of the thin young teller with the high cheekbones and auburn hair. But observing the fierceness of her gaze and the clench of her teeth from behind the bars of her teller's cage made him think about the tiger cages in Viet Nam and made him wonder whose safety it really was that needed protecting. Then she spoke and there was something about her voice that gave him the oddest sensation that they had met before. A premonition, like a shiver, ran up his spine—he knew this was no chance encounter.

"Look, I know you don't know me from the man in the moon," he said with uncommon directness. "Actually, right now, I feel like a man *on* the moon! Forty-eight hours ago I was flying in a helicopter over the Vietnamese jungle, newly liberated from a tiger cage in a Viet Cong prison..."

Grace Wolowski had not expected this, and Grace Wolowski was the kind of person who preferred to be prepared rather than surprised. The handsome young man with the terrible haircut saw her eyes widen and her jaw drop as the façade of bravado on the face of the brand-new junior teller began to crumble. Nervously she looked around to see if a superior was watching. "I spent twenty months in Viet Nam," he was saying, "because I was born on the wrong day of the wrong month of the wrong year." A warm smile spread slowly across his face. "Now I'm standing in front of a woman who lives in a cage, and I'm wondering whether I'm still in the jungle and dreaming, or if maybe being born on the wrong day has finally paid off."

Despite herself, Grace could not resist the impulse to smile back. There was something just so charming about him—forward and vulnerable at the same time. "You're not from around here, are you?" She had noticed his accent as soon as he spoke.

"Yeah, I told you I was from the moon," he said smiling, and his eyes looked so luminous when he spoke to her it made her think that perhaps he really was from outer space. And so she agreed to have coffee with him on her lunch break, and to give him some pointers about surviving in the city because Paul Burrows was a country boy—a country boy with less than half a college education and no work, just plenty of determination and a dream to get into the newly emerging field called computer electronics.

If nothing else, it was this sheer determination that won the day for Paul when only three weeks later he broached the question of marriage. During their lengthy courtship, he finished his degree and found himself a decent job. But one serious problem remained to be solved: he wasn't Polish and he wasn't Catholic, and in the eyes of Grace's mother, he might just as well have had horns and cloven hooves. Exercising the skill of adaptability he had honed in Viet Nam, he reasoned that although he couldn't change his ancestry, he could at least go through the motions of changing his faith—not that he really had a faith. In his cage he had never repeated the Baptist prayers he learned as a boy.

Paul saw his conversion to Catholicism as a means to an end and was even happy to learn all he could about his fiancée's religion. Being a practical man, he knew things would go far better for him with the Wolowskis if he simply "joined the team", a phrase he privately used to describe his conversion, and the fact that he knew the demands of religious practice for the men of the family were few, made him not only happy but confident he could make the plan work. *"A good plan is a plan that works,"* thought the survivalist. All he had to do was complete his catechism classes and put up with confession until the day he was confirmed, and he and Grace could be married in the Church. Out of respect for her beliefs and practice, and with a clear understanding that religion constituted a minefield as dangerous as any he had encountered in the war, Paul carefully avoided any discussions of religion and would not let himself be drawn into questions of theology. When the twins came along, he was happy to accede to his young wife's desire to raise them in the faith. Ronny seemed to inherit some of the best traits of his mother's religious nature, but when over time he saw that Anita seemed to embody more of his agnostic bent, he was secretly not at all disappointed.

Like many other Viet Nam vets, Paul did not want to talk about the war—"time to look forward, not back," he would say; "time for me to get on with my life." And get on with it he did, unpretentiously making a solid future for himself and his young family in the boom of the computer age in the eighties. But the world came unhinged that hideous day in February 1995, when he returned from work and found the fifteen-year-old Ronny hanging from a rafter in the garage behind the house, the cincture from his altar boy's alb around his neck.

Paul had seen many horrific things in Viet Nam—mutilations, torture, innocence violated. Somehow, he had managed to keep an inner detachment from the depravity and never lost hope in the possibility of the future; but seeing the dangling broken form of his son—this was just too much. An unspeakable, unthinkable, anguish engulfed him and a mournful cry issued from deep within his soul—a guttural animal noise, a crescendo of woe—drowning out all other sound. Time stopped, and in deathly slow motion, Paul righted the stool, climbed up with pocketknife in hand, cut the cincture and stumbled to the ground with the lifeless body in his arms. It took just seconds. Paul had known at first glance that Ronny was gone; still, he could not stop himself from beating on his son's chest and blowing into his lungs—over and over—until the counting and repetition induced a trance-like state of near exhaustion. Only when the paramedics arrived and gently pulled him away was the spell broken.

And that was the moment Paul Burrows became weary of life and all its broken promises, and though he worked hard to keep up an appearance of strength for his darling Grace and his beloved daughter, the luminosity disappeared from his eyes and darkness took hold of his soul, extinguishing the light of all his hopes and all his dreams. His family needed his strength, his love, to be able to believe in a future worth living, and so he would have to find the strength somewhere, somehow, the strength he had seen in the war, the strength that comes to the well-trained soldier when he realizes his life is over. He met the challenge as best he could for seven long years.

But in fact, Paul Burrows did not have too long to wait before he met his liberator. At first he tried to pass off the symptoms as signs of getting older, though deep inside he knew it was more than that, but the day he stood over the toilet bowl and watched with horror as it filled red with his blood, he knew his time had come. The next day he went to see the doctor, who examined him and immediately referred him to a urologist. In typical fashion, Paul said nothing of any of this to Grace or Anita while he waited a week for the test results. When he finally heard the report, he was stunned but not surprised.

Paul had taken a taxi to the doctor's office but walked the four miles back to his home. All the way his thoughts were turning, but they were not for him. His mind was focused on practicalities: they owned two properties outright—that was good; a few smart investments were yielding healthy dividends—those assets could easily be sold if needed; there was a small life insurance policy, and there would be a widow's pension—financially, at least, he would leave them in good shape. He comforted himself knowing there wouldn't be any large medical bills for treatments he had no intention of undergoing. In all honesty, he felt relief to know it would all be over soon enough. But the thought of the unresolved torment caused by Ronny's suicide—especially Anita's anger and alienation from her mother—contorted his mind in agony. He longed to be able to set it right before his passing, but how?

Soaking

"A warm bath might help... and another scotch." Already upstairs in her mind, Anita imagined the comfort and relief that awaited her. "I'll put lavender in the water, light some candles and just soak." She looked down. "What do you think, Mitsy? Think that'll do it?" Anita addressed her miniature Labradoodle as she poured herself a glass of scotch. The little white dog, all eyes on her mistress, sat attentively at her feet, seeming to consider the question. "Good thing I have you, Mitsy... where would I be without you? Let's go, sweetie," she said and set off to the bathroom with Mitsy trotting at her heels.

Waiting for the old claw-foot tub to fill, Anita busied herself measuring out the lavender in precise drops and lighting the candles and incense she had bought from the new boutique in the neighborhood, then she slipped off her robe and stood before the mirror. "Not bad, not bad at all," she said, looking at her flat abs and toned thighs. She turned to the side. "Nice ass too," she said while nodding in approval. "This jogging thing is really beginning to pay off, but just look at this hair," she said while fingering a few limp strands. "I really need to do something with this."

When she slid gently into the warm water, Mitsy settled herself comfortably on the bath mat beside the tub. In no time at all, the warmth, the candlelight, the aromatic vapors, and not least of all the scotch, began to work their magic. But in spite of her best efforts to relax and forget the ugly scene with her mother, her thoughts kept returning to the kitchen table and the argument earlier in the day.

What good is all this therapy anyway? Anita thought. *One damning glance from my mother, and I go from being a competent adult to being a frenzied child! I should be doing better than that by now, shouldn't I? How many more hundreds of dollars do I need to spend and how many more weekly sessions do I have to attend? Is it all just a crock?*

"Well I guess I have to deal with this," she said out loud to Mitsy. "There's no denying it; I really blew it." Mitsy twitched an ear, exhaled and went back to her dozing.

Anita watched the wheel of her thoughts continue to turn, shifting the blame back and forth from her mother, to her past therapists, and ultimately, to herself. She was the bad twin, the one who always questioned why things were and weren't what they were, especially when it came to religion. Ronny, on the other hand, was the good twin, the one who always seemed to know the reasons why, especially when it came to religion. Anita felt herself cringe at the painful stab of guilt that somehow made its way past the buffer afforded by the scotch and the two valiums she had taken before getting into the tub.

How many times had her brother told her, with an apparent certainty she could never fathom, "It is what God asks of us, Nita. We need to love one another—why can't you feel it?" he would say while refusing to be drawn into any childhood feuds or feelings of "righteous" anger.

It made her want to scream because all she could ever say was, "I don't know why; I just can't!"

Sometimes she cried in frustration, praying that someone, or something, would come to help her, but nothing did. Still, she adored her brother and tried to be patient, telling herself that if she could just watch him even more closely, then maybe she would catch a glimpse of the secret source of the conviction he lived but would not, or maybe could not, articulate. Then she might understand.

Anita sighed as her mind drifted back to that Sunday evening nine years ago, their thirteenth birthday, when Ronny announced at dinner, "I'm going to become an altar boy. The monsignor himself asked me to."

"The monsignor himself!" Her mother looked like she was going to explode with pride.

"Anything for the monsignor," said her father without taking his eyes off the plate of beef stew in front of him.

"Paul! Please, this is not the time for sarcasm," Grace said impatiently.

Anita looked across the table at her father because, in spite of the sarcastic tone of his voice, she could tell he was actually pleased by the news. She, on the other hand, was mystified and more than a little confused. She knew Ronny was very conscientious and quite sincere about the rituals of the church, but he had never aspired to be an altar boy, never wanted to be standing in front of an entire congregation doing anything, let alone washing the hands of the priests, whom he held in awe. They had even joked about it. "What if I tripped?" he'd say. "What if you farted?" she'd say, and the matter would end in giggles.

"The monsignor wants to meet with me every day after school starting tomorrow," Ronny continued. "He says I need a crash course, since I am starting so old, but he says I'll be very good and could start serving at the altar in no time." Ronny was beaming with joy over the attention the most important cleric he had ever met was offering to bestow on him. He glowed.

At the recollection, Anita felt a wrench of nausea pass through her as tears welled up in her eyes and dropped, like rain, into the bath water.

"That's wonderful, Ronny. I know you will make us very proud," Grace assured him.

"As long as you don't fart." Anita immediately regretted the comment—not because her mother lashed out at her for "foul talk," but because Ronny didn't laugh this time. He just looked pained, and the joy that had been beaming from his face seemed to vanish. Anita sighed again and slid deeper into the water's soft embrace.

Just try to let it go, she thought to herself; *just let it go*, she repeated as she attempted to regain her refuge of candlelight and lavender, but nothing was helping. Her tears grew into deeper sobs. Mitsy, balancing on her back paws against the side of the tub, tried to comfort her. "He was so sensitive, Mitsy, so gentle," she said to her little companion and rested her head on the side of the tub while Mitsy gently licked her forehead. "You're such a sweetheart, Mitsy. What would I ever do without you?" she said as she righted herself in the tub.

"Maybe that's what's changing, Mitsy—maybe I can still feel this pain but learn to let it go—learn to forgive myself." As Anita reached for her glass of scotch, the voices in her head were as loud as when she first heard them: "It takes a year at least," friends told her. "Give it time." "The sense of overwhelming pain is normal," the bereavement counselor said. "It's different for each person, of course, but there are common stages in the grieving process." She remembered how she had pictured a Grieving Checklist in her head: Denial: tick. Anger: tick. Bargaining: tick. Depression: tick. Acceptance: tick. When after a year she still felt numb and the world continued to feel empty, she decided to accept that too. Tick.

Taking another healthy swig of the scotch, Anita continued to remember. Five years passed. She celebrated her twenty-first birthday with a referral to a psychiatrist. "No, you are not going insane, Anita," he said to her during their first session. "We understand more about the grieving process these days than we did when Kubler-Ross put forward her stage theory." The doctor spoke over his horn-rimmed glasses and she liked him immediately. He was warm and friendly, with eyes like a puppy, and, well, he was also young and very attractive. She felt her body respond to the memory with a little shudder. She drew a deep breath and felt the warm water against her skin, embracing her.

"Here's to you, Dr. Luscious," she said out loud and raised her glass to toast the smiling vision she imagined standing at the foot of the tub. Draining the last of her drink, she held the liquor in her mouth, feeling the warm smoothness grow in intensity. She liked the sensation. "If only our work together had been as beautiful as you were," she said to her vision, and then smiling at her own cleverness added, "but alas, neither the therapy nor the romance ever led to a fulfilling climax, did it?"

"And so it goes, Mitsy, simultaneous titillation on two levels: the perfect man. Pity I chose the wrong guy, huh girlfriend? What's that? Yeah, I guess you're right; thanks to him I discovered I wasn't dead yet. Yep, here's to you, Dr. Luscious. At least you always listened to me."

And that was her doctor's immediate charm. He wasn't like the family counselor, who always seemed determined to convince them that everything would be all right in due time—as if she could promise them out of their agony; Anita had never felt heard by her. "What was it she used to tell me, Mitsy? Ah yes, 'Try to find your happy place.' What kind of bullshit was that? At least our Dr. Luke listened and I stopped crying all the time. He sure seemed all ears… and more!"

Anita closed her eyes and took a deep breath as her hand slipped under the water. She parted her legs and let her hand slip between her thighs, then checked herself.

"Not now, my dear," she told herself. "This is an important memory you need to explore." She smiled again—perhaps a little too broadly. "Now where were we?" she said, conjuring up his voice, attempting to cut through the fog emerging from the concoction of pills, alcohol and warm water.

"It's a complicated process, Anita," he was saying. "Your loss was tremendous—he wasn't just your brother, he was your *twin!*" The way Luke would say that word always seemed to hint at implications of great symbolic importance, unfortunately just beyond Anita's grasp.

"Too bad I never understood what he meant, Mitsy. Hell, I still don't. What was it he always said? Ah yes, 'He is your counterpart—the other half of you. You were intimately connected. Yet he abandoned you and you hate him for that, and feel guilty for hating him. It makes me wonder how this plays out in your relationship with your mother…' Well, he may have had something there, but I never really got it. I took it in like a child being told a fairy tale—still, I could have gone on listening to him forever. That voice, his eyes, and how he moved. It's no wonder that within six months I was madly in love with him. And, Mitsy, it wasn't just one-sided. I knew he looked forward to our sessions—always scheduling me for his last appointment of the day, letting me run on past the end of our hour until the little dipstick started feeling all guilty and made up that bullshit about his supervisor insisting he refer me to someone else. Of course, girlfriend, I had some pride—just told him I understood, not to worry, it would be fine… probably for the best." Anita sighed. "What's that you say, little one? Denial is more than just a river in Egypt? You're as wise as you are cute, and let me add that repression is vastly underrated. Asshole," she said loudly, not really sure whether she was referring to Dr. Luke or to his supervisor. Unsteadily she reached for the bottle of scotch she had carefully balanced on the rim of the tub and filled her empty glass.

"But that led me to Dr. Carol Sands, and that has been good, right, Mitsy?" Mitsy raised her head off her paws and looked at her. "Right away I really loved how she would always check in, as she called it, on our relationship. It made me feel that her concern was genuine and that she respected me. I have to admit we've done a lot of good work together on my automatic self-defeating thoughts. And the way I always judged myself—I was definitely a real mess when we started, huh, sweetie? Dragging myself through life? And that mantra of hers—how I love it—'Where is the evidence? Is there another possibility?' I remember once telling her that I was the one who deserved to die, not Ronny—that I was the flawed one. And do you know what she said to me, Mitsy? She asked me if I knew where and how this maladaptive schema, this distorted sense of who I am and what the world is like came into being. Yes, we were doing so well. I felt I was finally on the right path—a real journey of self-discovery. And thank God I'd stopped spending all my weekends lying in bed. I was growing stronger until…"

Anita squirmed in the tub. She felt her body tense and her jaw clench when she remembered finding Ronny's diary a few weeks ago. She had never known why he did it—why he killed himself. Now at least she knew, and with her knowing, her long-festering grief gave way to rage—rage against the monster who had abused him, the church that enabled it, and most of all against her mother, who stubbornly and without any rationality maintained its innocence at the expense of her own son's memory. Even her father, the one she could always count on, the one who was always her strength and balance, retreated behind a façade of denial and avoidance.

"I thought they'd want to know the truth. Whoa, did I ever get that wrong, huh, Mitsy?" Mitsy looked up into her eyes. Anita took another gulp of scotch and added some warm water to the bath. "I love you, Mitsy," she said. "You're my very best friend in the whole world. You never judge me. You're always here for me— now dear, where were we? Ah yes, sharing the truth. That didn't work out quite the way I thought it would." Anita closed her eyes and slid lower into the tub, her chin touching the water. The bath, the pills and the alcohol now completely enfolded her, blunting the pain. She stood outside of herself, a fuzzy vision like the doctor she had seen at the foot of her tub. She had become a passive observer of the past that continued to roll through the fog into her dreamlike present; she had no cares or thoughts of the future—no future even existed in this moment. Her sense of disassociation was so strong that her instincts began to kick in, and she attempted to regain the thread of her own narrative.

"So where was I, Mitsy? I was getting kind of lost there. Yes dear, I remember now, Mother was sitting there denying everything. Why does that not surprise me?" Anita slapped the water in the tub. Mitsy gave a little groan and resettled herself with her head where her tail had been. "Sorry dear, didn't mean to splash you," she said as she recalled the bitter sound of her mother's voice.

"Where did you find that?" her mother demanded, trying to imply the journal wasn't really Ronny's. "And what do you mean he was taking drugs? He would never do that. And where would he have gotten them?" she said while staring hard into Anita's eyes, her tone sharp and accusatory. "Don't tell me the monsignor was giving them to him! I should slap you!"

"Slap me?" Anita fired back. "You have the nerve to think I'd give him drugs? That is so like you, Mother, turning everything around to what you believe! But not this time; this time I'm telling you the truth and you have to listen!" Anita remembered how she stood up without giving her mother another look and stomped out of the house; she could still hear the sound of the door slamming behind her. Anita recalled how the next day she described the whole scene to her therapist...

"So, it didn't go too well, Dr. Sands."

"Do you remember what you were thinking when you fled the scene?"

"About a thousand different things, but mostly that it was all hopeless; Mother would never listen to me, especially if it challenged her precious Church. Why bother, she'd just wind up hating me."

Anita remembered how Dr. Sands had leaned closer to her and asked, "Reflecting on those thoughts now, do you think they are accurate? Where's the evidence? Let's start with the first: It's hopeless. So, you're saying your mother is incapable of learning, of changing, in the face of new information. Is that a fair appraisal of your mother?"

"No, of course not."

"Okay. So what about her 'never' listening to you?"

"Yeah, wrong..." Anita conceded.

"And then you said, 'especially if it challenged her precious Church' and 'she'd just wind up hating me'. What are you really saying here, Anita?"

"I'm saying," Anita hesitated, "Jesus, this is hard for me to say; I am saying the Church means more to her than I do. She loves the

Church more than she loves me," and she began to cry.

"How much that must hurt, Anita, to believe your mother cares for an institution more than her own daughter, her own flesh and blood. I wonder how this belief came to be born in you. Can you recall a time, in your childhood perhaps, when you had this feeling?"

Anita could still remember how her head began to swim with memories of her mother leaving her behind as she headed off to yet another service, or guild meeting, or bible study group, and how one memory suddenly floated to the surface, diminishing all the others in importance.

"I was six," she said, meeting her therapist's eyes. "I was skipping home from school and tripped and landed on my tailbone," she said slowly and softly. "The pain was excruciating. My mother said she could hear me wailing all the way down the street—even though she never came off her damn porch to help me. It was only after I managed to drag myself to the house that she had me lie on my bed and put ice on the bruise. Then she told me to stop crying because the priest would be here any minute and she had to meet with him about arrangements for... for flowers, I think it was. Anyway, she said she didn't have time for such nonsense now—it was time for me to calm down and keep still. And she got up and left, closing the door behind her."

"Can you think of any other explanation for your mother's behavior than that she loved the Church more than you?"

A long silence followed as vague thoughts swam through Anita's head until one appeared that pushed all the others away. The thought was like a light, a bright searing light, dispelling all shadows—all darkness. "She was afraid... afraid of being judged and found wanting," Anita said with conviction. "She was the one who felt unworthy—unlovable. And I took it on board..."

"That was quite a moment, Mitsy. What a release it was. Too bad I couldn't remember anything of that today—poor Mother... poor Nita... poor, poor Ronny."

Slowly, Anita slid lower into the bath water until she submerged herself completely in the quiet world beneath the surface. She welcomed the eerie sounds that closed in on her and the candlelight shimmering above her—like beacons illuminating her way to another world, another place free of pain, free of discord. The water was soothing, inviting her into peaceful oblivion. *Yes take me*, she thought as she closed her eyes, wanting to sleep... forever...

Anita surfaced with a great explosion of water and gasping, drenching Mitsy and frightening her into startled yelps.

"My God, Mitsy! That was just a little too close!" she said as she realized how near she had been to yielding to her spiraling suicidal thoughts.

"Better call it an evening." Her voice was shaky from the realization as she pulled herself out of the tempting water and grabbed a towel. Anita caught sight of herself in the mirror and stopped to look deeply into her own eyes. It was all there, and more. They reminded her of Ronny's as they were in those last months: vacant, hurt, scared, lost.

"I need more than Dr. Sands..." she whispered to her reflection. "I need more," she repeated with conviction as she blew out the candles and then made her way to the bedroom, where she crawled into bed without even removing her robe.

The Dream

Emotionally drained and physically exhausted, Anita fell asleep the moment her head hit the pillow, but her scotch and valium-flooded brain could not rest and continued to conjure dreamy thoughts and images of being in the tub surrounded by candles and the scent of lavender.

The warm water embraced her, caressing her, arousing her, exploring all the intimate secrets of her body. She closed her eyes, yielding to her watery lover. "Oh, Luke, sweet Luke, my beautiful Luke," she moaned as he slowly untied the sash of her robe, exposing her nakedness. They were in her room now, on her bed. She opened her eyes to see him, powerful in his black cassock, the shadow of a huge cross behind him radiating a malevolence that made her want to turn, to protect herself, but she couldn't move at all; he was on her now, holding her down, penetrating her. The metallic boom of a church bell filled the room—its plaintive call ringing inside her.

"Shame, shame on you, you wicked ones! God will strike you down to Hell!" shrieked her mother as she turned, breasts exposed, from the shadowy figure of the monsignor, whom she had been fondling in the darkness in the corner of the room. Luke leapt to his feet as Anita grabbed at her robe, trying in vain to hide herself.

"I repent! I repent! Oh dear God have mercy upon me!" cried Luke as he turned and fell to his knees before the cross. "Forgive me for yielding to her wickedness!" he begged while Anita's mother and Monsignor Aleksy echoed like a medieval chorus, "her wickedness, her wickedness, her wickedness."

Anita was sobbing, "I am not wicked! I am not! Love is not a sin! Love is not a sin!"

"Stop it now! Leave her alone!" A child's voice rose above the cacophony. "You hypocrites, leave her be!"

"Oh Ronny!" cried Anita as her dream abruptly changed and the two of them were standing alone under their favorite tree in the back yard. "It's you... isn't it?" she said.

"Yes, Nita, it's me—don't you recognize me?"

"Yes, yes, of course I do, it's just that you look different."

"Much has happened since I passed to the other side, Nita. I'm not the same as before, but I am still your Ronny, and I love you. Don't be afraid," he said as he took her hand and began walking toward the garage. "I have something I want to show you, Nita," he said tenderly.

"Yes?" she said, and it was as if they were both young again and they were sharing a special secret. Her heart filled with joy and anticipation as he gently led her through the door, but upon crossing the threshold, she sensed a foreboding and stopped in her tracks. Ronny tightened the grip on her hand and pulled her inside.

"Ronny, stop it! What is this place?" she cried as she saw the cross in the far corner of the empty room. It had an eerie glow and he was pulling her toward it, his grasp even stronger now. Anita was terrified. "Stop, you're hurting me!" she cried.

She heard a sound above her head and looked up—a body swayed from a heavy rope, and as it turned in the ghostly light, she saw the face: her own. She gasped and struggled for breath as a heavy blackness began pressing her into the ground.

Anita awoke screaming, her body drenched in sweat, heart pounding through its bony cage. She lay perfectly still in the darkness, shivering, listening to the sound of her breathing as it echoed in the depth of the silence that surrounded her.

"Only a dream, only a dream," she repeated over and over in an attempt to free herself from the grip of the images that continued to replay in her mind. She was awake now, tangled in the twisted robe she still held in her tightly clenched hands.

"Only a dream," she told herself again, "but Ronny was here; I could feel his hand… it was so real." Her hand reached down to stroke the little dog curled up at her side.

"Did you see him too, Mitsy? Did you see him too?" she mumbled before yielding to the arms of a deep and dreamless sleep.

***

Anita woke with a start.

"Oh my God, it's nearly seven-thirty!" She glared at the alarm as if it were to blame for not setting itself, then threw back the covers, jumped out of bed and nearly toppled over.

"Steady there, girl, you seem to be a bit wobbly this morning." She knew this state only too well—internally shaky, as if she were being held together by frayed string. Mitsy was right at her heels.

"Come on, Mitsy," she said. "I'm so late." Despite the fog of sleep that would not take its leave, and the visions that still called to her from her dreams of the night before, she willed herself to do what she had to, charging around her house like a mad woman, somehow managing to get herself out the door, into her car and onto campus only five minutes late for her eight o'clock Constitutional Law class.

But Anita was still far from fully functional, and her awareness of the lecture was touch and go at best. She looked around the hall at her fellow students. *I hope someone's taking better notes than I am*, she thought.

At the break she made a beeline for the coffee shop.

"Double shot of espresso, please," she said, trying to sound calm but unable to conceal the tone of desperation that managed to creep into her voice.

"No one better get between you and that coffee today. Late night?"

Startled by the man's voice behind her, she shot a quick glance over her shoulder. *Nice!* she thought, taking in the dark wavy hair and large brown eyes set in a chiseled face.

"You got that right," she said. Anita didn't recognize the face, but there was something definitely familiar about the voice. She turned to get a better look.

"You don't remember me, do you?" he said when she squinted her eyes and pursed her lips.

"Nope," she said playfully and turned to retrieve her coffee from the counter before turning back to face him again.

"Maybe after you take a few hits of that coffee you might recognize me," he countered with a smile. Anita leaned forward; it was the smile she recognized.

"Jake...?"

"Yep, alive and in person," he quipped. "So, how long has it been?"

"Um, like maybe seven or eight years?"

"A long time for sure, and I know I didn't have this when Ronny and I were altar boys," he said as he stroked his three-day shadow. Anita could feel the smile drop from her face as he mentioned her brother's name. Memories, like old photos falling out of an album, tumbled from her mind.

"Gee it's so good to see you, Anita," he said, not seeming to notice her change. "Do you have a minute?"

Anita felt conflicted; she was interested but at the same time wanted to flee—she simply was not up to the challenge of dealing with Jake and all that he represented and reminded her of.

"I only have a couple of minutes before class resumes," she said, "so it's not really a good time."

"Well how about after class then? We could get a bite to eat," he persisted. "Come on, Anita, for old times' sake?"

"Old times were really not that good for me, Jake," she said, but in the end she reluctantly agreed.

Anita might as well have skipped the rest of the lecture for all the buzzing in her head. Struggling in vain to pay attention to the droning of the professor, the flood of memories and emotions kept getting the better of her. Jake O'Brien was a year older than they were, so while she and Ronny had known who he was, they only became friends when Ronny joined him as an altar boy.

"Not that O'Brien boy?" Grace said when Ronny first mentioned wanting to invite him to dinner. "You know I don't approve of him. Mabel Petrovsky told me that since his mother died, he's become a real problem. His father, poor soul, does the best he can, but just look at him; I saw him at the grocery store—all scruffy and wearing an earring. Merciful Lord! I'd rather you had nothing to do with him, Ronny, and I certainly would not want to sit across from him at my dinner table."

Initially Anita disagreed with her mother. She saw no reason to dislike Jake and even tried to find reasons to be around the older, good-looking boy when he was visiting her brother. But as time went on and the friendship between the two boys deepened, it became obvious to her they shared something intimate and important, something she was not privy to, and she began to grow uncomfortable about being left out. Gradually this discomfort found refuge in her mother's view, and she adopted her opinion that Jake was indeed "bad news"—a view that gained strength when after Ronny's suicide Jake didn't even bother to come to the funeral...

***

Anita made her way to the small Italian restaurant just off campus. At first she walked quickly, energized by the fact that the seemingly interminable lecture was finally over, but as she drew closer to her destination, she began to feel heavy and slow, like lead had been poured into her legs, and a nameless dread began to grow inside her. She stopped walking, leaned against a lamppost and began to entertain thoughts of turning back. But it was already too late; Jake had spotted her.

"Hey, you okay, Anita?" he said as he approached her. "You don't look good—I mean..." Anita grinned in spite of herself at his ambiguity.

"I know what you mean, Jake," she offered. "I guess I don't feel too good. You know it's quite a shock to see you."

"I suppose… kind of like seeing a ghost maybe?"

Anita gave a wan nod.

"Look, I'm sure a little wine and minestrone will get the blood back into your face… and it'll be good to talk." He took another step in her direction, but when he reached for her arm, she took a step back.

Jake stopped in mid-movement and buried his hand in his pocket. The awkward moment would have allowed her the opportunity to demur—Jake felt it—but Anita decided to go, and to execute the plan she had been formulating on her walk to the restaurant. She could see it all clearly in her mind, a way to strike back at all the wrongs he had done to her and her brother, wrongs that had surfaced so powerfully since she had seen him in the coffee shop. She would keep her cool, listen to whatever he had to say, and then with all the dignity she could muster, tell him calmly she had not the slightest interest in ever seeing him again and once and for all to stay the hell away from her and her life. Then with exceptional poise, she would place her napkin on the table, stand, give him one last venomous look and turn to make a regal exit from the restaurant and Jake and all he represented….

"How about that table in the back?" he asked chirpily.

Could he really be that oblivious? she thought as she walked stiffly to the table. *And if he has any idea to put a move on me, I'll castrate him with my fork!* Contemplating the absurdity of the image, Anita smiled in spite of herself. Jake saw her expression, but being oblivious of the intention behind it, smiled back.

Jake's attempts at chitchat at the too small, too secluded table flowed like ice. The level of Anita's discomfort was nearly intolerable until the wine arrived.

"Anita, are you angry with me?" Jake said as he took the carafe and poured them each a glass. "Did I say something wrong?"

Anita took a large swallow, and for the first time since they had been seated met his gaze. He was searching her face with such open sincerity that it threw her off. He really didn't get it, she realized. He really didn't have a clue. Her eyes began to well with tears.

"Ronny..." was all she could manage to say.

Jake was silent for a moment. "Of course," he whispered, looking down at the table. Anita watched as he tried to gather himself—appearing to physically pull himself together with tiny twitching movements. Then he looked up and into her eyes again. "It was not my fault," he said quietly. "I knew the talk—that I was a bad influence, that I encouraged him to do drugs—but that isn't what happened. When he... when he did what he did, it nearly killed me."

"I suppose that's why you didn't even bother to come to the funeral." Anita's sarcasm erupted so quickly it surprised them both. "I'm sorry, Jake. I really am," she said when she saw deep hurt in his eyes. "I've just been so messed up since I recognized you this morning... actually, I've been messed up for a long time now... but I promised myself I would hear your story. You and Ronny were so close... or at least I thought you were."

"We were."

The soup arrived and was ignored—neither was very hungry now. Jake ordered a second carafe and poured more wine.

"Look, Anita," he said haltingly, "Ronny had good reason to want to die—so did I. When I found out he had hanged himself, I went looking for my father's gun. He caught me just as I was loading up." Jake was now fully engaged in the conversation, his own repressed and forgotten memories, the source of the pain and guilt he experienced every day of his waking and dreaming life, were streaming to the surface. Anita, touched by the sincerity of his story, felt a strong need to connect with him and considered sharing what she knew from Ronny's diary but decided instead to wait.

"I was totally gone—beside myself," Jake was saying. "I was crazy with fear and guilt and sorrow. My dad threw his arms around me and held me so tight it was like I was in a straitjacket. I couldn't talk. I was sobbing and thrashing around. I was totally out of control and couldn't stop. Dad said it lasted almost an hour. When I finally got exhausted and fell asleep, he called the doctor. Anita," he paused and looked back down at the table, "I wasn't at Ronny's funeral because I was in the hospital on a suicide watch. When they released me after six weeks, Dad shipped me off to his sister's in Indiana. It was more than he could deal with on his own."

Listening to his story, Anita became aware of a curious feeling—like privilege or gratitude. She felt she was being given a rare opportunity, as if she could speak to Ronny himself, through Jake, about his anguish. Obviously, Jake had been abused as well. Why hadn't she realized that? She chose her words carefully; she did not want to blow it.

"Jake, Ronny had a journal. I found it only a few weeks ago."

Jake looked alarmed and his face became noticeably pale.

"Please, Jake, listen. There were a lot of pages torn out. I think he wrote things in it just to get them out of his head and then destroyed them. But there were still enough pages left for me to figure out the monsignor was not by any means the saint he tried to make everyone believe he was, and Ronny was obviously tormented and deeply conflicted by their relationship. You have no idea how glad I am that bastard of a priest is dead." Anita smiled in a way that made the hair on Jake's neck stand up. "If he weren't," she said softly, "I really don't know what I might be capable of doing. And," she added with a touch of irony, "me, studying to be a lawyer." Jake smiled and nodded his head.

"Yeah, and I wanted to be a priest," Jake said, and then quickly added when he saw the stunned look on her face, "gallows humor, Anita, gallows humor."

"Not funny, Jake," she said, but Jake could tell she actually was amused.

"But in fact, there was a time I really did want to be a priest," he continued. "Ronny and I used to talk about it. I don't think that's so unusual for altar boys… in the beginning." Suddenly Jake paused. "Sad to say, probably not that unusual for certain altar boys even later. They call it 'identification with the aggressor.' It's a way of coping."

Jake saw immediately that his remark had pushed Anita to a point she was still very far from being able to see, let alone accept. To break the tension, Jake made another attempt at levity.

"So, Anita, when the Dream Police come to arrest me, will you be my lawyer?"

"Dream Police?"

"Oh yeah. I have the most vivid and sometimes terribly violent recurring dreams, and, more than once, I've told my analyst I was glad there were no Dream Police. His comeback is usually something like, 'The only thing criminal about your dreams is that you haven't been given an academy award for them.' He finds them creative and meaningful, of course he doesn't have to experience the pain, but I do have to admit that working with them has helped me in ways I could never have imagined."

"Really?" Anita was both intrigued and skeptical, especially with her previous night's escapades still darkening the corners of her awareness. She decided to risk some additional self-disclosure. "Remember how you asked me this morning if it had been a late night?"

"It seemed like a reasonable way to open a conversation—not too rude, I hope?"

"No, not at all; it's just that it was no average 'late night.' Things have been getting even more intense for me since I found Ronny's journal. I've been arguing with my mother like you wouldn't believe, and I'm haunted by dark thoughts."

"Like suicide?"

"Like… like maybe slipping away," she said softly and sighed.

"Slipping away? Away to where?" he replied with a sense of wonderment since he too was no stranger to dark thoughts, but he was afraid—afraid of death, afraid even more of damnation. But "slipping away," there was something about the way she put it that had a different feeling.

"Tell me more, Anita."

"It happened big-time last night. You sure you want to hear about this?"

"I'm all ears," he said while making big circles around the sides of his head. "I'm sorry," he said when he saw the terse look on Anita's face. "My way of coping."

Anita nodded in response. "I'm no stranger to that," she responded.

"Please, Anita, tell me about last night."

Anita nodded again. "I was in the tub, and it would have been so easy to just let myself slip away," she said, remembering how she came so close to letting go. "But I pulled back." Anita and Jake could only stare into each other's eyes. It was obvious to them both they could not be closer; they could not be sharing a more intimate moment. Both saw it so clearly; they were joined, they were one, they shared the same hell. It was a profound moment, powerful and complex and had they been lovers, or siblings, or parent and child, they would have embraced and held each other close in this oneness. But here, stranded in this void of intimate strangeness, they were frozen, unable to move, unable to offer the comfort of closeness.

"Will you tell me more about the journal?" Jake finally said, attempting to reach out across the abyss of separation.

"Not here," she said softly. "Maybe it would be better if you read some of it yourself."

"Yeah sure, Anita; I would like that." But there was more hesitation in his voice than enthusiasm. "Do you have it here?"

"It's at home. We can go there now if you like."

"Okay, I mean sure, let's go."

The Journal

Jake's attempts at more conversation during the drive to her house fell flat. Anita gripped the steering wheel with both hands and kept her eyes glued to the road while he went on and on about how he happened to be on campus to hear a lecture recommended by his analyst—something relating to trauma by some renowned psychoanalyst—and how he had really looked forward to it, but it was cancelled because of illness, and how he was hoping it would be rescheduled because he really was interested in the topic. But Anita was entertaining her own thoughts and heard almost nothing of what Jake was saying. She was frightened, and she didn't know why. *Maybe this isn't a good idea,* she thought. *Maybe Jake can't be trusted; maybe he is too unstable to help me; maybe showing him the journal is a violation of Ronny's privacy; maybe all three of us have been damned and Mother is right after all...*

"We're here," she said as she pulled to the curb.

"This your place?" he said with surprise as they came to a stop. "Yeah, pretty spectacular for an unemployed law student, I know. My dad bought it as an investment long before I was born—well before this neighborhood became so gentrified. Later, when I got into Northwestern, he decided he could afford to turn the place over to me so I could be closer to campus."

"Some graduation gift!" Jake said as they mounted the steps to the old three-story greystone. "And you have this whole place to yourself?"

"Yep," she said, "all for little old me—and Mitsy of course."

"Mitsy?"

"My dog."

"Is she friendly… I hope?" Jake said with a hint of seriousness.

"Very friendly, most of the time—just like me," she kidded. Anita unbolted the solid wooden door leading into the vestibule.

"Daddy didn't do anything much to the place, you'll see. It still has its Victorian charm, cracks and all."

The tiny entry was dimly lit by a wall sconce, and beyond the interior glass door with its lace curtain, Mitsy was making her presence known. Luckily for Jake, Mitsy greeted him almost as warmly as she greeted her mistress.

"Wow, Anita. What a beautiful piano!" Jake was peering into the living room as Anita hung her coat on a hook by the door at the foot of the staircase. "I remember Ronny used to brag about how well you played. Do you still play?"

"Not really; not in years. And I don't know that I ever played that well when I was younger, but it's very sweet to hear that Ronny bragged about me." Anita continued to talk about the piano. It felt like a safe subject and a way to avoid for a while the real purpose of Jake's visit. For his part, Jake too appreciated the distraction. And so Anita continued on, telling Jake how the piano had been owned by one of her father's wealthier business associates who had needed to upgrade and was looking to rid himself of the piano "right at the peak of my childhood career" she joked, "so Daddy got it for next to nothing."

"It's beautiful," Jake repeated.

"It's a Steinway baby grand, you know, and even though I haven't touched it since forever, I can't bear to part with it."

Jake continued to stare at the piano looking somewhat mesmerized, but, in fact, he was just struggling to get his bearings—everything seemed to be happening so fast.

"Well don't just stand there," Anita said, "it's not going to start playing itself for you." Jake turned to her with a smile.

"I don't know about you, but I could use some more wine," she continued. "Come on, I have some back here," and she proceeded to lead Jake down the long hallway, past the darkened dining room, and into the coziness of her well-lived-in kitchen at the back of the house. Anita slid a bottle of wine to the front of the marble countertop.

"Here, open this," she said after placing the corkscrew next to the bottle. "I'll go get the journal. The glasses are up there."

Jake looked at the bottle and the corkscrew. He wasn't very experienced with opening wine bottles that didn't have screw-on tops. But he said nothing.

Once upstairs in her study, Anita's hands trembled as she lifted Ronny's journal out of her desk drawer. "God help me," she whispered and wondered why she had said it. But deep down, deep inside, she realized she was staring into the shadowy unknown world of her own future, and she was deeply shaken. She quietly closed the drawer, and clutching the tattered book against her chest, slowly descended the stairs and made her way back to the kitchen.

Anita stopped at the doorway, transfixed by the sight of Jake O'Brien at the table looking sad and lost and every bit the sixteen-year-old boy she remembered from her childhood. He looked so young—young and out of place beside the wine bottle he had struggled to open for her and the two glasses he had carried to the table. Resisting the urge to rush across the room and comfort him, Anita uttered a slight cough before approaching the table and quietly seating herself in the chair across from him. Jake looked up as she carefully placed the journal between them.

"You seemed to be a million miles away..." she said and picked up one of the glasses of wine.

Jake slowly nodded his head. "You know, Anita, life is so full of surprises. Who could have imagined this morning that we would be sitting here this evening? Anyway, so this is it?"

Anita could see the mixture of hesitation and curiosity reflected in the features of his face—the youthful appearance now turned gaunt and worn like the tattered journal before him.

Anita chose her words carefully. "If you don't feel up to it, Jake, you don't need to open it."

"It's not that, Anita," he said while carefully sliding his wine glass a safer distance from the book. "I just don't want to rush into it. After all, a journal is such a private thing—a place where you can pour out your heart and your most intimate thoughts and secrets. Ronny was the closest friend I've ever had, and he never even mentioned this to me. So maybe there are things he didn't want me to see. I would hate to feel later that I'd invaded his only refuge—so much has been stolen from us already, maybe I shouldn't…"

"I know. I was stunned when I found it. At first, I could hardly contain myself. But then I had similar thoughts. I was afraid of what might be in it. I thought maybe reading it was just another violation. But in the end, it was almost as if Ronny himself were crying out to me to read it. I felt he wanted me to understand; he wanted me to know the truth, otherwise, why not destroy the entire thing and not just tear out certain pages?"

Anita could see the anguish on Jake's face and how his hands shook when he reached for the book. Carefully, he picked it up with both hands, set it closer to him on the table, and then simply stared at it with tear-filled eyes.

"Jake, I've read every page, and I believe Ronny would want you to as well. There are things in it I don't understand, but I think you might, and maybe somehow it will help—and if that were to happen, I know in my soul, Ronny would be glad." Anita did not know how such certainty had crept into her words, but she deeply felt the truth of what she said.

"I'll be right back," Anita said when she felt Mitsy squirming at her feet. "Oh, sweet pea, of course you need to go out," she said, and after grabbing her glass from the table, she stood up and headed for the back porch with Mitsy in eager pursuit. "Take your time, darling," she said as the little dog scampered down the steps to the yard. "Let's give Jake a few minutes—let's give us *all* a few minutes." Mitsy hit the yard first and scampered off to the bushes to do her business. Anita managed to navigate the steps without spilling her wine and took a sip as she waited beside the little stone statue of St. Francis.

The night was clear, and the brisk Chicago air felt sharp and cold against her face. *Should have grabbed my jacket,* she thought as she gazed up at the moon and stars. "Life is a Dream," she whispered aloud, remembering the title of a book she read years ago. "It sure the hell is," she said to herself. "It sure the hell is."

When she returned to the kitchen, Jake was sitting very still, bent over the open journal on the table. Wishing not to disturb his reverie, she quietly went about preparing Mitsy's dinner then slid onto the barstool next to the counter, pretending to be busy arranging the pens and pencils in the old Marimekko coffee mug.

Jake, oblivious to his surroundings, suspended in the half light of a dream-like interface between the present and the past, regarded his friend's handwriting—the neat handwriting of a child:

Again I wait
"Dear Lord" I pray
Who hears?
Silence

Muffled footsteps approach
The darkness grows
Cold fingers grip my soul

I pray, I pray, I pray
My prayer is all I hear
All I feel

Then Silence
No answer
I am alone

Though the handwriting was familiar and brought back the sound of Ronny's voice, the words revealed a side of his friend he had never known. Yes, Ronny could be serious and Jake always knew how deeply his friend revered the Church, but the tone of despair, the desperation and the silent calls for help, these were things Jake had never seen. *Maybe if I hadn't been so self-absorbed...* his thoughts trailed off in quiet recrimination.

Jake continued to read—he really had no choice—but reading was sickeningly painful, like pulling a thin scab off a festering wound. Each sentence reawakened memories Jake had kept buried deep within himself for years. He turned the pages slowly, touching them with the respect accorded a sacred object, his fingers moving from page to page, from memory to memory, as if on tiptoe, trying not to disturb a sleeping baby.

Watching him out of the corner of her eye, Anita observed the procession of expressions playing across his face, the little movements of his lips as if praying, and the opening and closing of his eyes, like sentinels at the gate protecting his heart from taking in too much. When Jake's body shuddered—like from an electric shock—and his breath caught in his chest, she knew whatever it was he had just read must be something very powerful indeed.

"What is it, Jake?" she said, unable to resist the impulse to ask. Jake turned sharply to look at her.

"Man, I was so lost I forgot you were even here."

"Sorry, Jake, I noticed your reaction. What did you read?" Jake said nothing at first, just turned back to stare at the page.

"The Elite Sacrament," he mumbled to himself so softly Anita could not hear what he said, but she stopped herself from asking him to repeat himself.

"The Elite Sacrament" was written boldly across the top of the page. Jake knew the term well; the other boys used it in hushed conversations with each other. He remembered how they often laughed about it to cover their fear and their shame. No, Ronny had not, by any means, been the only one. The boys spoke about the Elite Sacrament with a sense of instinctive sin veneered with vanity—for were they not the chosen ones? For them it was a secret esoteric ceremony to which only they were privy. A feeling of terror and disgust enveloped Jake as dark memories stirred in him. He stopped and was not sure he wanted to read what followed. He closed his eyes for a moment as he took a deep breath, and then he read on.

Raise the fallen Christ
With the touch of virgin lips,
Resurrect His strength.
And when He offers you
The holy elixir
Do not hesitate to drink it down.

Jake had not been "invited" to this ceremony, only learning about it from the other boys. He never guessed Ronny was involved. In fact, Jake had been envious of the other boys. He felt left out, even though Monsignor Aleksy did call upon him for other favors. Jake's body tensed at the recollection of being called to the monsignor's study where he was compelled to hold on to the back of the couch while being forcefully penetrated—again and again. He remembered the searing pain and the musky smell when his face was pushed against the old upholstery. Later, under the delusion of his own twisted thoughts, he would think with envy about the Elite Sacrament and wish he too had been chosen to arouse the monsignor and taste the milk of the Lord. He had rationalized his situation by thinking it was because he was younger than the other boys, but now he knew Ronny had been chosen even though Ronny was even younger than he was.

From across the room, Anita saw him squirm and heard the little moan that came from deep inside when he realized that even now, so many years later, he was still, at some level, in some twisted way, envious.

"Are you okay?" Anita said as she walked over to the table. This time she did not resist the urge to comfort him. She walked behind him and looked to see what he had just read. Then she placed her hands on his shoulders.

"I never understood that part. Jake, do you know what it means?" She could feel the tenseness in his shoulders—they felt like stone.

"Yes," he said softly, "but not now, I can't right now."

Anita understood; this was enough for both of them. She

walked around the table and closed the journal.

"We really didn't have much at the restaurant," she said in an attempt to break the moment's spell. "I have some leftover quiche—it would be enough for the two of us."

"I don't think I could eat, Anita. But thanks," he finally said after a long pause.

"I guess I'm not really hungry either," she said, "but come with me, I think we need to get away from the kitchen."

Jake nodded vaguely and followed her down the hall to the living room.

"Do you mind, Anita?" he said, pointing to the piano in the corner of the room. "Might calm me down a little."

"By all means," she said and with a little smile added, "I would love to hear you play."

"I hope you're not disappointed. I really just tinker at it for myself."

"No matter," Anita said as she settled herself in her grandfather's overstuffed chair near the fireplace. "I could use some calming down as well."

"Okay, no pressure then," he said.

Anita watched as Jake adjusted himself at the piano bench, and though she could just barely see his shoulders and face from where she sat, she noticed he had an extraordinary look about him. His eyes were downcast as if he were studying the keys intently, but his posture and everything about him suggested that once again, like when she had entered the kitchen and had seen him sitting over Ronny's journal, he had gone to some place far away. But this place seemed different. Anita felt it was lighter, happier.

Jake was absolutely still and appeared to be in deep reflection; then he made the slightest movement, closed his eyes, and touched a key. The whisper of the single note filled the room, and as it died away, it left in its place a profound silence. Another key was touched, ever so slightly louder, and again, as the sound faded, a profound silence engulfed the room. Jake continued, eyes closed, listening intently—*to what?* Anita closed her eyes as well, listened and continued to wonder as seemingly random notes were struck, tumbled over one another, died out, and were re-born. When the music stopped, she opened her eyes. Jake was sitting quietly at the piano, watching her. "Looks like I put you to sleep."

"More like into a trance. I never had any idea you played."

"I don't, I mean I've never had any lessons or anything like you did, but sometimes when I'm around a piano I just... I get attracted to it. When I sit down the sounds just come out and I listen."

"That's interesting, Jake; it reminds me of when I was a little girl and would sit at the piano. Have you ever considered taking some lessons?"

Jake tilted his head and furrowed his brow. "Yeah, I've thought about it but never have."

"Well, maybe you should; you have such a natural ability. Your playing seems to come right from your heart."

When the clock chimed midnight, it surprised them both and Jake accepted Anita's offer to sleep in the guestroom without an argument. They had drunk a lot of wine and were both emotionally spent. Anita accompanied him to his room and got the extra blanket out of the closet. After getting him situated, she bid him a good night as she closed his door and headed down the long hallway to her room. Once inside, she had barely enough strength to undress, too tired to do anything with her clothes other than let them fall in a heap on the floor. She collapsed onto her bed and immediately fell asleep only to awaken about an hour later, cold and scared and feeling very much alone. She slipped on her robe and went to the bathroom to get some water, but did not return to her room. Instead, she headed for the guest bedroom. Trembling slightly, Anita eased the door open. She knew what she was doing but had no idea why. She could hear the heavy breathing and knew Jake was asleep. Relieved, she entered the room, slid under the covers and curled up next to him—her back against his chest.

The Morning After

Anita was careful not to disturb him when she got into bed. It wasn't sex she needed, it was nearness—nearness to his life; and perhaps it wasn't even nearness to *his* life she needed, just nearness to the glow of life itself. But Jake was aware of her presence from the moment she stepped into the room. Instinctively, he too knew it was not about sex, but her physical proximity—her warmth, her scent, the rhythm of her breathing—did excite him and kept him from sleep until she finally slipped out of the bed just before dawn...

***

Jake awoke to the aroma of strong coffee. Feeling dazed and vaguely sick, he pulled on his clothes and followed the trail down the back stairs to the kitchen. Stumbling through the door, head pounding from too much wine and too little sleep, he found Anita wrapped in a thick terrycloth robe perched on the same stool by the counter she had sat on the night before when he was reading Ronny's journal. She was clutching a mug in both hands, blowing across its rim.

"Some coffee?" she asked as he entered.

"I could really use some," he responded enthusiastically, relieved to be talking about anything but the night before—Ronny, the journal, or Anita in his bed. "What time is it?" he mumbled, trying to sound even groggier than he really was. Anita held out a steaming mug. She could see the slight tremble of his hand as he reached out to take it. Jake turned slowly and carried it safely to the table.

"Nearly seven-thirty." Anita stole a shy glance at him as he chose a chair just beyond the periphery of her stool. Jake had that tousled morning look of an innocent and vulnerable little boy.

"Nearly seven-thirty!" he said and turned in his chair to look at her. "Anita, are you nuts? It's Saturday morning!" he said loudly, waving his hands in the air over his head in mock alarm. "Don't you know it's illegal to get up before eleven o'clock on a Saturday?" he persisted. But Jake was no actor; his words came out sounding far too loud, his gesture awkward and forced. Realizing his attempt at humor had fallen flat, he slumped heavily in his chair and began quietly nursing his coffee.

Anita had been rehearsing all sorts of speeches, all manner of excuses, explanations, apologies she thought might erase what, in the light of the morning's relative sobriety, she now considered an embarrassing display of pathetic neediness. *Crawling into Jake's bed— Jesus, what was I thinking?* She shuddered at the thought.

They continued to sip in silence, the kind of tense silence that echoes louder than any sound, but as the moment began to stretch into minutes, Anita realized that Jake too was in no hurry to bring up the evening's taboo. *Perhaps*, she thought, *he really was asleep all the time and had no idea I was ever in his bed.* Breathing a sigh of relief, she regarded him out of the corner of her eye. *I really should say something*, she thought.

"Remind me, you were on campus yesterday for what?" she said, trying to latch onto something safe.

Feeling grateful for the choice of a somewhat neutral topic, Jake looked up and launched into his explanation. "Yeah, so during one of our sessions, Sam, my analyst, told me about a public lecture at the Feinberg School of Medicine by a Dr. Anne Rose. I guess she's some sort of authority on trauma, and I guess he thought I might find it interesting, maybe even helpful. But when I got there, it had been cancelled. I think she was sick. Anyway, I took the opportunity to have a look around the place because I've been considering going into medicine—that is if I ever finish my bachelor's degree."

"You're a student too?" Anita was intrigued. Somehow Jake didn't fit her stereotype. She had always been driven in her studies, full of purpose, but Jake seemed so solitary, unconnected, drifting.

"Not at the moment," he diverted his eyes to his coffee cup. "I'm on one of my typical unscheduled breaks. I have a lot of trouble staying with it for some reason," he gave a small chuckle. "But somewhere along the line, I got it into my head to become a cardiologist. Probably because of my mom—she had heart problems—maybe just another one of my silly dreams. I'm sorry; you've probably noticed I have this habit of rambling sometimes."

"Well yes, I have," she said and smiled, "but go on; it's very interesting." When Anita shifted on the stool she felt her robe loosen around her legs, a fact not lost on Jake who tried not to stare. Anita reached down and pulled the fold over her exposed leg. Jake cleared his throat.

"Okay," he said, his voice a little more shrill than a moment ago, "well, so anyway, I've been working on a degree in philosophy for like…forever, but study is even harder for me now — it always has been a bit of an effort… I guess now they'd call it ADHD, you know Attention Deficit Hyperactivity Disorder, but that was in a former life. These days it's even worse. Sam says it could be Post Traumatic Stress Disorder—and I've never even been in a war— sorry, that was just a joke."

Daddy, tell me about when you lived in the tiger cage. Jake's attempt at humor had stirred some distant memories of her father and his inability to talk about the war. He never did, always finding some reason to change the subject.

"Anita, are you okay?"

"Yeah, sorry. Something you said made me think of something else—it wasn't important. Anyway, I've picked up a few labels myself—bereavement became Adjustment Disorder then Clinical Depression, which became Major Depressive Disorder, and now the latest one is Bipolar II…"

"I suppose it helps to have names for our misery...anyway, where was I? Yeah, about studying... still, when I'm really into the material, I can't think of anything else. Then I start doing really well, and about that time I just... I lose the plot."

"Lose the plot?"

"Yeah, like I'll take a paper I've worked on for weeks and toss it in the garbage on my way to turning it in. Sam says I'm terrified of success—that the mere possibility of succeeding is intolerable, as if I believe I really don't deserve it." Jake hesitated, after last night he had wanted to stay away from any sort of heavy conversation, yet here he was knee deep in one. He gave a little shake of his head and got up.

"I'm sorry, Anita. I didn't mean to get into a heavy conversation this morning. I have so many things I need to do today; I better get going."

"Me too," Anita replied. "I've got a to-do list a mile long."

Jake stopped where he stood at the sink ready to rinse his mug and turned back to face her. For a moment they simply looked at each other, taking each other in—all the unspoken fears written in their eyes and on their faces suddenly clear for both of them to see.

"Anita, what I said was true, but I was not being totally honest with you either. What I really need to do is get out of here."

Anita felt the all too familiar burn of rejection. "It wasn't that awful, was it?" she fired back while squeezing her robe tighter against her chest.

"God, did that ever come out wrong. I have to learn how to speak up and say what's on my mind, but it's still new to me. What I really mean is that last night was pretty overwhelming. I see so much pain in each of us, and yet there were moments between us that would count among some of the most wonderful I've experienced in a very, very long time. I just need some space now to absorb it all."

Anita nodded her head. "Jake, I totally agree, and I admire your courage to be so honest. It's something I need to learn to do myself—to express myself without feeling a need to defend myself."

Jake nodded his head several times. He wanted to say more but knew the timing wasn't right.

"Come on, I'll walk you to the door," she said.

As he stood in the vestibule putting on his coat, a look of inspiration spread across Jake's face. "Would you be interested in going to the lecture with me when it's on again?"

Anita hesitated; she wasn't so sure about the lecture, but she was absolutely certain she wanted to see Jake again.

"Yes Jake, I would like that very much," she said and then added, "that is, if I can."

"It's a lunchtime lecture series, Anita."

"That could work; even we aspiring lawyers are allowed to eat."

"Good, I'll give you a call as soon as I know the day."

"Well then, it's a date," Anita said enthusiastically, then felt her face flush with the forthrightness of her remark. But apparently her confession was lost on Jake, who simply turned and headed off down the steps.

Standing in the doorway watching him go, Anita felt frightened. *I don't even know where he lives,* she thought and flinched at the confession of her neediness. "Jake O'Brien," she said aloud so softly it was almost more of a thought than a sound. *Was he even here at all or was it just a dream?*

But after closing the door and stepping back into the hallway, she noticed the wine glasses and remnants of food in the living room. Releasing a long sigh, she crouched down to pet her little dog, sitting in rapt attention at her feet. "Oh yeah, he was here all right. Dreams don't leave dirty dishes." Anita was surprised at the amount of effort it took to get back onto her feet. "Wow, Mitsy, I'm really exhausted. C'mon, let's deal with the mess later; better for us both to take a little walk and get some fresh air. Let's go get dressed," she said as she turned to go up the stairs, Mitsy bouncing along behind her, tail wagging happily.

The crisp autumn air helped clear Anita's mind and the longer she walked, the lighter she felt. The events of the past thirty-six hours had definitely shifted something in her, and she felt she was looking at things with fresh eyes—even hearing things in a new way.

The more she walked, the more the colors took on an incredible vibrancy. Tuned to the energy of the awakening city—her awareness flooded with the voices of the people, the honking cars and the braking buses—she began to walk faster and faster, little Mitsy already struggling to keep up with her pace. Anita was losing control; she couldn't have stopped if she wanted to. Compelled to keep moving, she disregarded traffic signals and walking lanes, dodged people and cars. The pressure of life, its demand for expression through action, its demand for recognition, drove her from within. She had merged with it, become one with it, but it was all too much. She was as helpless as a raft in a storm at sea, buffeted by the gale winds, tossed high and low by the raging waves. Anita broke into a run—the drumbeat of her running shoes on the concrete pulsing in her ears, the rhythm of her breath driving her sails.

"Hey!" she heard a voice. "Hey lady, stop!" Anita turned to see a man screaming at her. "Look what the hell you're doing! You're going to kill her!"

"Oh my God!" she said when she looked down at her little dog staring up at her with a panicky look in her eyes, panting heavily, her small tongue drooping from her mouth. "Oh dear God, Mitsy!" she cried, and scooping up the little creature, she snuggled her under her sweatshirt against her chest. Overwhelmed with exhaustion and gripped by a strange sense of desperation, Anita sank to her knees on the spot, weeping bitterly.

"Can I help you, miss?" Anita looked up at the cheerful Salvation Army matron who had pushed through the small crowd of people gathered around her on the street.

"I don't know if anyone can help me." Anita heard her own voice as if from a distance; the hopelessness it betrayed surprised even her.

"There there, dear. It can't be that bad. Let me help you over to that bench." Anita allowed the kindly lady with the sparkling eyes and gray hair to help her to her feet. They sat on the bench beside each other, little Mitsy resting on Anita's lap.

"Here," said the woman as she offered Anita her handkerchief. Anita stared at it blankly. It took a moment before she realized what to do.

"Thank you. You are so kind," she said as she dried her eyes with shaky hands, trying to regain some sense of composure.

"What can I do for you, dear?" the lady was saying with the voice of an angel.

"I'm okay now, just exhausted, and need to get home. I had no intention of walking this far and didn't bring any money with me. If you could lend me bus fare, I'll return it to you."

"Oh, don't worry about that," the matron said as she waved down a passing cab.

"Here," she said, pushing a small wad of bills into Anita's hand. "No no, take it, I insist. You'll pay it back to someone else who needs it, I know you will. Now on your way—God bless you." And before she knew it, Anita was back on her front step fumbling with her keys, having left the cabbie with a generous tip courtesy of the Salvation Army.

Once inside, Anita managed to get Mitsy watered and fed and bedded down with an extra blanket in her doggie bed by the heating vent in the kitchen. She sat down heavily on the floor next to her and tried to comfort her, apologizing over and over again for her selfishness, though, truth be told, her little dog had weathered the ordeal far better than her mistress, and within minutes, the little trooper was fast asleep. Anita breathed a sigh of relief, and it was only then that she became aware of the sound of her beeping answering machine. Summoning what felt like the absolute last reserves of her energy, Anita quietly rose from Mitsy's side and tiptoed to her phone. It was a message from her therapist.

"Hi, Anita, Dr. Sands here. We had an appointment at ten o'clock. Just wondered what happened…"

A shockwave reverberated through Anita. She winced and suddenly felt ill. How could she have totally forgotten they had re-scheduled their regular appointment time for today, Saturday?

Anita derided herself for being so irresponsible though, in all honesty, she had no desire to see Dr. Sands or to go over all she had been through in the last few days.

"Hi, Dr. Sands. It's Anita. I'm so sorry I missed our appointment. I totally blew it. I got caught up and just forgot."

"Are you okay, Anita? You sound a bit shaky."

"No, I mean yes, I'm fine. Just totally embarrassed to stand you up, I guess."

"Don't give it another thought. Remember, I'll be away for two weeks, so shall we plan to meet on the Monday I get back, at our usual time?"

"Excellent. Yes. I'll see you then. Have a good trip."

"Take care, Anita. Bye."

Still feeling disordered and disconnected from her body, Anita reached out to the comfort of habit and began to busy herself by tidying up from the evening before. As she gathered up the empty glasses, bottle and plates from the living room, her eyes came to rest for a moment on the piano. A vision of Jake sitting at the keyboard in quiet concentration flitted into her mind. *It feels like that was a million years ago,* she thought as she released a heavy sigh and headed for the kitchen.

"Well, got to keep moving forward, right, Mitsy?" she whispered as she re-filled Mitsy's bowl. Then noticing Ronny's journal still sitting on the table, she walked over and picked it up, holding it to her chest for a moment before unplugging the phone and slowly climbing the back stairs to her room.

When she replaced Ronny's journal in her desk drawer, she gave it a kiss. "I miss you," she said aloud and headed for the bathroom.

Anita sat on the floor of the shower and let the water pour over her. Twenty minutes later, she dragged herself out and crawled into bed. The numbers on the clock on her nightstand glowed "1:00 PM." It occurred to her that two weeks from now was another anniversary of Ronny's death. She made a little sound—something between a sigh and a whimper—and yielded her consciousness to beckoning sleep.

The Invitation

Jake was struggling—distracted and troubled—ever since spending the night at Anita's. Even on a good day, he had had a hard time with his part-time job at the hardware store. He was completely out of his element selling lawnmowers and tools he really knew nothing nor cared anything about, and the already strained relationship with his manager had only gotten worse. Mr. Kloss was always on him about something or other, always looking for opportunities to criticize, always finding and inventing meaningless tasks to keep him busy. But now when there weren't many customers and his boss was occupied with other things, Jake felt totally lost. When there was nothing for him to do, nothing to divert his attention, he would stand beside the lawnmowers like a ghost, neither in this world nor the next—thinking thoughts he was practically oblivious to, responding to them at some inarticulate emotional level, his heart being pushed and pulled, up and down like a leaf in the wind. He was used to feeling ambivalent about school—that was nothing new—but now he felt dissociated from his whole life, simply going through the motions, somehow making it from day to day. In his infrequent moments of relative lucidity, he recognized that the real source of his discomfort lay in the memories of his childhood, Ronny's journal and his recent conversations with Anita; sadly, the power to do anything about it did not come with this knowledge.

At home in the evening it was not any better. He would look for the easiest way to get himself fed then slouch down on the living room couch in the gloom of the dim shadows cast by the light he had failed to turn off when he left the kitchen. Leaning his head back, he would close his eyes and let the feelings born of his thoughts carry him away until his body and mind yielded to the temporary respite offered by the oblivion of dreamless sleep. There were moments when he felt he couldn't take it anymore and wanted it all to end. He remembered then how Anita spoke about just slipping away—more than anything, he wanted to just slip away. But now there was Anita herself, and he was not alone anymore. In the midst of the gloom of his dark thoughts, he remembered her often and she became for him a beacon of hope for something—he knew not what, but something—better. And so he checked every day to see if the lecture had been rescheduled, and then he would have an excuse to call her. It was only two weeks, but for Jake it seemed like a lifetime.

***

Anita had not slept well. Today was the eighth anniversary of Ronny's suicide. She had tossed and turned most of the night and only fallen into a deep sleep just before dawn.

"Hello?" she said after managing to find the ringing phone on the nightstand.

"Anita?"

"Yes," she said, still struggling to untangle herself from the fog of sleep.

"It's me, Jake O'Brien. Do you remember?"

"Of course, Jake; of course I remember."

"I woke you, didn't I?"

"It's fine Jake, I need to get up anyway, but this is not a good time for me to talk. I'm never at my best when I first get up and..." her voice trailed off as she remembered it was now the anniversary of her brother's passing—an event she preferred to commemorate in solitude. There was silence on the phone.

"Anita, are you there?"

"Yes, Jake." Anita was trying not to sound irritated.

"You were talking and then you just stopped."

"I'm sorry. It wasn't important."

"That's okay. Listen, Anita, I won't keep you then, but I do have something I want to tell you." The excitement in his voice was obvious.

"About the lecture?"

"Well yes," Jake hesitated, "that and also I wanted to tell you I took your advice." Anita's mind went into reverse.

"Advice?" she said.

"Yes, about the piano lessons. I just came back from my very first piano lesson. I took your advice and found someone who lives in the neighborhood."

"Ah, the piano lessons; I forgot I even said that. How did it go?" Anita said, hoping her question wouldn't launch him into a long description.

"It was awesome!" he said, his voice bursting with enthusiasm. "His name is Victor, and he is the most amazing man! I was scared, you know, being a rank beginner and all that—and I suppose because I really wanted the experience to be good I had the old battle of whether I had any right to it—you know, was I worthy?"

"I understand," she said, trying not to sound insincere; her hopes for a quick exit from the conversation dashed, she let her head fall back heavily onto her pillow.

"Anita, listen to me going on and on about it like a kid. I must be boring you to tears."

"Well actually," Anita bit her bottom of her lip. "Well actually," she rallied, resisting the opportunity to cut him off, "I'm really very interested in your story."

"Really? Good, I hoped you would be."

Anita grimaced and could not repress the impulse to comfort herself after she absentmindedly allowed her hand to slip between her thighs.

"Okay, well anyway," he was saying as she touched herself gently, "from the first moment I felt like I had known him all my life—he made me feel that comfortable—and he seemed really interested in me. He asked me what had inspired me to call, and what kinds of music I liked to listen to, and even what kinds of books I liked to read. He seemed very interested when I mentioned sitting at your piano and just letting the sounds find their way out. He asked me if I would show him on his piano. Of course I was really nervous, but I did it, and before I knew it, he was sitting right next to me and we were playing together, you know just letting the sounds come. Anita, it was awesome."

"Jake?"

"Yes?" Jake wondered at the sudden softness he could hear in her voice.

"What did you say his name was?" she said while her fingers continued to evoke little waves of pleasure.

"Victor, Victor Linton."

"That's a nice name. What does he look like?" she asked, her voice soft and a little breathy.

"Well he's tall, taller than me. He's thin and his face is kind of elegant, I guess you would say. He has graying hair…"

"Oh he's older?" Anita said, trying to square the image of the man with her object of satisfaction.

"Yes, but he doesn't seem old if that's what you mean," Jake replied, still clueless as to what Anita was doing. "He's full of energy; he's pretty powerful actually." Anita gave a gentle sigh.

"I can't really describe it, Anita, but it was just so beautiful, even when the notes clashed, so to speak. Really, it was all perfect," Jake said, returning to his narrative.

"Really?" Anita replied, feeling the rush toward completion.

"Yeah. Victor talked about how dissonance, as well as consonance, was a part of harmony—how it mirrored the perfection of life. He said something about the chords of our humanness, and then asked me if I had ever read *Damien* by Herman Hesse. Anita, did you ever hear of Abraxas?"

"Not really, Jake." Jake could hear her heavy breathing now.

"Are you okay, Anita?"

"Oh yes. I'm really good."

"Good. Well, I hadn't either; I ran right out and got the book after the lesson. Abraxas is the God that has both consonance and dissonance—angels and the Devil…"

"Whoa, hang on, Victor, that's really deep stuff and you're starting to lose me."

"Anita, you just called me 'Victor.'"

"Victor," Anita repeated softly as the final wave climaxed on the shore.

"Yeah, guess it was because I was talking so much about him. We both know how easily I get carried away. Anyway, the lecture I called to tell you about is this coming Friday at noon. Do you still want to go?"

"Yes, of course, Jake. I'd love to go."

"Good. Then why don't we just meet outside the auditorium at about 11:55? That should be enough time for you to get across campus after your class, right?"

"Perfect, Jake. See you then."

Anita was in no real hurry to get up. She lay in bed allowing her thoughts to vacillate between Jake and Ronny—Jake and Victor—the present and the past—the misery of life and the pleasure of her fantasy.

Better get up, she thought, *there's work to do,* and feeling the dampness on her thighs, she headed for the shower.

After a short walk with Mitsy and some toast and coffee, Anita went to her study and turned on her computer. Staring blankly at the screen, surrounded by an array of books and papers on the desk and the floor around her, Anita struggled with the problem of putting her thoughts into words. Her treatise on the prosecution of sexual abuse within the priesthood was faltering. *Far too emotional— lacks the compelling power of objectivity,* her professor's voice echoed in her head. *Find your legal voice, Anita. Remember your audience. This is not an article for the Washington Post.*

"It damn well should be," she answered aloud and got up. "I better give it a rest," she told herself and wandered over to the bookcase. Taking a small framed picture from one of the upper shelves, she gently caressed the smooth metal frame as she gazed intently at the familiar image of Ronny and her when they were only six, on the day of their first communion. They were dressed up like a miniature bride and groom. *Perfect for the top of a wedding cake,* Anita thought with a smile as she pictured the two of them standing ankle-deep in cake icing—Ronny looking perfectly angelic, she looking perfectly devilish. Anita's smile broadened as tears began to cloud her vision. "Oh Ronny—what can I do? It was all so wrong; can it ever be made right?" She returned the picture to the shelf and went to retrieve the journal she had been carrying around since she got out of bed. Randomly turning to a page she read:

> *He tells me it is God's will, but I don't understand*
> *how God could will such a thing?*
> *He tells me to accept that the Lord works in*
> *mysterious ways; that it is not for me to understand.*
> *God is supposed to be love, but I don't see love*
> *in his face when he touches me.*
> *I feel dirty and puke and cry all night.*
> *When he hurt me today and I cried, he held me and said,*
> *"Let us pray, for Christ died for our sins."*

"Right, Christ died because a boy cried when you abused him. Is that what you tried to make him believe? You hypocritical pervert, He died for your sins, not my Ronny's, and if there is any justice in His love, you will rot forever in the worst hole of hell." Resisting the impulse to slam the book shut, Anita closed it carefully and placed it back on the desk, then sat down again in front of the computer. Struggling to formulate her thoughts and feelings in the appropriate language of legal argument, she started writing with a vengeance:

What would Thomas Jefferson have to say about the modern-day distortion of the separation of Church and State woefully apparent in the polemics of certain religious leaders defending their right to act as judge and jury when it comes to criminal behavior among their own? I am not arguing against the inalienable right of the individual's beliefs and religious practices within our society, but, is it not also obvious that if ever those practices exceed or pervert the very laws that secure and protect them as a collective within society, that they cannot claim transcendence over those same laws? Put simply: in a nation of laws, not privilege, who can be above the law, and where is the law more clear than in the area of child sexual molestation and abuse?

Anita continued to write feverishly for hours, happily losing herself in her own passionate argument about patterns of accusation and cover-up that reached all the way to the office of the Pope himself; about legislation and the woeful lack of prosecution of the sexual abuse of minors within religious institutions. There were judicial and cultural taboos abounding, she believed, that had colluded for far too long in preventing an open and honest investigation into the matter.

***

Two days later, it was finished. As she held the completed document in her hands, Anita felt for the first time that perhaps she had actually accomplished something for Ronny. She had decided to take a page from Jake's book and do something outrageous. "No, Mitsy, I'm not going to toss it in the garbage, but even if Professor Schmidt hates it, I'm going to find someone to publish it!" She was quietly confident, however, that she had included a sufficient number of legal citations to impress even her stuffy old professor.

The Lecture

Anita could see Jake pacing at the entrance to the auditorium, looking anxiously in her direction as she approached.

"Sorry, Jake," she puffed as she ran up to him, "I had a paper I needed to turn in."

"Just in the nick, Anita. Let's grab a seat."

Anita was surprised; only about fifty people were dotted around the auditorium, and by the look of them, Anita guessed they were mostly students, interns, residents, and perhaps a smattering of staff doctors and therapists. Equally surprised, and feeling a little self-conscious about possibly exaggerating the speaker's reputation, Jake fumbled for an explanation.

"Sam tells me analysts don't always draw the big crowds—but they are a dedicated bunch."

"Great popularity sometimes indicates a low common denominator," Anita replied.

"Wow, cool—very profound, Anita. How about sitting over there?" he said, indicating two seats comfortably back from the podium, yet still close enough to be able to make out the speaker's features.

The auditorium lights were already beginning to dim as they settled into their seats and a bearded middle-aged man in a crumpled suit and tie stepped to the podium. Leaning down a little too close to the microphone, it barked in protest as he began to speak. Repressing the urge to snicker, Anita leaned over and whispered to Jake, "Why do people always have to do that?" Jake smiled and shrugged his shoulders in response. He was feeling happy —happier than he had for weeks.

Anita's spirits were also high, though not totally free of ambivalence. She had been looking forward to seeing Jake though felt conflicted about the lecture itself, and upon hearing the announcer's slight German accent confirmed her most negative preconceptions about psychoanalysts.

The man pushed back a little from the microphone and began to speak. Dr. Anne Rose's credentials were indeed impressive: graduate of the New York University Psychoanalytic Institute, psychoanalyst in private practice since…, adjunct professor at…, consultant to…; the list went on, but the stuffy tone of the man struck Anita as authoritarian—in the same way that the Church was authoritarian—and it made her feel a bit edgy.

She began to seriously doubt the wisdom of accepting Jake's invitation and hoped she wouldn't embarrass herself by dozing off right in front of the speaker, whom, by now, she envisioned as a sixty-something European matron with grey hair severely pulled back into a bun, cold piercing eyes and a droning voice. Apparently Jake had shared her vision because they simultaneously turned to each other when a petite brunette, svelte in a figure-hugging deep red suit, strode confidently to the podium from the other side of the stage. Anita guessed her to be in her late forties. She wore her hair piled high on her head with a few stylish wisps framing her attractive face. Anita leaned forward in her seat to get a better look. The woman's presence and appearance embodied both competency and accessibility. She seemed completely at ease in her own skin and walked purposefully to the podium in her three-inch heels. Anita's interest had definitely been piqued; she was all ears.

In most other circumstances, Jake would have been quite pleased to gaze at such an attractive woman. Beginning with the red high heels, he let his eyes wander to her shapely calves and up her legs to disappear under the clinging red skirt. *Nothing wanting on top either,* he was thinking when Anita whispered to him, "I never thought she'd look like that, did you?" Jake placed his palm across his eyes and stretched out his thumb and forefinger to massage his temples.

"Ah, no," he mumbled, but there was something oddly familiar about her.

Dr. Rose took a moment to compose herself and then briefly gazed out over her audience. Anita was relieved the moment she began to speak—it was immediately apparent she knew how to handle a microphone. She liked her strong clear voice—a voice that reflected her confidence but without any hint of sanctimoniousness—and she found its gentle melodious quality engaging and relaxing.

"Trauma is something we all can relate to because in the course of human life its occurrence seems inevitable—a conclusion I have arrived at based on my own personal experiences as well as those of my friends, colleagues, and patients alike. Trauma spares no one. Rich and poor, female and male, educated and uneducated, no one is exempt from its potentially debilitating effects. This is why I have chosen to speak to you today about *Breaking Through Traumatic Dissociation* from a psychoanalytic perspective.

"But first, before getting too deeply into the subject, I feel it is necessary to make a few general remarks about psychoanalysis. I say necessary because looking out at you—the audience—I see a number of notebooks in the hands of people in their early twenties, and so I'm assuming many of you are students who may associate the term psychoanalysis with descriptions such as archaic, unscientific, and irrelevant. You may even think the whole subject of psychoanalysis is boring—or worse—that it is all a bunch of bullshit, to borrow a colloquial expression."

"Thank you," she said in response to the quiet chuckling she heard from different corners of the hall.

"I know many of you are here because you are expected to attend—because it is part of your training—and yet I also have no doubt that among you there are a few who value the traditional as well the modern incarnations of the rich history of investigation into the human psyche psychoanalysis represents. Don't worry," she said, bringing her open hand to the side of her face, "your secret is safe with me."

There was more chuckling from the audience, this time a bit louder. They were warming to her and she could feel it. Even Anita was surprised to discover how much she was relaxing. There was something about the presence of the speaker—something about her openness that engendered trust. "Weird, Jake," she whispered, "I can't believe how safe she makes me feel. I can feel my tension just melting away." Jake nodded without removing his eyes from the speaker. Apparently, Dr. Rose was having a similar effect on him. Anita liked everything about the woman—even her gestures and her movements because there was nothing extraneous or contrived about them, and the sense of calm she projected seemed to be affecting the rest of the audience as well.

"Now with regard to those individuals who belong to the first category I described, I am hoping that what you hear from me today might create a crack in this well-defended armor against psychoanalysis. And even a tiny crack is all we need. To quote Leonard Cohen, 'that's how the light gets in.'"

The audience waited expectantly as Dr. Rose took a sip of water.

"Decades ago, long before any of us were born—1917 to be precise—Sigmund Freud wrote in his *Introductory Lectures to Psychoanalysis* that trauma 'shatters the foundation of life.' He then went on to postulate that this trauma causes the traumatized person 'to abandon all interest in the present and future... to remain permanently absorbed in—stuck in—the past.' Like so many of Dr. Freud's conceptualizations, this assertion has been studied, modified, re-stated, renewed... but not entirely rejected because it contains a truth that even today, in these more, so to speak, enlightened times, we are still forced to confront the fact that psychic trauma can shatter a human being by destroying the foundations upon which that person has built their inner world—just as surely as physical trauma can kill a human body."

When the speaker paused to allow her audience to absorb what she had said, Anita took the opportunity to open her purse and take out a small notepad and pen, placing them at the ready in her lap.

"You *are* a serious student, aren't you?" Jake whispered to her.

"Got to be prepared," she whispered back as she wrote, *"Psychic trauma as destructive as physical trauma."*

Dr. Rose silently regarded her audience. She was not afraid of silence; indeed she was highly skilled in making use of its power, and her timing was impeccable. Taking another sip of water, she returned the glass to the lectern, let her eyes scan the audience and said, "I think at this point it might be helpful to offer a working definition of 'psychic trauma' to guide us here. This definition is drawn from the definition of 'trauma' found in *Psychoanalytic Terms and Concepts*, published by the American Psychoanalytic Association in 1990, edited by Moore and Fine. 'Psychic trauma is the mental-slash-emotional experience resulting from stimuli—internal or external—too powerful to be dealt with or assimilated in the usual way. What often follows such stimulation is the feeling of being overwhelmed; a state of helplessness, ranging from apathy and withdrawal to an emotional storm accompanied by disorganized behavior bordering on panic, results.'

"Let me repeat for emphasis: When an individual experiences something originating either internally or externally that is *too powerful* to be dealt with or assimilated in the usual way, he or she feels *overwhelmed*, and a state of *helplessness*, ranging from *apathy* and *withdrawal* to an *emotional storm* accompanied by disorganized behavior *bordering on panic*, results."

I can't believe it, thought Anita as she grabbed her pen to make a few more notes—less for their content than to ground the already escalating intensity of her emotional state. *That's me!* she thought. Dr. Rose's words had become like arrows straight to her heart—stirring feelings, opening old wounds, making them bleed fresh blood. She dabbed under her eyes with a tissue.

"Are you okay?" Jake asked.

Anita nodded in affirmation though in truth she was feeling

neither normal nor okay. Her mind was beginning to speed up, and there was a dream-like quality to her thoughts that made it hard for her to stay in her seat. No longer totally at the lecture, she was moving into some emotional juncture where the public lecture became a private session and the doctor was now speaking directly to her, about her. Instinctively she placed her hand on Jake's forearm.

"It is the nature of human individuality," the doctor was saying, "that the experience of psychic trauma—its intensity and duration, as well as its outcome—will be different for each person. For some, a traumatic event can mark the end of healthy development, leaving the person vulnerable to further and repeated trauma, while for others, it can elicit a different response—strength, improved adaptation, a leap forward in development—all depending on one's biology, psychology, and social, or if you prefer, environmental, circumstances.

"Researchers across the fields of psychology, psychiatry, and psychoanalysis tend to agree—it is not the event itself, but an individual's reaction to it that matters most. For example, I have worked with clients who have witnessed the torture and killing of many people, who themselves expected to die, and who still function more adaptively than a client robbed of fifty dollars at gunpoint."

She paused again to let the significance of her remark sink in. *The woman is a gifted speaker,* Jake was thinking, his observation serving his need to create some distance between himself and the topic for, like Anita, the topic was beginning to strike a little too close to home. Being with Anita was enough to bring back the memories of her brother, and with those memories came memories of Monsignor Aleksy and the sexual abuses he suffered in those dark musky rooms and halls of the church. Lightly he placed his hand over Anita's, which still rested on his arm.

"I don't think I am telling you anything you don't already know, but what I would like you to consider in a new way is the unique difficulty that can be observed in, and later described by, traumatized individuals in the throes of struggling to assimilate their traumatic experience. I suggest this difficulty presents itself in the form of a psychological wall that prevents the individual from being able to deal with their experiences the way one normally assimilates experiences; in fact, the existence of this psychological wall can even be considered the *signature* of emotionally crippling psychic trauma. You know," she said in an almost off-hand manner, "our signature is how we are known to ourselves and each other. A signature defines us—summarizes us." Gently withdrawing her hand from Jake's, Anita scribbled on her notepad, *"What is my signature? Who am I?"*

Dr. Rose paused—but this time it was not for the sake of her audience as much as herself—to gather herself for what would be difficult for her to speak about.

"Of course, the question becomes: if this wall exists, then how can it be approached and how can it be breached? In order to illustrate the process with more than theory or speculation, I will draw examples from my own life's experience." There was something in how she said it that everyone in the audience felt— some level of intensity that hadn't been there throughout the lecture that made them sit up and take notice. The speaker was turning the ship into the eye of the storm.

"Nine years ago," she said more slowly and deliberately, "when my son was fifteen, he was involved in a boating accident while we were on vacation in Martha's Vineyard. He was out sailing with some friends when they lost control of the sail in a gust of wind. The boom swung around violently and knocked my son overboard, unconscious." The mention of her son stirred two memories in Jake: the last time he had visited Ronnie's grave and… *Oh my God!* he thought, *the woman at the cemetery was Dr. Rose.*

"We, my husband and I, had just finished lunch and were reading quietly in the living room of our vacation cottage when a police officer and a priest appeared at the door. From that moment everything changed. Time changed; light and sound changed. I felt cold and my mouth went dry; my heart pounded. I wanted to run, but I was frozen to the spot; my husband had to open the screen door for them. 'No, no, no. No! Not my Nicholas,' I heard a woman's voice protesting. The sound was unnatural—almost otherworldly. I had no idea the sound was coming from me. I saw my husband turn to me from what seemed a great distance. There was an expression of horror on his face. Only later did I discover that it was more the sound of my voice than the news of the tragedy that had brought on that look.

"I did not cry, though some part of me, some voice in me, told me I should but I was numb—my psychological defenses were trying to protect me, to keep the reality of the news from destroying me. All I wanted to do was lie down and go to sleep."

There was pin-dropping silence in the hall when she paused. For Anita the intimacy of the story and the feeling of the doctor speaking directly to her made everything feel too close and closing in—pressing heavily on her chest and making it hard for her to breathe. Jake too was caught in the moment; his body felt hot all over and his face was flushed, little beads of perspiration appeared on his forehead. Placing both of her hands on the lectern, Dr. Rose leaned closer to the microphone.

"We can call this state 'shock', but that hardly covers it. It is, *this* is, the inner experience of being overwhelmed and responding with apathy, withdrawal as mentioned in the definition of trauma," she said, her voice having regained a measure of professional objectivity.

"The priest stayed behind when my husband left with the policeman to officially identify our son and claim his body. Just listen to those words, *identify our son and claim his body*. The very formality of the statement is an attempt to create distance, to disassociate oneself from the experience. To this day, I remember how the officer said it, how it in no way connected to what I was feeling. Although the priest remained with me, his presence could not console me. I felt utterly alone—an empty isolation unlike anything I had ever known.

"In an attempt to deal with my anguish, my mind sought refuge in the details of practicality—what needed to be done—but it was a mechanical reaction; there was nothing of me behind it. I started thinking about how I would tell my mother, what we would have to do to get back home—cold details. But the mechanism was not working. I was engulfed in a pain I could neither identify nor escape—a pain greater... different—than anything I had ever experienced before. I wanted to escape, but couldn't; I felt like an insect pinned to a board. I was immobilized—helpless.

"I remember the priest speaking to me in a quiet voice, but I heard nothing. He might as well have been miming. He had no relationship to me. I had no relationship to him. God did not exist. I closed my eyes. I had never felt so tired in my entire life."

Anita's pen slid off her lap onto the floor, but she didn't notice; she was totally absorbed in the story and was still having trouble breathing. She felt like she was suffocating. Jake was shivering and could feel the cold sweat soaking his clothing. He bent over and retrieved the pen, placing it back on Anita's notepad without making eye contact.

"When my husband returned, he had a shattered look on his face, confirming the worst—confirming what we had both known from the beginning. The priest offered a few more words of consolation and left. Frankly, neither his presence nor his absence made any difference to me. Like a robot, I decided to attend to the necessary phone calls. My mother was first. When I heard her voice, the sobbing suddenly cut loose from the depths of my soul. 'He's gone, Mom, our Nicholas is gone... drowned... in a boating accident... he's gone.' I collapsed onto my knees on the floor, and my husband took the phone."

Dr. Rose scanned her audience again. Some were looking down, others were staring at her. On some of the faces she could read shock, in others pain, and in a few something she took to be genuine empathy. There were some blank faces as well. She had seen that before and knew her story had touched them in a way they were not prepared to experience.

"This is the material of traumatic loss," she continued. There was nothing personal in her voice now—no self-pity or sentimentality. "How does one recover from that? How can one re-emerge from what is, in many ways, an experience of profound estrangement—from others, from oneself, from life itself—re-emerge from what is, in essence, an annihilating isolation?"

Anita recognized herself in each nuance of Dr. Rose's agony.

"Yes, how?" Anita pleaded silently.

"'Profound estrangement,' 'annihilating isolation.' I don't use these words casually; they are powerful and effectively represent intense psychological states. These words are drawn from the vocabulary of psychoanalysis. It is a vocabulary imbued with a richness I feel is vitally important to keep alive. Unlike some of the mechanistic language of so-called 'objective' modern science, the sometimes-poetic language of metaphor and ambiguity used in psychoanalytic discourse deeply nourishes our inquiry into the human condition. It is experiential; not merely descriptive. It is a language that speaks to us simultaneously on many levels.

"But to return to the question at hand: What is it then that supports a return to vitality, to life, once a person has become dissociated from themselves? What is it that breaks down the protective wall constructed by the ego to segregate itself from the effects of past traumatic experience and guard itself against future assaults? There are no one-size-fits-all solutions, of course. But time and again, in my study, in my research, in my practice, and in my life, I return to the power of 'attunement.'"

"Yes I know, the word sounds so," she said as she lightly traced little circles with her index fingers in the air around her ears, "so psychobabble." Her timing was perfect. The audience spontaneously burst into laughter, a welcome relief from the depth of feeling they had been experiencing. Even Anita and Jake turned to each other and smiled.

"These days," Dr. Rose continued in a more serious tone, "the neuroscientists speak of mirror neurons that fire in our brains in response to witnessing another's behavior. They speak of this as the possible foundation of what psychologists refer to as empathy.

Empathy: this is another important word—it is about the capacity for insight into another person's world. It is what I saw in some of your faces when I told you the story of my son. Psychologists agree to define it as the ability to experience another's emotional state without losing the awareness of our own. The word I used, 'attunement,' has many of the same qualities as empathy, yet connotes another level of response. Attunement, in the way I use the word, suggests the capacity to bring oneself into resonance with another—to know and feel what another is knowing and feeling from the position of being that other. It is the experience of 'you and I are not we, but one.' Attunement is a process of actual matching—harmonizing if you will—the tuning of one's own frequency to another's vibration.

"We have all heard people say things like, 'I get exactly where you are coming from' or 'I am with you.' These statements can have extraordinary power, but they can also sound trite and even enrage the person they are directed at. The difference in their effect is directly attributed to attunement or the lack there of. Ordinarily we see things from our own perspective—from our own shoes—and statements coming from that perspective can, at best, have only the most limited positive impact, but when one cultivates the ability to see and feel things from the shoes of another, then the effect of these statements can have extraordinary power and can facilitate incredible positive change. I see the difference as being the difference between pity and compassion.

"I believe a musical analogy can serve us well. In music, two different sounds can be played together, resulting in an interval. They are different sounds, but sounding together they form a unity—a single thing—a relationship. Relationship," she repeated for emphasis, "makes one thing out of two, and every relationship has its own unique qualities. What we are communicating to a person when we are attuned to them is, 'We are different, but we are vibrating together in harmony. I am sounding one note and you are sounding another and together we create an interval.'

"Now not all intervals are consonant—representing agreement.

Some intervals can be quite dissonant—representing disagreement. What we learn from music is that all good music embodies and controls both consonance and dissonance. A mistake often made is that people consider consonance good and dissonance bad. But a composer knows the value of both, and when he accomplishes the right balance, he produces a masterpiece. Attunement can have elements of both. The composer—the therapist—knows how to create a functional productive harmony using all the elements available to the situation. This harmony, created from the unique experiences of both the patient and the skillful and attuned practitioner form a certain something representing another, higher place, where hope lives and can be reborn. Together they can create something that neither of them on their own could create. This genuine attunement of which I speak can break through the isolating barrier traumatic experiences create. It can be that powerful. I am living proof, and I am not alone. Are you with me?" she asked, with a sweeping gaze across the audience.

"Are there any questions?"

"It just makes so much sense to me I need to meet this woman," Anita whispered to Jake while quickly scribbling something on her pad.

"Yes," Jake replied. "I was just talking about consonance and dissonance with Victor the other day at my piano lesson. It was like she was speaking directly to me."

"I have a question, Dr. Rose." A female voice came from the back of the auditorium and all eyes turned to a young woman wearing a grey lab coat.

"Dr. Rose, I don't really doubt or disagree with anything you are saying, but I must admit to having a problem with psychoanalysis and what I believe to be Freud's sexist approach to women—not to mention his downright bizarre notions of the Oedipal complex and hysteria."

Dr. Rose moved to the side of the podium to see the questioner more clearly. "Yes, please go on," she said encouragingly.

"Thank you, Doctor. Yes, well, I had to undergo analysis for a certain period of my training, and I found the whole experience horrifying. I never felt so lonely in my life, like I was out there on a limb, exposed and vulnerable, and all the analyst would say was 'hmmm, and what do YOU make of that?'"

There was silence for a moment, followed by a quiet, nervous laughter as the audience wondered how the speaker would respond to the woman's confrontation. But the doctor seemed completely at ease. Anything but intimidated, she appeared to be genuinely interested, encouraging the woman with a warm smile. She walked back and took the microphone from the podium and then moved toward the front of the stage in the woman's direction.

"There are a couple things I would like to say to that," she said softly. "First, I am so pleased you raised these issues. I could feel your sincerity and earnestness when you spoke. I like that, and I am truly sorry for your painful experience. I am not going to try to change your mind, but will you allow me a moment to see if we can keep the baby from being thrown out with the bathwater?"

"I would appreciate that." the young woman said sincerely as she resumed her seat.

"Let me first respond to the claim of Freud's supposed sexism. I'd like to remind everyone here that the criticism needs to be discussed in light of the prevailing cultural views at the end of the Victorian era. I ask you, is it not reasonable to expect that even a great mind, an independent thinker like Sigmund Freud, would still have to be influenced by the views and mores of his time? I am not saying this to make excuses for Freud, only to supply some context to his conclusions and try to find what is relevant in all this to us within our current cultural context.

"From this perspective, let me suggest that the real issue here has more to do with how analysis is understood and practiced today. Unfortunately, as a result of your encounter with one unskilled practitioner, you have decided that psychoanalysis is all rubbish, and though your conclusion is understandable, I would suggest you try to see that it is not professional. I see your lab coat, so I am speaking now as one professional to another. On the personal side, it is true that we all tend to gravitate to people and theories we feel comfortable with; there is nothing wrong with that, but the imperative—the challenge—is to keep an open mind towards those people and ideas to which we are not naturally drawn. Our likes and our dislikes need not change—and in my opinion they usually don't—but we do need to expand the domain of our appreciation in order to take in new things. Exercising the attribute of appreciation leads us to the state of impartiality which is the true cornerstone of genuine professionalism."

She paused and then looking to the woman at the back of the auditorium said, "I am deeply sorry your experience was so painful—I would go so far as to say it bordered on abuse—abuse of the power of relationship," then almost to herself she added, "There is a lot to answer for."

Her pronouncement went through the audience like a shockwave. Dr. Rose lowered her eyes momentarily and then walked back to the podium. Placing the microphone into its holder, she continued, "I know we are running out of time, but before I close I would like to take this opportunity to say something about Freud's writings. Firstly, most people, unless they are training to become psychoanalysts, have never read Freud. They may have read interpretations or opinions of interpretations, or opinions of interpretations of opinions of Freud's writings, but not Dr. Freud himself. Secondly, for those of us who do not speak German, there is the problem of the English translations. Arguably the most widely accepted and influential translation currently used in this country was done by the English psychoanalyst, James Strachey, and published in the 1960s. The undertaking was monumental, and there is no doubt the English-speaking world owes him a debt of gratitude for his efforts, but controversy rages over the accuracy of his works.

"Freud apparently had a very well developed literary style, relying heavily on imagery, metaphor and ambiguity. The only award he ever won for his writings was the Goethe Prize for Literature—that should tell you something. It was Strachey who took common words Freud used, such as 'slips' or 'mistakes' and coined terms like 'parapraxes.' He has been accused of falsely 'scientizing' Freud's works, and as the saying goes, something was lost in translation. These works are currently being re-translated, and while subject to the same laws of subjectivity, the newer translations will hopefully bring more of the true flavor of the man and his ideas into popular culture.

"I hope you can forgive me for making this one final attempt to persuade you to reconsider your understanding of psychoanalysis. I can assure you, psychoanalysis is very much alive and well in its continuing evolution. You may be surprised to learn of the existence of the *Journal of Neuro-Psychoanalysis*, for example, which has been around for decades. If I have inspired you to find out more about current practice in psychoanalysis—which ranges from object relations to self psychology to intersubjectivism and all the wonderful permutations in between—you can pick up a list of recommended readings from the table just outside the door." She held up several pages of densely typed bibliography. "Just some light reading in your spare time."

Everyone laughed, including Dr. Rose.

"Now, I would like to conclude by saying thank you to all of you who have come here today. You have been a very attentive and responsive audience. No speaker could ask for more."

The applause was enthusiastic. Anita continued to applaud vigorously as she made a beeline, with Jake scrambling behind her, for the steps beside the stage where Dr. Rose was already speaking to an earnest-looking young man. Anita nervously awaited her turn, not sure what in the world she would say, or even why she was standing there. But she was calmer now. The unreality of the state she had begun to feel during the lecture had abated, and in its place was left a firm determination to move forward, to face what needed to be faced, but when Dr. Rose turned to her with her full attention, Anita found the closeness to be momentarily disconcerting.

The doctor, recognizing the earnest expression on Anita's face, was the first to break the silence.

"I hope you enjoyed the lecture."

"Oh, yes. Really... I... it... I was wondering... if you were accepting any new patients. I was wondering if... I'm sorry, I don't mean to stand here babbling in front of you."

Dr. Rose regarded the attractive young woman standing before her. Then she smiled warmly and slowly nodded her head.

"Sometimes it is difficult to find words to express powerful feelings. I understand, and if you like, I would be happy to arrange a time for us to meet to see if we think we could work together—if that's what you would like to do?"

"Yes." Anita released a sigh of relief. "Yes, yes. That would be great. Thank you."

The Crux

It was early in the session; Anita was reclining on the couch.

"Well it was a story about a man who is looking for something under a streetlamp," she said. "A passerby asks him what he is doing. 'I lost my key,' the man replies. 'Here under the streetlamp?' the passerby asks. 'No,' he answers, 'I lost it back there in the yard—in the dark.' 'Then why are you looking for it here?' the passerby asks. 'Because the light is better,' replies the man."

"And how did the story relate to your piano lesson?" Anne asked, controlling her tone, not wishing to appear more interested in the story than her patient's experience.

"Well I played a piece of music—something by Franz List—and when I finished, he looked at me and said it came off sounding mechanical, like I didn't understand it. He said it seemed to him that I wasn't really there at all, wasn't engaged with the music, and then he looked at me, like some giant bird—a crane or something—and then, just like that, my whole life's history, the whole thing, just poured out of me—about Mother and Daddy, Ronny, even you—all of it."

"And after that he told you the story?"

"Yes, he told me the story, and at first I thought it was only a joke to cheer me up. I laughed when it was over; I had no idea he was connecting it to my situation. But then he asked me why I was laughing. I told him it was funny, and he replied that in the East, humor is sometimes used to convey a deeper truth. In this case, he said the man was a real teacher and not a fool, and what the story conveyed to those who could *hear* was that truth, being of the nature of light, is never found in darkness. 'Truth,' he said, 'is always found in the light.'" Anita's voice was calm and matter of fact, but Anne observed the curled toes through the openings of Anita's sandals—a sure sign of her patient's tension.

"And that makes two of us," Anne thought to herself, surprised at how irritated she felt about what Anita was telling her. Certainly it wasn't just about the story; she had heard it before and even used it with certain patients to illustrate the foolish ways people attempt to avoid examining their issues. But the way the piano teacher used it, claiming the man was correct, even some kind of wise man, was ridiculous. His approach, if she could even dignify it by calling it an approach, flew in the face of all her training as an analyst—so much of which was aimed precisely *at* getting her patient back into the yard and bringing the light of awareness to those dark places where balance and mental health had been lost. But this session was for Anita, her patient, and her own issues would have to wait for another time. Exercising the self-control of her training and the practiced manner of an experienced therapist, she swept aside her own considerations and merely asked, "Well, what do you think?"

"I don't know what to think, Anne. I feel confused… and a bit annoyed, I guess."

"Annoyed?" Anne said, concerned that perhaps she had not concealed her own reaction as well as she thought and was subconsciously influencing her patient.

"Well, I don't know. He is a very gifted teacher, and so warm, but it felt like he pulled the rug out from under me when he said I was looking for answers in the dark—and I felt criticized…"

"And tell me if I'm wrong here, Anita, but perhaps you think he was out of bounds to be commenting on your personal situation— even if you were the one to bring it up in your lesson."

"I think that may be part of it," she said as she pulled a strand of hair away from her forehead and tucked it behind her ear. "It was more about… well… that he wasn't supporting me."

"After all, how could he say your efforts were misdirected, a waste? What does he really know about what you have been through and what you have gained?" Anne realized her question was giving voice to her own reaction, still she felt she knew her patient well enough to be able to speak to the appropriateness of her comment.

"That's it exactly!" Anita responded. "Still, to be perfectly fair, he never did say I had been wasting my effort." Anita closed her eyes, trying to remember exactly what he said that bothered her so much. "He said, and I remember it pissed me off at the time, that my efforts could be considered an *unnecessary necessity*. Yes that's the expression he used, but I didn't say anything at the time."

"No, I wouldn't think so..." Anne stopped herself from saying anything more, realizing it wasn't the time for touching on father-figure/transference issues. Another opportunity would certainly come. *Unnecessary necessity* she hastily scribbled on her note pad. The remark intrigued her, but what in the world did it mean?

"So tell me more about your confusion, Anita—you said it felt as if he pulled the rug out from under you..."

"Yeah, I can't describe it exactly, but it felt bad and kind of reminded me of how I felt when I left the Catholic Church."

"Like you had been betrayed? Misled? Didn't know what to trust?"

"Sort of, though I really can't say I felt any malevolence or agenda behind his remarks; still, I guess I could say it rattled my belief in the value of what we have been doing."

"Does that scare you?" Anne noticed the stirrings of apprehension within herself, but could not discern its source. Was it coming from Anita's experience or was it from her own—or a bit of both?

"Yes, I guess it does. It makes me wonder, have I have been deluding myself?" Anne could feel in her patient's question a reaching out to her for an affirmation, but not wanting to close down the opportunity the question afforded, she decided to explore it further.

"This really is an important question, Anita; I'm glad you've brought this up. How can you know whether our work *is* accomplishing anything or merely producing imaginary successes and imaginary gains? It does go to trust, doesn't it? What or who can we trust, and why do we need to look to others for confirmation?"

Anita nodded her head. "Well I guess I have to learn to trust my own experience. Doesn't it just come down to that?" Anita gave a little laugh and added, "You see how screwy this is? Now I'm seeking your agreement again. Why would I need it if I really believe that my own experience is all I need?"

"It is an irony, isn't it?" Anne replied neutrally, though she was really quite pleased with her patient's insight—a patient who seemed to be more with it at the moment than she was. Anne knew she wasn't on her game today. She found the remarks of this piano teacher surprisingly unsettling, like the feeling one gets from the chill of the first north wind that blows on a late summer's morning heralding the march of the seasons, reminding one of the inevitability of change. Anne gave an involuntary shudder and made another note before ending the session.

***

Later that evening, while sipping wine in the refuge of her living room, Anne felt relieved to have the opportunity at last to reflect on her session with Anita. It had nagged at her the rest of the day during sessions with other patients; it was in the back of her mind while responding to phone calls and correspondence. No doubt, if it weren't for her continued agitation, she would have eaten more than a snack of crackers and cheese when she got home, but from the moment Anita had left her office, Anne knew all she really wanted to do—all she had to do—was explore her feelings and her unusual reaction to their session. Why had it disturbed her so much? She took another sip of wine and closed her eyes. All she could see was a shadowy faceless figure whose name was Victor. *Unnecessary necessity* it repeated and Anne could discern a knowing smile, coolly aloof and just a little too self-assured. She took a deep breath and, resting her elbow on the arm of her chair, lightly cradled her chin between her thumb and the side of her index finger. *Okay,* she thought, *what's really going on here? So this Victor sounds arrogant and his opinions contradict my own, but is this enough to explain, let alone excuse, the intensity of my reaction?* She answered herself with a gentle shake of her head. "Again I ask you, kiddo, what's with all this defensiveness?" she said aloud.

Anne placed the side of her index finger between her lips as she found her thoughts drifting back to her college days and a similarly unsettling story in a book a young philosophy student had given her. *What was his name? Was it Dennis?* Anne moved her hand back and forth, allowing her finger to lightly caress her lips. They had met only once, in the park on a warm sunny afternoon, and she never saw him again. She was wearing a colorful, flower-print summer dress, sitting in the grass under a tree reading a novel. He had approached, and she had been a little annoyed, but he did seem nice enough, and he certainly wasn't obnoxious. He smiled a lot and presented himself with the right mix of confidence and deference, and while attempting to engage her in conversation, he never let his eyes wander from hers. Recalling the moment, Anne allowed her fingertips to trace the memory of the plunging neckline of the little sundress.

What the hell am I doing? she thought. *I can't believe I'm thinking about this guy and getting myself turned on!* Anne gave her head an involuntary little shake and took another sip of wine. *And why in the world did I even start remembering that day in the first place? Ah yes, it was that parable in the book Dennis, or whatever his name was, gave me. I must have read it a hundred times.* Anne knew exactly where it was; she walked over to the bookshelves and took it down. It opened right to the story and she began to read:

Nuri Bey was a reflective and respected Albanian who had married a woman much younger than himself. One evening when he returned home earlier than usual, a faithful servant came to him and said, "Your wife, our mistress, is acting suspiciously. She is in her apartments with a huge chest, large enough to hold a man, which belonged to your grandmother. It should contain only a few ancient embroideries. I believe that there may now be much more in it…"

Anne returned the book to the shelf. She remembered the story only too well. Nuri Bey had confronted his wife with the servant's suspicions and asked to be allowed to open the chest. "Because of his suspicions, or because you do not trust me?" was her response, and before he could answer her, she gave him the key to the chest and left the room. Nuri Bey sat with the key for a long time and then called his servant and the gardener. Together they picked up the chest, carried it to a distant part of the estate and buried it. The story ended: "The matter was never referred to again."

The story still made Anne uncomfortable. How could they all go on after that: she, never knowing if he had opened the chest; he, never knowing if there had been a man inside of it? *Was this a supreme example of denial, or was there something else to it—like the damn little story of the key and the streetlamp?* she thought. *And so, dear, here we are again right back at the beginning. What is bothering you about all this? It's not about competition with this piano teacher; you know enough to realize that these stories can have many meanings, and there's no need to prove the validity of your interpretation.* Anne took another sip of wine and then walked slowly across the room to the window. Her attention was drawn to Venus twinkling in the darkening evening sky. Day was exchanging its dusky cloak for nighttime indigo, and the vastness of the universe began to weave its magic spell upon her. Anne watched as one by one the stars revealed themselves in the arching firmament. The room darkened and disappeared around her as she was drawn up and inwards. "We are the stuff of stars…" she said aloud and tilted her head to gaze higher into the firmament. "So, my brothers and sisters, speak to me."

She placed her glass on the table beside the window and felt a current of relaxation flood her body. The tenseness in her stomach she had been carrying unnoticed eased, and the entity within her she had come to call "the witness," appeared. She became aware of her inner and outer worlds and watched her thoughts appear and disappear as her attention probed the deepening darkness of the sky, where suddenly a veiled star came into view—a star that had been there all along—like the key in the shadows.

Could empathy be the key here? she wondered. *To understand his position, I need to stand in his shoes. I need to be able to consider him in his entirety—as a whole—from the inside. Now how am I going to do that since I don't know anything about him?* Softly, so as not to re-awaken the world, Anne opened the French doors and stepped onto the balcony. The cool of the evening engulfed her as she settled into her favorite deckchair to listen to the chorus of thousands of voices singing their praises to the night.

This is how she did it now. No longer did Anne attend church services where she would squirm with anger and grief. No more weeks spent on spiritual "intensives" that left her exhausted and frustrated. No more tedious lectures from dreary, po-faced philosopher analysts. That was all so far away now. The fruits of the decades of discipline remained within her, but the structures evaporated as if they had never been... *because they never were.* So ran her thoughts. Now she communed directly with... with what exactly? Anne would be hard-pressed to elaborate, to even explain to herself what she did. It was something about opening, without effort, allowing influences, higher influences, to reach her. But there was no need to explain, to her or anyone else. This was so personal—and not just about her mind. Her whole being was involved—the spiritual and the mundane, her celestial self and her womanhood, aspiration and sexuality. There were no conflicts here—conflicts she learned from the church, conflicts tacitly implied by so many teachings. She took a deep breath and heard her inner voice, *We are united in trauma—in suffering—but our nature is joy.*

The Challenge

It was five past the hour when Anne heard the door of her waiting room open and close. It was not like Anita to be late. She rose from her chair, ready to greet whatever might be waiting there for her—it didn't take long for her intuition to be confirmed. Standing quietly in the office doorway she watched unnoticed as her usually graceful patient struggled with her hat and coat and then all but slammed them down over the back of the chair. Anne could read the irritation in every movement Anita made.

"Good morning, Anita. You okay?" she called from the office door.

"Oh, hi, Anne, you startled me. Yeah I'm okay."

"Well come on in and we'll get started."

"I know, I'm sorry I'm late—definitely a little distracted today—but my tardiness can be blamed on God," she said, attempting a thin smile.

"Let's talk inside," Anne replied and stepped aside to allow her patient to precede her into the office. Anita went directly to the couch, where after adjusting the skirt of her tailored brown business suit, she reclined in her customary position with a deep breath.

"That a new vase?" she asked while pointing across the room at the little table near the door.

"Actually it's been there for a while," Anne said as she settled herself on the nearby big leather chair.

"But you moved it from somewhere else, right?"

"It's always been right there, Anita; I guess you just missed it," Anne said with a little smile. *This is definitely not the Anita I usually see,* she thought.

"Well I am a little discombobulated—those holy rollers really piss me off," she said while tugging at her skirt, which had crept up her thighs.

"I think it might be a good idea to start from the beginning." The doctor's voice was gentle yet subtly probing. "You said when you came in that God made you late today; how so?"

"Well, it was kind of a joke, but not really—first, I slept through my alarm, and that started it, and of course, because I was running late, I got stopped just as I was heading out the door by the holy rollers, you know, the Seventh Day Adventists. They always seem to appear at the worst possible times; it's like they have radar or something," Anita said with a little laugh. Raising her palm up next to her head she continued, "Had I been on time, they never would've caught me."

"Hence your statement that God was to blame."

"Well, as I said, it was just a little joke, but you know, it's odd; those people really do piss me off."

Anne was quick to recognize the opportunity presented by the verbalization of such a strong emotion; it spoke to her of a willingness in Anita to examine her complicated and deeply conflicted relationship with religion, God, and religious practice. "What is it that pisses you off?" she asked, her tone of voice perfectly attenuated to encourage her patient to venture into the tangled undergrowth of her inner world.

"Well, for one thing, they're so… so… *clean*. And I always get a weird feeling from them like they aren't quite human—you know—there's something robotic about them. Anyway, there they stood blocking my door—a young man in a dark suit and two young women in those black coats they always wear—asking me if I have God in my life." Anne picked up her pen and pad from the table beside her.

So clean and robotic, she wrote. The choice of words was

significant. *Sees church people as clean… implies she sees herself as dirty? Robotic—an internalized belief indicating the faithful are something less than human?* Anne placed her pen and pad on her lap.

"And so…" she said lightly, not wishing to interrupt the flow of her patient's narrative, knowing from experience that people reveal much more about themselves than they realize when they are talking about others.

"Yeah, well you can imagine what I said."

"Tell me," Anne encouraged her.

"I'm afraid I was a bit rude," Anita paused.

"Rude?" Anne said softly, realizing that to say more at the moment—to exercise the influence of her own authority—could risk bringing premature closure to the issues—effectively burying rather than unearthing them.

"Yes, I was so annoyed that these total strangers had the nerve to confront me with such a question. I told them that as a matter of fact, God was in my kitchen drying my dishes, and if they wanted to speak to him, they would have to come back later when he wasn't so busy; meanwhile, I was running late. And with that, I pushed past them, slamming the door behind me."

"I like that." Anne gave a slight chuckle. "I'll have to remember your line the next time they knock on my door."

"I want credit for it," Anita joked.

"Of course," Anne joked back but was quick to respond when Anita's expression abruptly faded from a smile to a frown.

"What is it?"she asked.

"I started thinking about why I slept through my alarm this morning. That doesn't happen very often, and I didn't have a particularly late night either. I guess I didn't sleep very well."

"Oh?"

From the beginning, Anita always found her therapist to be genuinely interested in her as a person and because of that, she was able to be more open with Anne about her inner life—more open than she had ever been before in therapy. But this morning she was finding it difficult.

"Bad dreams," was all she said before retreating once more into her private reverie.

Anne was patient and willing to wait; it was an ability that served her well with her patients, but she also knew that in this situation, if she remained silent too long, Anita could drift beyond reach and a real opportunity could be lost. So after several minutes, she ventured an interpretation. "You know, Anita, we've often talked about the theory in psychoanalysis that there are no accidents. I'm wondering if sleeping through your alarm was an unconscious act of defiance, or rebellion—perhaps you really don't want to be here today at all." There was no hint of judgment in her voice because there was no judgment to be made—Anne was simply wondering aloud, so Anita's defenses were not put on alert, but her message apparently got through loud and clear. Anne watched as her patient's shoulders began to tremble as heavy sobs rocked her body. Gently offering her a tissue, she sat back to wait as Anita dabbed at her eyes and then blew her nose.

"Well, just look at me going all to pieces," she suddenly blurted out. "There I was, well and truly off in my own world, playing out the scene with the Seventh Day Adventists all over again, when I began thinking about all the 'churchy' people I've known in my life, and I felt myself getting more and more annoyed. And then, for some reason, I remembered one of my dreams…" Anne felt they might be getting to something important but chose to remain silent.

Anita hesitated then turned onto her side, propping herself up on her elbow. "It was shocking because I was having sex with Ronny—and believe me, there was no way I was going to tell you about it—but then, what you said about maybe sleeping through the alarm was defiance or rebellion on my part—it was like you were reading my mind…"

"But why the sobs, Anita?"

"Because I saw so clearly that you 'get' me, and yet, I never feel like you judge me. I've never experienced this in my life…" she murmured as the sobbing broke through again. "With you, I always feel," she hesitated, "accepted…"

"I'm glad you feel that way, Anita; your feelings are not misplaced," Anne said with a warm smile, handing over more tissues. "And why the sigh?" she asked simply when Anita stopped crying, taking care not to probe too deeply too fast.

"Yes, well I guess since I brought it up, I should probably tell you about the dream."

"Okay," Anne said, reaching for her pencil and pad. "I'm ready."

"Well, I don't remember the whole thing—mostly just the end. I was in the church where Ronny and I grew up. I was the only one there, and I think it was night because all of the stained-glass windows were dark and the lighting in the church was very harsh. I was standing in a place towards the front of the congregation where all the pews had been removed. I remember thinking how awful it looked—the floor was so ugly, linoleum had been laid over the wood and it looked old and dirty.

"Anyway, I was just standing there looking around, and then I realized my lover was there with me. I couldn't see him, but I knew he was there. Then the scene shifted and we were on the floor behind the altar having sex. It was very dark, and it was very exciting because it was so forbidden. And then he turned so I could see his face, and it was Ronny—my own brother! He was laughing and he said, 'Fooled you. You're it!' and that's when I woke up."

Anita rolled off her elbow onto her back, breathing rapidly, her hands laced over her stomach.

"Any thoughts?" prompted Anne after she finished her notes.

"Well I'm thinking I had the dream because I had read a bit of Ronny's journal last night. Not that I was ever as religious as he was, but as a child I always did find the church rather beautiful and otherworldly. The whole nasty business with Ronny and his suicide certainly altered my view of the church, so in the dream it's barren and tacky—I mean, what could be tackier than a linoleum floor?"

"Quite so, and what about the lover and the sex behind the

altar? Anything come to mind about that?"

"I guess in some way my feelings for Ronny were as close as I've ever been to having feelings like someone might have for a lover. I don't know; I definitely have a lot of resistance to going there—I mean, thinking about having sexual feelings towards my own brother is rather… awful."

"Understandable, though, as you said, the sex in the dream may simply be a symbol of the closeness you feel towards him."

"That does make sense to me. I certainly can't remember ever having sexual thoughts about him—not consciously anyway. It also makes sense I'd expect to find Ronny in the church—and finding him and being with him would make me happy. And he did used to tease me too—'Fooled you. You're it!' That would make sense coming from his mouth."

"I can see that Anita; is there anything else?"

"Not really… not now anyway."

"Shall I tell you what occurred to me?" Anne ventured.

"Absolutely!" Anita said as she shifted into a sitting position on the side of the couch—better able to see her doctor's face.

"Like you," Anne began slowly, "I was struck by the fact that the church is barren and tacky—right down to its foundation; and I agree with your analysis that its symbolism is consistent with the transformation in your attitude towards the church after you discovered the abuses Ronny suffered. I also find it significant that the stained-glass windows are all dark, the lighting is harsh, and that you mentioned no beautiful or inspiring images of Christ or the saints. Thinking back to your comment about me not judging you, this 'harsh' suggests to me how you feel you've been judged all your life. And yet, before you discover your lover, you're completely alone in this room. It makes me wonder who it is that judges you so harshly. Could it be you who is your own harshest critic?"

Anne stopped for a moment to observe how her patient was taking in her suggestion. Her expression seemed serious, thoughtful, but not defensive. She decided she could continue.

"And so in your dream, you interject the presence of your lover—again, perhaps it's something in you, with which, in this case, you need to connect. And you do, in the darkness behind the altar—which is interesting because isn't that where the priests usually stand?"

"Yes, I hadn't considered that."

"So, it's complicated. You said you were excited because it's forbidden. Maybe something in you thinks you shouldn't be connecting with this loving part in yourself, and another part of you, a more defiant aspect of your personality, turns this into excitement—turns it into a game, as opposed to the serious business it is for you. And then, it literally becomes a game, because now it's hide and seek: 'Fooled you! You're it.' I can't help but think it suggests you are both the one who is hiding and the one who is seeking yourself."

Tears were trickling down Anita's cheeks as she lifted her eyes and turned her face towards Anne. "But Anne, what about making love in the place where the priest stands?"

Anne nodded her head slowly and in an even softer tone said, "I suppose some might say this represents your own dark, disavowed desire to have with your brother what the priest had with him—but I don't buy that."

"Why not?" Anita asked timidly, feeling somewhat relieved.

"Because your brother did not experience love in the sexual acts he was forced into—there was no love, ever, expressed in them. I'm more inclined to think that this scene offers something of a solution to your situation." Anne momentarily debated with herself whether to continue. She felt the certainty of truth in what she was about to say, but was not altogether sure whether Anita was ready to hear it. She decided to take a risk.

"Again, these are just my thoughts. You are free to disagree. What popped into my head was the juxtaposition of meeting with your lover and being in the priest's 'place.' Maybe this harsh critic you have inside needs to give way to love—not only towards yourself, but also towards the priest." She could see Anita's entire body stiffen and a subtle glow of anger in her eyes. "Remember, Anita. There are many layers of meaning in any dream, and anything I say might reflect only a small part of what is going on; so even if what I suggest doesn't resonate within you, don't immediately reject it. I'm not saying to accept it either, just try to figure out why you are reacting to the statement. This can really help."

"Well, Anne, until that last bit, I was feeling like you were really onto something, about the harshness I deal myself and my need to find and embrace the loving part of me..." Anita took a deep breath and gathered herself before she continued. "But to tell me I should put love in the place of hatred towards the priest really pisses me off." She slammed her mouth shut so as not to explode in a full rage and say things she knew she would regret.

"Anita," Anne's voice was soft and soothing. "I am not telling you to do anything. I am only telling you what I thought your dream might be saying—in other words, what you are trying to tell yourself to do. And if I'm wrong, I'm wrong. Really, you and only you know what the truth is."

"Okay," Anita replied, sounding unconvinced.

"These things take time, Anita. We can only go as fast as we can go; the seed breaks ground in its own time, grows stem and leaves in its own time, and flowers fully in its own time. We can nurture, we can protect, but the plant grows and flowers by virtue of its own intelligence. You have brought a lot here today, and we are now out of time—I believe at the right time."

Anita looked surprised. "I totally lost track of the time, but you're probably right that it's a good place to stop. I don't think I could give or take any more right now."

Anne smiled. "Any more today would probably be less," she said.

"I agree. Thank you, Anne."

As Anne watched Anita depart, she noticed the change in her patient's demeanor from when she first arrived. Although the edge was gone, in its place she could read uncertainty. *Will she be able to digest all this or is it too soon yet?* she thought. *Well, we'll see. This could be a very significant time for her,* she thought. She released a long sigh—a sigh that spoke of hope and concern and the challenge that lay ahead for her patient.

There but For the Grace of God Go I

He noticed it as soon as she came in for her lesson: her typically vibrant youthful complexion now pale and drawn, the tight clench of her jaw, something cold and seething in her eyes. She all but stomped through the room on her way to the piano, sat down hard without even taking off her coat, and then jerked her head around to face him.

"Hi, Victor," she said, pretending a smile—a smile like her mother's, a smile so fake that beyond its obvious dissimulation it would not convince anyone of anything. He met her eyes but said nothing, gestured nothing. Quickly turning back to the piano, she lifted her briefcase from the floor and busied herself finding her music.

"Well, should I play the Bach?" she said while staring at the piece of music in front of her. *Shit,* she thought, *I knew I should have cancelled this damn lesson.*

Her teacher remained silent, simply walked over to the old stuffed chair and sat down.

"Okay," she said and put her hands on the keys and began to play. Two measures into the piece she stopped and started again without pause. Then she stopped again. It was a simple minuet she had played a hundred times.

"I'm really sorry, Victor; I knew I shouldn't have come today— I have a lot on my mind."

Still he said nothing. He had that power—the power to say nothing—the power of silence that could evoke a response in ways which words could not.

"I've had a very difficult day," she continued, still not taking her eyes away from the piano. "I should leave now; I shouldn't have come." The silence was getting to her; she felt herself becoming even more annoyed.

"Of course I'll pay for the lesson. I'll be okay by next week," she said, turning to face him.

He continued to look at her; it wasn't a stare, it wasn't a glare, it was neither probing nor vacant, it was just nothing, and it only added to her discomfort. Anita had never known a look like this. It was impossible to read him—definitely not her mother's stony silence—not even her analyst's silent invitations. No, Victor's silence was empty—like consciousness directed at nothing; and it was this emptiness, this consciousness with no aim beyond itself that opened her up in a way that nothing else could.

"I've just seen Anne, my analyst, and we've been working through stuff connected to my brother Ronny and his suicide... no... his murder!" she paused and then added, as if rendering her final verdict, "Yes, murder by that pervert priest who abused him. He's as responsible as if he had put the noose around Ronny's neck himself. I hate him! I hate the idea of him!" Anita placed the tips of her fingers to her lips and held her breath. Her teacher took it all in—what she emanated, what she said.

"God, I'm a mess today," she continued, her voice sounding more vulnerable, more desperate now. "How could he have gone on living, spreading evil wherever he went, after Ronny paid for his abuses by hanging himself? I just don't get it. What about the hypocrisy, the lies, the cover-up, don't they need to be addressed?"

Her teacher continued to watch, absorbing it all—the words, the hunched shoulders and clenched fists, the throbbing artery at the side of her neck. Only when she was totally spent and lapsed into a mute silence did he finally speak and in a voice that was barely a whisper. "There, but for the grace of God, go I," he said.

Anita wasn't sure she had heard him. "What?" she shot back.

"There, but for the grace of God, go I," he repeated. She heard him this time, and she didn't like it. Not that she knew why, she didn't even know what he meant, but something about the remark rekindled her rage—like gasoline on smoldering embers.

"And what exactly do you mean by that?" she said sharply and shook her head with disgust. "No, I mean I need to go," she said brusquely as she grabbed for her sheet music and began stuffing it into her briefcase. *How dare he judge me!* She was fuming inside. *Not him, not my mother, not the fucking Church*—nobody can do that to me. Anita was up and nearly at the door when she felt his hand lightly touch her shoulder. She spun around, ready to speak her mind, ready to fight, but there was something in his gaze that made her fall silent, inside and out. Suddenly she felt deeply ashamed.

"Sit for a moment," he said and pointed in the direction of the old couch by the door. Anita could do nothing but comply. She walked to the couch, sat down heavily and placed her briefcase on the floor at her feet. He followed her to the chair nearby and after seating himself uttered a deep audible sigh.

"You asked me what it meant," he began slowly, "the statement 'there, but for the grace of God, go I.' It is the game of King and Beggar, nothing more." His voice was soft and gentle, seeming to come from somewhere far away.

Anita shook her head. "I have no idea what you are talking about," she murmured.

"I know," he replied. "Let me try to explain. In this game, the king is a haughty king—quite taken by himself and his position. One day he's looking out of a palace window and he sees a nearly naked beggar in the street. 'Look at that miserable wretch,' he says to himself, 'what arrogance to lie out there in front of the palace where I may see him!' You see, Anita, this king, because of his pride of being a king and his disgust for the beggar, has sowed the seeds for his next lifetime as a beggar."

"I don't know what you are driving at, Victor," she said defensively, "and I don't know that I even believe in 'a next lifetime.'"

"Well you can take it as a parable to explain relationships. The king and the beggar are in some sort of a relationship, yes?"

"I guess," she said while crossing and uncrossing her feet. "Okay, so go ahead."

"Are you sure?" he asked gently.

"Yes," she responded without conviction and then added, "Perhaps I'm meant to hear it." Victor pressed his lips together and tilted his head a little to the side.

"Perhaps," he said softly. "And it so happened that when the king saw the beggar in the street, the beggar in the street looked up into the palace window and saw the king in all his finery and began to lament his poor and miserable life. 'Oh, if only I were a king and not a wretched beggar,' he thought—his heart filled with envy and hate for the king and all his fortune and superiority—and thus did the beggar sow the seed for his next lifetime as a king.

"Of course, at some point they both die and the beggar takes his next life as a king and the king returns a beggar. Now in their new lives, the beggar turned king is haughty and the king turned beggar is envious and thus a relentless pendulum of exchange is established that continues to swing for lifetimes on end."

"How horrible!" Anita said, warming to the story.

"Horrible," Victor repeated. "I would say vicious because the law of cause and effect is vicious in its impersonality. But see how it goes, the story is not over, for one day after many lifetimes of exchanging their roles, the king looks out the window again and sees the beggar, but this time he is no longer haughty. Many lifetimes of being both—playing both parts—have loosened his attachment to his role and consequently weakened his pride. Now, when he sees the beggar he says to himself, 'Oh, look at that beggar, is there really any difference between him and me? Both beggar and king I have been—in fact, I am really neither.' Meanwhile, at the same time, the beggar looks up and sees the king in his palace and says, 'Oh, look at the king, is there really any difference between us? Both beggar and king I have been—so, in fact, I am really neither.' And at that moment, the vicious pendulum of cause and effect is broken for them both; the law that is called *karma* has been satisfied, and they are both free. Anita, can you see what I am saying?"

Her head was swimming. "I don't know," her voice wavered so she hardly recognized it herself. "It makes me feel strange, this story, and I really can't say why. I understand that it's about reincarnation, but like I said, I don't know anything about that. So it speaks of relationship and attitudes, and the traps we create for ourselves by our attitudes. But how are you applying it to me and to Ronny and to the priest?" She was gaining momentum. "Are you saying I've been an abuser or Ronny was, so he got abused, or maybe the priest had been abused so he had to become the abuser? I can't accept any of that, but even if I did, so what? Are you saying I'm supposed to forget all about it, not hold him accountable?"

"Anita." The steadiness of her teacher's voice made her stop. "These questions—your questions—arise in your mind as thoughts, but thoughts are the wrong instrument—too slow and clumsy. What thoughts can't know, cannot reach, the heart knows. You said the story makes you feel strange. Perhaps it touched something deeper—some real feeling."

Maybe it was how he spoke as much as what he said. Something about the quiet surrounding him and the quality of his voice—soft yet piercing—held her usual defenses in abeyance. They simply didn't function—didn't seem to need to because they couldn't find anything to hold on to.

"Whatever it is, it is a stranger to me," Anita said. "Still, I agree, I am feeling something different now." This was new territory for Anita and but for the sound of her teacher's voice, she had no compass. The echo of her own voice in her ears sounded childish, shrill, and annoying. She was beginning to feel remorse. The word "sacrilegious" floated into her mind, but she pushed it away. She was observing herself now from a new vantage point, an open space deep within, viewing herself as if from a great distance. She was no longer judging, merely seeing.

Suddenly she was aware of her teacher's voice. "I will try to speak to your questions," he said. "It seems to me we can boil them down to these two: What is this story about, and why are you telling it to me? You are correct that I am bringing up the subject of relationship: in this case, the relationships that exist between you and Ronny, Ronny and the priest, you and the priest, you and your mother, Ronny and your mother, and your mother and the priest. I am suggesting, by my story, that the 'fates' of all of you are bound together and also, and this is perhaps the more difficult idea to accept, that for any one of you to become free, all of you must become free, and for this to occur, all of you must first see yourselves in the others.

"In my story, it was necessary for the king and the beggar to exchange roles many times before they were able to dissociate themselves from these roles. When I first heard your story, I said, 'There, but for the grace of God, go I.' I tell you truly, I seldom use this kind of biblical reference. Perhaps I was just picking up on the whole Church tie in? I really don't know, it just came out.

"But Anita, I have had the good fortune in life to meet some remarkable people. I have learned a lot from them, still I stand before you incomplete and flawed. I see myself as being surrounded by angels and heroes, but I don't mistake what I've learned from what I am. I could never ascribe blame to you or to anyone else. I can't read the karmic footprints that have led you all to this place, but I do know this, unless you all can put yourselves in the other's place and see each other with compassion, you will never be free, which is why I offer this story to you now."

These words had an unusual effect on Anita. For a moment, her thoughts and feelings became quiet: the briars and tangled vines of her anger and sorrow had been swept away. There was no argument, no division in her now. She remained quiet and still for a long time. Victor was silent too, profoundly so…

Gradually, Anita became aware of the ticking of the grandfather clock in the hallway. "There isn't enough time in one lifetime for all that," she heard herself saying, "and what about the two players who are gone? Ronny and the monsignor are both dead."

"Perhaps, but wouldn't you agree, the relationships still exist? A wise woman, Simone Weil, once wrote that following the loss of someone, 'his presence is now imaginary, but his absence is very real: henceforward, it is his way of appearing.'"

Anita struggled to take in what she had just heard. Her thoughts had become distracted when her teacher mentioned the "wise" woman—it was a reaction she had acquired to anyone and anything she identified as authority—but the words 'way of appearing in the present moment' had caught her.

"I'm sorry, Victor, what did she say, that woman?"

"Simone Weil," he said and slowly repeated the statement.

"Yes, who is she?"

Victor closed his eyes and for a moment saw himself as a little boy at his grandmother's house.

"Who's that?" he said, pointing to the photograph of a woman with dark hair and remarkable eyes that seemed to be greeting him from behind a pair of wire-rimmed spectacles. "Is it you?" Victor remembered the amused look on his grandmother's face when he asked.

"No, darling," she had said, "but she is a special friend of your Zadie and me."

"Can I meet her, Bubby?" he asked.

"Yes, dear, but now you can only meet her in her absence." Victor hadn't understood, but neither did he ever forget his grandmother's words.

"Victor, are you okay?" Anita asked. She had never known her teacher to drift away like this.

"Yes, I'm okay," he said softly, his eyes still closed.

"You became so quiet; did you fall asleep?"

A gentle smile played on his lips. "No. I was just recalling an old memory."

"You were telling me about Simone Weil," she prompted.

"Yes," he repeated, his eyes now half-open, his voice sounding as if it were traveling to her from some distant place. "It has been said that the present exists to repair the past and to prepare for the future. I find a great deal of hope in this assertion." His eyes were now fully open as he looked at his student. "Do you, Anita? Do you think we can change?"

Anita felt his question resonate throughout her whole body and the way he looked at her, what was it she saw in his eyes? *Is this compassion?* she asked herself.

The Party

Anita's life was on an upswing—something she hadn't experienced very often in the troubled years since Ronny's death. Sessions with Anne were going well, and she was making real progress. Her piano lessons with Victor had become less turbulent and her piano playing was really improving—even Jake could hear the difference. She could finally see the light at the end of the tunnel with school, and she was already exploring options for after graduation. All this and more: spring had grudgingly come to Chicago—the weather was mild, trees and shrubs were blossoming, daffodils were peeking out and crocus was in full bloom. Yep, it was definitely time to have a party, her first since childhood. She would think about it on her morning run.

Anita felt good on the inside and wanted to look good on the outside as well. She chose the black sports bra and little running shorts she knew were sure to draw a few admiring glances and decided to let her hair be free. She had recently splurged on a soft perm, her first, and had the stylist put in some red highlights. When she stood in front of the closet mirror, she liked what she saw, and after turning to the side for a final glimpse, she was off for her run.

Bouncing down the stairs and out the front door, she decided to take a different route through the little side streets to the park that runs for miles along Chicago's lakefront. It was a bright sunny day. The temperature was perfect, her body felt rested and strong, and her breathing easily fell into harmony with the tempo of her movements. By the time she hit the path along the lake, she was in full stride and quickly closed on the figure jogging in front of her. "Check that out!" she said to herself while admiring the well-toned shirtless body in tight running shorts. *Nice ass! Bet he would be fun in bed—let's pass him and give him something to look at.* Anita smiled and said, "Hey," as she ran past him. She felt his eyes follow her after she cut in front of him, and she could not refrain from a little grin of self-satisfaction. Through the trees she caught glimpses of Lake Michigan, sunlight sparkling on the calm blue water. The park was filled with other runners, walkers, bikers and people playing every sport known to a ball.

After her usual two and a half miles, Anita turned back toward her house and began thinking about the party. Who would she invite? Some friends from law school, her neighbors, Claire and Eric, who lived in the greystone next door, Anne, Victor, and of course Jake. *I'll fill in some others as it gets closer,* she thought. By the time she arrived home she had already figured out what she would serve and how she would decorate the house. She decided on a Saturday night three weeks away. *Yep, I can get it all together by then,* she thought. In the mood she was in today, nothing would be impossible for her.

By the end of the three weeks, it was an entirely different story. The day of the party, Anita's initial exuberance had long since faded, replaced by a mixture of stress and anxiety. Well into her second vodka over ice, she was putting the final touches on the three trays of hors d'oeuvres when she heard the doorbell. She hoped it was Jake—he had told her he would try to come a little early to help out—but it was Gracie's voice she heard on the intercom.

"It's us!" Gracie chirped, followed by a nervous giggle. *Where the hell is Jake?* Anita heard herself think. "Hey, Gracie!" she said instead. "Is that Eileen and Rodger I hear in the background?"

"Sure is," they chorused in unison. "And I dragged Joe along too," Gracie added with a sound like a little snort.

Gracie was a laugher; one form of chortle or another seemed to punctuate the end of all her sentences, but tonight, even with the distraction of Anita's own worries about her party and her growing irritation with Jake's tardiness, she could hear the strain in Gracie's voice. Perhaps it was because Gracie had recently come to confer upon her the role of an older, wiser sister and confidante. Things between Gracie and her new boyfriend Joe were getting pretty serious and tonight she would be introducing him to Anita.

"I'll buzz you in; I'm taking something out of the oven so just follow the hall back to the kitchen."

"Mmm good! I'm starved," Gracie said. Anita hit the buzzer and followed her guests' progress by the advancing sound of Gracie's gleeful giggles. *As long as he can put up with her constant cackle, I think the boy will do just fine,* Anita thought but could not stop herself from grinning as she pictured him walking into the kitchen with bright orange earplugs stuffed into his ears.

Turning to greet them as they filed through the door, Anita could not resist sneaking a peek at Joe's ears. It was all she could do not to burst out laughing at her own little joke.

"Well you sure look happy for your party," Eileen said as she approached Anita with a hug followed by two giant air kisses aimed in the general vicinity of Anita's cheeks. Anita's face was still stuck in an ear-to-ear grin, trapped by the vision of Joe and his earplugs, and she knew that if she said anything at all to Eileen she would totally lose it. She turned away quickly and pretended to occupy herself by straightening the two trays of hors d'oeuvres on the counter.

"You look smashing, girl!" Gracie exclaimed. "Just look at you! If the slit on your dress were any higher and the neckline any lower, they would meet at the pass. Is it silk?"

"It is Gracie, thanks. I got it at the boutique," Anita managed to reply after taking a few deep breaths to pull herself back from the brink of hysterics at the image of Joe in glowing earplugs. Remaining careful to avoid any eye contact with Gracie or Joe, she pointed to the open bottle of wine on the counter, "Hey, Rodge, will you bring some glasses from the dining room?" she said and then mumbling something about the music, she grabbed her drink and headed to the living room to turn on the stereo, Mitsy at her heels.

More guests began to arrive. The neighbors, Claire and Eric, came through the back door, bottle of wine in hand; a few more people from school wandered in along with the chic French woman with a short European-style haircut and her husband with the shaved head and gold earring, owners of the trendy boutique on Halsted Street where Anita had only recently started working part-time. Of course, Mitsy was all excited attention, greeting each newcomer with a friendly quick bark and wagging tail, and busily working the crowd. It was now nearly seven-thirty, and the fact that Jake was still nowhere to be seen weighed more and more on Anita's mood. She thought about calling him, but decided against it, then tried to put him out of her mind. She certainly wasn't going to let him ruin her party.

Somehow both Anne and Victor arrived without her knowing it and surprised her in the dining room when they approached her to say hello. *Did they come together?* she wondered and began to look for any tell-tale signs that would indicate whether their joint appearance was a coincidence or something more. Knocked off her game by the thought, Anita immediately went into 'figure-it-out mode.' She knew they had met at her first piano recital, but had no inkling it had gone anywhere from there. She was both stunned and confused over the possibility it had and didn't know whether she liked it or not. *No,* she very quickly decided, *I definitely do not like it.* She felt somehow betrayed, though she didn't know why exactly, and she still couldn't tell whether they had actually come together or not. Of course, Anne the woman and the therapist immediately picked up on Anita's discomfort and the expression of suspicion on her face.

"Anita," she said warmly, and taking her hand added, "what a beautiful home you have here."

"Yes, people don't really expect me to have such a nice place," Anita replied, responding with a grimace to her own awkward remark. Anne smiled; she knew not to mix business with pleasure. Anita diverted her eyes up to Victor's.

"Thanks for coming," she said with a smile, attempting to regain her seriously crumbling poise. "Did you have any trouble finding the place?"

"Thank you for the invitation, Anita. Actually, your directions were quite good, and we had no trouble at all."

We! The word pierced her like a dagger. *So they did come together.* Anita could feel her face flush as she darted her eyes back to Anne, who met them with another friendly smile.

So that's it, she thought, easily reading Anita's mind. "You look great tonight, Anita," she said, "that dress is perfect, and I love the accessories. Where did you find the earrings and necklace?"

"Well… thanks. Remember I was telling you about my part-time job? I got them there—at the boutique." Then seizing the opportunity to make an escape from what she felt was an increasingly awkward situation, she added, "That's Nadia and Paul over there, the owners. I'll introduce you."

"Nadia," she called out, taking a quick step in her direction, "come here. I want you to meet someone." Nadia, with Paul in tow, joined them by the table. "Nadia and Paul, this is Anne and Victor." Anita shot another quick glance up to Victor, who was not surprised to see the reflection of anger and betrayal in her eyes.

Despite the capable and sometimes "spiky" personality she tried to project, Victor, from the beginning, had no trouble reading her fragile vulnerability—her damage. It was his gift and his curse—this ability to see beyond the surface of people and things. He was born with it and as a child it had caused him much suffering. Were it not for his grandmother, who shared the same ability, his plight would have been even more dire. With her help, he eventually became skilled at living in both the visible world that others saw and the invisible world that most people did not. He became adept at recognizing and respecting people's boundaries and not revealing he was privy to places he had not been explicitly invited to enter. Still, for all his efforts, others instinctively sensed there was something different about him—even when he wasn't saying anything—which unnerved some and attracted others.

Anita shifted her glance from Victor to Anne and back to Victor.

Oh my God, she thought, suddenly feeling naked and exposed before them. *Every silly little neurotic thought, feeling, or action must be lighting up on my face like a billboard.* Seeking strength in defiance, she went on to herself, *Well, and so what? What have I got to hide or be afraid of anyway? And what difference does it make if they are together?* But no amount of bravado could erase how miserable Anita felt. *Shit,* she said to herself, *here I am feeling jealous over this guy, and he's old enough to be my father.*

"Anne was just admiring your jewelry," she choked out reflexively to Nadia as she sneaked another quick glance up to Victor, who had begun a conversation with Paul.

"Hey, Victor!"

Anita turned quickly as Jake heartily announced his arrival, walking toward them from across the room. Anita stood in frozen disbelief as Victor responded with an enthusiastic embrace and "Hey, Jake." She could feel the sting of tears about to overtake her and wanted to stamp her feet and throw her glass on the floor. *"What about me?"* she wanted to shout at them. *"It's my party!"*

She felt Anne's hand on her wrist and turned to face her. The warmth in Anne's expressive eyes seemed to be saying, *I understand—I've been there myself—I understand.* "Men can be so insensitive at times," she said, without a trace of enmity. Then sliding her hand gently up to Anita's elbow asked, "Is there more food to bring out?"

Anita nodded mutely. "In the kitchen," she said, her voice sounding flat and disconnected.

"We'll be back," Anne said cheerily to Victor and Jake. "Come on, Anita; let's get the rest of the food."

They were no more than halfway to the kitchen when they heard Jake calling as he ran down the hall. "Gosh, Anita," he gushed when he caught up to them, "I'm really sorry. I didn't mean to be rude—it's just that Victor's so tall and he was the first person I saw when I came into the room."

"He is tall," Anne interjected, but Jake was still speaking a mile a minute.

"And so I called out to him and then we were talking and…"

"You're late!" Anita snapped at him. "You said you'd be here early to help me."

"I know, I'm really sorry, I took a nap before the party and then overslept and just woke up half an hour ago."

"You should have set your alarm clock," she shot back, "and I was getting worried." Anita felt the tears begin to well up in her eyes.

"Jake, Anita could use some help with the food—perhaps you could give her a hand?" Anne said, attempting to guide the situation.

"Yeah, of course," he responded. "I'm sorry, everything was going really fast… I didn't say hello to you either, Anne."

"Well, I'm not as tall as Victor," she quipped. "Don't give it a second thought. Perhaps Anita can find you a glass of wine while I go see what Victor's up to."

"Yeah that would be great," he said, and turned to Anita. As they headed off to the kitchen, Anne found her way to the living room where Victor was standing near the piano, talking to Claire and Eric.

"Yes, well it was Kabir, the great mystic poet and master who said, 'Until one experiences it, it is not true.'"

"So, truth is not absolute?" Eric replied.

"Well of course there may be a distinction between Truth with a capital 'T' and truth in the sense that a carpenter's line is true; still there is a connection—oh excuse me," he said to Eric when he saw Anne approaching. "Ah, there you are. Did you get the food out?" he said with a wink.

"Yes, Jake is helping her now," she said with a look that told him much more than her words.

"Ah good," he replied and smiled. "Anne, I would like you to meet Claire and Eric Davies. They live next door. We were just talking about the relationship between truth and experience."

"You're so good at this light, superficial party talk," she joked, then turned to shake hands with Claire and Eric. "Please don't let me interrupt the conversation," she said.

"Claire and Eric brought a very nice bottle of Australian Shiraz to the party, and we began talking about the connection between the wine and the wine glass. It turns out that Claire and Eric are very knowledgeable on the subject and Eric was explaining how the characteristics of the wine are affected by the characteristics of the glass it is served in."

"Somehow that led us to the question of the difference between knowledge and understanding," Claire chimed in, "and then Victor mentioned this fascinating quotation from… um…?"

"Kabir."

"Yes, thank you, Eric; Victor mentioned this quote by Kabir. Well, Victor had made the point that hearing about a place from someone who had actually been to that place would have a totally different effect than hearing the same words from someone who has only read about the place."

"Interesting," Anne said thoughtfully—the conversation about the difference between knowing and experiencing having caused her to recall an event from the day before…

She had received an urgent request to join an interview a colleague at the university counseling center was having with a new student. His specialty was adaptive technology, but he was very much at sea with this student's physical problems. The woman had a serious back condition which had required surgery to insert steel rods, leaving her freedom of movement significantly impaired. Anne and her colleague listened for about five minutes to the student's account of her back issues and what she wanted to accomplish from her study until it became apparent that the student's level of anxiety was rapidly escalating, her speech becoming more and more pressured. Instinctively responding to the woman's energy as much as her words, Anne raised her hand, stopping the woman in mid-sentence with a gesture of "enough," and began to speak calmly to her about the inner experience of anxiety—specifically the fear of not being heard or taken seriously.

She spoke from understanding, and although the woman had never mentioned anxiety as an issue for her, she listened attentively. As Anne continued to describe how anxiety can operate, how it feeds on itself and cuts one off from the world—drawing upon her own experience for descriptors—she paid close attention to the effect her words and her energy were having on the student, and by the time she finished, she saw that the woman's countenance had changed dramatically. Her posture, her face, her state, had all shifted. Staring open-eyed at Anne, she said, "I can't believe it, Dr. Rose, I suddenly feel so relaxed! That's really weird. I feel so relaxed." Then turning to the other consultant, she asked, "Why do I feel so relaxed? What happened?"

At the time, Anne had wondered as well. She had not been satisfied to attribute the change in the student's state solely to "therapeutic skill." There was, she thought, a missing piece of the puzzle somewhere. Now, hearing Victor's words about the difference between knowledge and experience caused Anne to revisit the question. The student's response was not the result of Anne's knowledge, but her experience, and perhaps the difference lay not in her choice of words, but what was being carried by those words. Anne didn't simply know about the student's anxiety, she had experienced the same state herself and had transformed it. Didn't that have something to do with her ability to do the same for this woman?

"It's an interesting coincidence," Anne said when she noticed the trio looking at her. "What you were speaking of triggered a recollection." Victor said nothing but his eyes prompted her to share.

"What kind of recollection?" asked Claire.

"Well, without going into the details—because it had to do with a patient—let me just say, it led me to a certain question which is one of my pet preoccupations. To put it simply, the question is:

What really changes with experience? Nowadays, technology provides us with evidence that experience changes brain structure, in other words, there is an organic change in us resulting from experience, but what interests me most is what actually changes in us that can be recognized by others when we speak from our experience. People obviously cannot see that the brain and its chemistry have changed; so what is it they are really perceiving?"

"Vibrations—like the hippies used to talk about," responded Claire as she swirled her glass of Shiraz.

"Exactly," Anne replied. "I actually like the term quite a bit. But what I want to know is the exact nature of this vibration. Is it physical, mental, emotional?"

"And what is it in us that perceives this vibration?" Eric added. Victor had been standing very still, watching and listening, saying nothing.

"Yes that is a very good question indeed," he said and closed his eyes. Anne turned to look at him; his lips were pursing—it was almost imperceptible—the pressing and releasing as if they were responding to some deep thoughts—like a tail wagging on a dog. Eric and Claire also were looking at him.

"It has been my experience," Anne said with a mischievous twinkle in her eye, "that when someone says, 'that's a great question,' what they really mean is they have a great answer." Victor slowly opened his eyes; his lips forming a wry smile.

"Would you like the party answer or the real answer?" he joked.

"Both," parried Anne, "and at the same time."

"Vibration is the manifestation of state," Victor responded without hesitation.

"And what is state?" Claire asked.

"State is the sum total of all those qualities that compose the wine glass."

"I get that," replied Eric, "but what about the wine?"

"Wine has no state; it has ipseity."

"Ipseity?" they chimed in unison.

"Yes, ipseity is perfection's individualized experience of reality."

"The characteristics of the wine?" said Eric.

"Yes, the characteristics of the wine."

Well I asked for this, Anne thought, when she felt herself becoming agitated. She looked at the open, almost yearning, expressions on Claire's and Eric's faces. Victor definitely had the ability to touch people in a special way. She had felt it herself from the very first time they met at Anita's piano recital. When he spoke, something inside wanted to believe everything he said was true, and this loss of objectivity—this suggestibility—went completely against both her nature and her professional training. It was very unsettling.

"And Eric's question about what it is in us that perceives and responds to another's vibration?" Anne asked as much in self-defense as in the spirit of inquiry.

Victor turned and looked directly at her. It was as if they were alone in the room. It was suddenly so intimate that Anne had to resist the impulse to look away.

"The tale of love," he said softly, "must be heard from love itself. For like the mirror, it is both mute and expressive."

***

In the kitchen, Anita was directing Jake with the final touches on the tray of quiches while she fussed with the carrot curls and parsley. Her silence and the tension in the air were making him increasingly uncomfortable. When the last carrot curl was in place, Jake turned to her, and gently taking her by the shoulders, looked into her eyes. Slowly and deliberately, and with a directness he seldom exhibited he asked, "Okay, what is it, Anita? I mean it. You know me; I've been late before. Why are you still so upset?"

The unexpected tenderness in his voice totally threw her, unleashing a thousand things she wanted to say—unfinished phrases like "I'm just so lonely... hurt... wanting you to want me... wishing for someone to be here for me... hating myself for being so needy...," but all she could do was look back into his eyes and let the tears roll down her cheeks. The look in her eyes spoke more to him than any words could.

"Oh, Anita…" he responded, and wrapping her in his arms held her close. Anita tensed, involuntarily.

"Let it go, Anita," Jake whispered to her. "Just let it go. I'm here; I'm here now."

Anita sobbed quietly, her head buried in Jake's chest, and an unusual serenity began to grow within her. Jake could feel her breathing becoming slower and deeper. His simple gesture had brought them both to a moment of closeness neither had experienced in their adult lives. They were still lost in this pure and timeless embrace, neither having any inclination for it to end, when Gracie entered the kitchen with a nervous giggle.

"Well just look at the two of you—just like some old romantic movie," she exclaimed as she grabbed a quiche from the tray and started munching. "Anyone would think you two were Garbo and Gilbert in *Flesh and the Devil…*"

"Yeah, right, Gracie," Jake made the effort to sound nonchalant, "and I'm sure you'll write a great review." Still holding Anita in his embrace, he turned his head to face Gracie. "But you tell me," he continued, "how would you comfort Anita after she'd put so much effort into this evening and only just now discovered she'd wrecked the profiteroles beyond repair?"

Relieved by Jake's ability to think on his feet, Anita chuckled quietly to herself, happy to stay hidden for a moment longer in his arms.

"See, I knew it!" retorted Gracie, as she sprang into action. "Oh, come on, sweetie," she said, while making an exaggerated attempt to disentangle them from each other's arms. "This is a super fantastic party. Who needs profiteroles anyway? Whatever the hell they are; you've got a ton of super great food here already," Gracie said in that high, obsequious voice adults sometimes used to speak to children. "It's no wonder I hate you, you perfectionists can be such a pain," she said before interrupting herself with another chorus of giggles and throwing her arms around Anita, who by now was laughing too. "But God, Anita, I think we'd better do a bit of damage control there on those eyes—the Cleopatra look is so yesterday…"

As Anita beat a hasty retreat into the powder room, Gracie swung around to face Jake.

"Okay, you bastard," she said in the manner of a cop in some second-rate police drama. "What did you do?"

"That's what I like about you, Gracie, you're so subtle. I'm telling you the truth. Anita is so wound up about this party she just needed to let off some steam."

Gracie winked and nodded her head. "Yeah right, and I'll buy that bridge you want to sell me." Then with a menacing step in his direction, she stuck two fingers into his chest and added, "But just remember this, buddy, she's my big sister, and I'll be watching you. Now, grab that tray," she directed, and picking up two bottles of wine from the counter commanded, "and let's go find my Joe."

Feeling relieved to be able to rejoin the others at last, Jake followed Gracie out of the kitchen and down the hall to the living room, where the party was in full swing.

***

Safely behind the closed door, Anita scrutinized her face in the mirror. "What a disaster!" she said aloud, then hearing the music and muffled voices in the background, she let out a little groan and said, "And just how the hell am I supposed to get through this party?" She rummaged through the vanity drawers. *No help here,* she thought, *I need to get upstairs.* Opening the door a crack, she peeked out and, finding the coast clear, made her move. Like a thief in her own home, she headed for the kitchen. After a brief detour to pour another drink, she made her escape up the back stairs, Mitsy scampering excitedly behind her. Reaching the upstairs bathroom undetected, she quickly closed the door behind her just as Mitsy managed to get the tip of her tail out of the way. She went straight for the medicine cabinet. "First, two of these," she said to Mitsy as she shook three Valium from the bottle. "Hell," she said, looking down at the extra pill in her hand, "two's good, but three's better," and swigged them down with the rest of her vodka. She hadn't felt the need for medicine in many months, "but tonight is special," she told herself, though the truth was she had been fighting the feelings now for some days—the blurring of the line between fact and fantasy—between functionality and dysfunction.

"Now to get to work on this mess, huh, Mitsy? Don't want to scare them all away. Off with the old," she said with a laugh that was a little too loud, as she applied the make-up remover, "on with the new." But her hands were unsteady and the eyeliner brush would not obey. It took several re-applications before she was satisfied.

"Did a number on my hair, too," Anita scowled while dampening her hair to try to revive the perm. "That didn't work," she said and added more water. "Crap, it's too wet now; I need a dryer…" Anita lost track of time as she compulsively scrunched and shaped and wetted and dried her hair. Nothing worked; in the end, she gave up. Staring blankly in the mirror, she told her reflection, "Hopeless. Just forget about it." Turning away in defeat, she headed back down the back stairs. Relieved to find the kitchen empty, she made a beeline to the bottle on the kitchen table.

Anita sloshed more vodka into her glass, filling it to the brim. "Quick, Mitsy, the coast is clear; let's make our escape," she said, retracing her path to the stairs where she plunked herself down on the steps out of view. Taking a healthy swig, she whispered to Mitsy, "Let's just hide out here a little longer until the guards sound the alarm and come to get us. At least I can always count on you, dear," she smiled down at her little dog, who had made herself comfortable at her feet.

***

Anne was only half listening to Victor's commentary now. Nadia had joined in the discussion while Paul had drifted over to chat with Rodger and Eileen. Her attention wandering, she scanned the room. Watching people in action always intrigued her. It wasn't a matter of psychoanalyzing—that required far too much effort—it was simply her way of taking it all in—the movement, the sounds, the impressions of humans "be-ing." It fascinated and soothed her at the same time, but something Victor was saying abruptly pulled her back.

"More wine?" said Victor as he held the bottle aloft.

Anne knew it was an attempt to get her to re-engage. Anne met his gaze. "Why not?" she said as she traced the flow of the deep red liquid as it glistened in the candle light. *Ipseity,* she thought. The word annoyed her for some reason. When Victor turned to fill Nadia's glass, Anne murmured something about needing to sit and quietly slipped away to the overstuffed chair near the fireplace. It was the perfect vantage point to continue her observations undisturbed.

***

"Better get back to it… what say, Mitsy?" Anita wobbled as she stood, then crashed into the wall. "Whoa, steady there, girl." Let's ditch these heels, she thought as she unceremoniously kicked off her shoes. Looking down at Mitsy, she had an inspiration. "Gimme a hand, little lady. The princess must make a regal entrance." Toppling forward as she bent down to scoop Mitsy into her arms, Anita straightened herself, and after regaining her balance, tried again, more slowly.

With Mitsy tucked safely under her left arm, Anita gingerly worked her way down the hall to the living room, using her right arm to steady herself along the wall. Propping herself up in the doorway she thought, *It's really hazy in here*, as she squinted into the room. *Is that Victor over there by the piano? Must be, he's towering above all those people around him. That man sure is a charmer.* "Look, Mitsy, our throne," she said when she spied the vacant window seat beyond the piano and began to work her way slowly across the room.

"Made it," she said after arranging the pillows and curling up with Mitsy on her lap in the corner. Gazing around the room, Anita marveled at all the people—gesturing, talking, laughing—*Like watching a movie,* she smiled to herself, her anxiety not even a distant memory.

"Hey, hon."

Anita swiveled her head just in time for Jake's friend Tim's kiss to find its mark on her cheek.

"Whoa!" she responded, "shouldn't be sneaking up on the princess like that. How's you doing, Timmy?"

"Anita, you look smashing as always, but I gotta say, your eyes do look a touch on the glassy side... been up to something?"

"Ooo. Just a little relaxation helper, Timmy," she said and winked. "Who's your friend?"

"Ah, I don't think you've met my boyfriend, Mark. Mark, this is Anita."

Anita raised her hand limply. Rallying, Mark took it gently, bowed chivalrously and gave it a kiss. He had sparkling blue eyes with the longest lashes Anita had ever seen. "Actually, I think we have already met, so to speak. You're a runner, right?"

Anita squinted up at the smiling face, trying to focus her blurry vision. "Turn around, Mark," she said. "Yep, I'd remember that ass anywhere," she said while feebly reaching out to give it a pat. "And so nice of you to remember me too, Marky."

"I may be gay," Mark replied, "but I'm not blind. You have a pretty memorable bum yourself."

"That was the day in the park I decided to have my party." Then turning back to Tim, she said, "Damn it, Tim. How come every drop-dead-gorgeous guy I meet is gay?"

"Yea, life's a bitch, but here's one guy who isn't..." Tim said as he glimpsed Jake approaching.

"I was looking for you, Anita," said Jake. "Hi guys, it's great to see you here. Glad you could make it. I thought you had another party?"

"Well of course we do, it's Saturday night—we're just getting warmed up," Tim grinned.

"Hey, c'mon. There's someone I want you to meet—remember me telling you about Victor, my piano teacher? You want to come too, Anita?"

"No thanks, Jakey, I'm a little dangerous on my feet right now. I think I'll just stay put for a while, but tell Victor I said hey."

"You got it," said Jake as he turned his two friends in the direction of the piano.

"Dude! You never mentioned your piano teacher was so, so—good looking," Tim said as they walked away.

"Tim, I swear...! You have a one-track mind," Jake kidded.

"I resemble that remark," parried Tim.

Anita watched them walk away and then closed her eyes.

Whoa, better not do that, she thought as the room began to spin madly out of control. She opened her eyes to see Gracie approaching.

"There you are!" Anita felt Gracie's laugh piercing through her fog.

"I didn't know you had a twin sister," Anita said as she tried to get her eyes to focus.

"Are you, okay Anita? You don't look so good."

"Thanks for the vote of confidence, Gracie."

"No, seriously, Anita, what's wrong?"

"Guess I'm a bit 'over-relaxed.'"

"Overdid it, huh? The vodka cure. Well, it just won't do to have the hostess snoring in the front room. I'll find my Joe and we'll get you upstairs."

"Need to make a pit stop first," Anita mumbled. But Gracie was already off in search of Joe.

Fortunately, Joe was strong and Anita was compliant, so they managed to get her upstairs and onto her bed without a scene. Jake appeared at the bedroom door moments after Gracie and Joe had gotten Anita settled.

"Poor Anita. Missing her own party," Gracie giggled. "I'll let everyone know—but it's 'party on!' for the rest of us, right, Jake?"

"It's what Anita would want," Jake solemnly pronounced, his right hand across his heart, head respectfully bowed.

"You're terrible!" Gracie howled, grabbing Joe by the arm. They disappeared out the door and down the front steps.

Jake lingered for a moment, watching Anita closely. He had never seen her face so relaxed, all the prickly edges of her distrust erased. He was struck by her simple beauty, but began to feel uncomfortable when he felt himself becoming aroused. Turning away abruptly, he left the room, pulling the door closed heavily as he went. When he reached the top of the stairs, he heard Gracie's voice above the crowd. "Ladies and gentlemen, your attention, s'il vous plait. Anita says she loves you all and she has gone to bed. Please continue without her."

***

"Need to make a pit stop first," Anita mumbled as Gracie and Joe helped her from the window seat.

"Well don't be long and don't fall in either," Gracie replied and laughed. "Need some help?"

"Nope, got it covered, I'll be right back."

"We'll be waiting right here for you," Gracie said as Anita stumbled off to the powder room.

A cacophony of weird music and eerie voices drifted through the closed door. Why had she done that to her hair? she thought as she regarded her partially shaved head in the mirror. Anita reached up to touch the bald patch but the spot felt funny on her head—like she could put her fingers into her skull and touch her brain. In horror, she pulled her hand away, her fingers covered in blood. Quickly turning on the faucet, she attempted to wash the blood away but was distracted by the sound of someone tapping lightly on the door. Anita turned off the water and opened the door. It was Anne standing absolutely still, staring menacingly at her. Anita stared back at the demonic presence. How could she not have noticed? It was suddenly all so obvious, the bright red lipstick, that too-sexy dress. Anne was not what she appeared—how could she have missed it? Anita's terror turned to rage. "How the hell could you do that to me?" she spat.

"What are you talking about, dear?" Anne said sweetly, but the venom in her eyes betrayed her. Anita shivered and took a step back.

"What do you and Victor do when you're together—talk about me while you're fucking? Do you laugh at me, compare notes?"

"Excuse me, I've got to pee," Anne demanded as she pushed Anita out of the powder room and slammed the door behind her. To Anita, it felt like a bomb had gone off. She began to shake. She was totally consumed by rage.

"How dare you!" she screamed at the door, then turned and raced down the hallway into the front room. Stopping at the doorway she looked at all the bizarre, evil cartoon characters talking and laughing. Then she heard herself screaming, "This party is over! Everyone, get the hell out of here! Now!"

Gracie immediately turned to Jake, glaring at him. Jake, terrified, was shaking uncontrollably, the glass in his hand spilling wine all over the floor. Claire and Eric looked shocked and were hurriedly moving toward the door. It was obvious even Victor's omnipresent serenity had evaporated. He closed his eyes and took a deep breath.

"You heard me! I said out!" Anita continued to scream, her hands squeezed into tight fists she shook in front of herself like a punch-drunk fighter.

She awakened with a start; her heart was pounding; she was drenched in sweat. She could hear Gracie's voice in the distance and realized she had been dreaming. Moments later, she was asleep again…

***

Everyone else had left except Gracie and Joe, who stayed to help Jake with the clean up. It was nearly two-thirty in the morning, and Jake was physically, mentally, and emotionally spent. He just wanted to be alone—needed to be alone—but he did appreciate them staying to help.

As Joe and Jake stacked the last of the dishes in the drain, Gracie appeared in the doorway. "What are you two grinning at?" she demanded as she lifted her chin and began sniffing the air. "Oh!" she said and started to giggle. "A little inspiration I see."

"More like motivation," said Jake.

"Say goodnight, Gracie," said Joe.

"Goodnight, Gracie," Jake said, and the two of them nearly fell over laughing.

"Not funny, you two clowns. Jake, can you stay here tonight? Anita is fast asleep, but I really don't think she should be left alone."

"No sweat, Gracie. Mitsy and I will take good care of her. I'd planned to stay anyway, to give her a hand in the morning—sort of my penance for not getting here early to help out. And the guestroom is very comfortable..."

***

The house was silent now. Jake walked around, systematically turning off all the lights and blowing out candles. Then he slowly ascended the steps in darkness. When he came to Anita's door, he opened it for a final check. He could see the outline of her body lying on the bed. Mitsy was curled at her feet. The puppy half stirred as he softly entered the room, but settled immediately when she recognized him. Jake stopped a few feet from the bed. Anita's breathing was deep and regular and he felt reassured. But he could not leave.

Anita lay on her back, her left arm lying across her stomach, her right arm bent upwards at her side, her hand gently curled against her cheek. In the light from the streetlamp outside her window, Jake could clearly see her breasts pushing against the confines of the dress Gracie had been unable to remove. Transfixed, he watched them rise and fall with the soft rhythm of her breathing. Unable to look away, he found himself exploring and caressing them with his mind; found himself becoming more and more excited at the erect nipple barely shrouded by the thin and clinging fabric. Fully aroused now, he imagined himself gently sliding the straps of her dress off her shoulders; imagined her breasts falling free of their constraint. He felt the warmth—the excitement— swelling within him.

Without shifting his gaze, he let his hand slip to the front of his pants and lightly fondle himself. Quietly kicking off his shoes, he fumbled with the button and then the zipper. Now, standing half-naked and fully erect in front of her, he began to tremble as he imagined rubbing himself against her soft lips. Managing to step out of his trousers, he cautiously moved a step closer while gently stroking himself. As he watched her breasts rise and fall, he imagined his tongue gently licking her nipples. He traveled in his mind to the warmth between her legs. The slit of her skirt was open wide and he wondered if the shadow he saw was her nakedness. He was sure it was... there... for him to enter, to be engulfed in its wet warmth.

His legs felt so weak he could barely continue to stand—his hand moving quickly now—the blood pounded in his ears. Mitsy stirred as he let out an involuntary gasp of release.

Afterwards, Jake stood absolutely still, tears streaming from the corners of his now clenched eyes. Recovering his senses, his sense of release gave way to terror. Involuntarily, he covered his eyes with his hand, then spreading his fingers he peeked cautiously through the crack. Though Anita was still sound asleep, he was overwhelmed with guilt. Quietly retrieving his pants from the floor, an alien voice spoke within him, telling him to clean up the "holy elixir." After using the bottom of his shirt to clean-up his transgression, he tiptoed slowly out of the room.

Though the sound of Jake entering her room had not awakened her, it had stirred Anita into another dream.

"Oh Ronny, is that you?" she said when she opened her eyes and saw the shadow in the doorway. She struggled to sit up, but her body was heavy and unresponsive and all she could manage to do was raise her head. The figure moved quickly to her bed.

"You little ungodly whore; just look at you!"

Anita recognized the hateful self-righteous voice. "Mother!" she cried. The figure was upon her now, clawing at her breasts with sharp nails. "Stop it!" she screamed. "You're hurting me." Anita felt the warm sensation of her own blood flowing over her chest. Another darker, heavier figure emerged from the shadows and stood gaping at her by her mother's side.

"*Cleanse her, Father!*" shouted her mother as she continued to rip at Anita's breasts with long black talons. Anita's eyes were wide with horror as she watched him part his robe and expose himself before her. She could hear his labored breathing as he stroked himself harder and faster. Anita tried again to move—to escape—but couldn't. The figure stepped closer to her. She could see the enormous red member.

"*The elixir of Christ's mercy will cleanse your sins,*" he growled.

"*Accept his love; he died for your sins,*" her mother shouted in chorus.

Anita felt his release—the thick warm poison mingling with her blood—like the confluence of two rivers—feeling it run down her breasts and over her body…

***

When Anita awoke, daylight was streaming through the bedroom window; her head was burning inside. It felt like her brain was as big as a watermelon squeezed into a skull the size of a walnut. Shaking, she tried to take stock of herself. Her sweat-soaked, crumpled dress was twisted around her. She felt disoriented and bewildered. Mitsy sat upright at her feet, all attention.

"Damn, Mitsy. What terrible dreams—at least I think they were dreams. I really am beginning to wonder what's real and what's not." Anita looked around the room. "And how'd I get here? Last I remember… I don't remember…" she said as disjointed scenes of her party mingled with her nightmares and began to take form in her troubled and confused mind.

"You awake?" She was startled to hear Jake calling from the bottom of the stairs.

"I think so," she said, and shuddered involuntarily as the sound of his voice stirred a recollection of the dark shadow's voice.

"Want some coffee?"

"Yeah… and a bullet for my head," she joked, though the thought of a quick end to all her misery was strangely comforting at that moment. Anita slid under the covers and slumped back onto the pillows. She felt heavy and drained—unable to move—her thoughts racing from one violent image to another. When Jake appeared with coffee, three Excedrin and an ice pack, she managed a weak smile but wondered at the cold chill that ran through her body in his presence.

"I thought I heard moaning coming from your room." Anita noticed the unusually cautious tone of his voice.

"I'm not surprised. I had the worst dreams. I feel terrible." Eyes closed, holding the ice pack against her forehead, she continued, "I don't remember how I got here... Joe was helping me... and Gracie... and I remember seeing you leaving my room. At least I think I remember it." Jake felt his blood run cold. His own sense of guilt kept him from recognizing how profound Anita's distress was.

"Jake, I'm really scared. I don't know what's going on. I don't think I can even get out of bed."

"It's all right, Anita," Jake said, trying to console her. "You had a lot to drink last night and with all the stress of the party—maybe you should give Dr. Rose a call."

"That's just it, Jake. I don't know if I can trust her anymore after what I saw."

"But, Anita, that was just a dream, you said so yourself. It wasn't real."

"I'm not so sure, Jake," her usually well-moderated voice now unusually tense and shrill. "I think what I saw about her *was* real," she said, and buried her head in her pillow.

In the Dark

Anita stood in front of the full-length mirror in her bedroom, mercilessly scrutinizing her reflection. What she saw horrified her. The lovely dress she had worn to her Big Party, only a year before, now made her look like a badly stuffed sausage—all lumps and bulges—and she couldn't even get the zipper all the way up over the flab. She squeezed herself out of it in disgust, and took another searching look.

Who are *you?* she thought silently. *What's happened to me?* The extra pounds and the puffy bags under her eyes were ample evidence that the past year had taken its toll on her. First Victor had left for India, and with him her interest in piano had also gone. Then her father became ill, and her interest in anything other than caring for him vanished as well. She had deferred her studies, so close to completion, because she could not focus. Exercise went out the window—even running, and she had so loved to run, to feel her body in motion, her breath. These days she felt too exhausted to contemplate running even a single block. Her father had been dead six months, but the wound had yet to heal, not even a scab, and she felt his loss as much today as she had the day he died—maybe even more now that the shock of the event had been replaced by the cold light of reality.

Of course the wound is fresh—today's his birthday, reasoned the voice of years of therapy. *Be kind to yourself, Anita, and a few extra pounds is not the end of the world...*

In the aftermath of her father's passing, Anita had vowed she would try to make amends with her mother. So on Friday nights she would go to her mother's house for dinner. But her mother never came to her house, making one flimsy excuse after another. *What the hell's her problem anyway?* she challenged the universe, as she fussed with her hair before the mirror. *And so what if Jake moved in; does she even care that he's such a big help to me?*

"No doubt she finds it unforgivably sinful," she said aloud, striking a seductive pose and grimacing mockingly. "And why is it any of her damn business in the first place?" she continued, as she dropped the pose and turned her back on the mirror. *Once a bitch, always a bitch. Why the hell do I even bother?*

Anita sighed, realizing little, if anything, had changed. Still, tonight, she had vowed, she would make it special. It was her father's birthday after all. So she rummaged in her closet until she came across a loose-fitting summer dress, threw a wrap around her shoulders to hide her cleavage, *the only respectable thing left about my body,* made a brave face and headed down to the kitchen, stopping there to pour herself a tumbler of vodka—*for moral support,* she thought. After tossing it back, she poured another. *Probably gonna need this…*

Anita grabbed a bottle of Chianti from the wine rack, stuffed it into her bag, and headed out. She was determined to make the dinner with her mother festive, a celebration, and why not? *It's Daddy's birthday.*

Her mother met her at the door with a forced smile and then immediately spied the bottle of wine sticking out of her daughter's bag. Anita involuntarily shuddered from the chill of her mother's disapproving gaze.

"Oh, Mother," Anita tried to be playful, "C'mon… it's Daddy's birthday."

"It *would* have been," Grace corrected.

Anita knew better than to argue and headed into the kitchen, led by the aroma of her mother's lasagna. A fresh salad was already on the table.

"What, no garlic bread?" Anita joked.

"I didn't think you needed it," her mother said coldly as she gave her daughter a onceover that would rival even the most unabashed construction worker.

Anita tried to hide the sting of her mother's criticism and said nothing as she foraged through the kitchen drawer, looking for a corkscrew. "*Oh Daddy,*" she said silently to herself while fighting back the tears—how much she missed his warmth.

How could he have loved such a bitch? she thought as she managed to fish out a corkscrew from the tumbled mess of her mother's drawer.

"What do you need?" Grace asked with an tone of impatience as she noticed her daughter beginning to search through the cupboards.

"Don't you have any wine glasses?"

"In the hutch in the dining room, where they always are," she said curtly.

Anita returned with two crystal goblets. "Were these a wedding present?"

"Of course," was all her mother said, as she lifted the lasagna from the oven and placed it on a potholder on the kitchen table.

Anita rinsed the dust from the glasses, filled one and handed it to her mother.

"That's too much—half that for me," her mother said, waving the glass away.

"Fine; here you go," said Anita as she poured a small amount into the second glass and placed it on the table in front of her mother's chair. Her mother, busy serving the lasagna, took no notice and held out the plate to Anita, now seated opposite her.

"That's too small; twice that for me," Anita said, trying to make light of her mother's comment about the wine and her own irritation that her mother insisted on doling out ridiculously small portions.

Her mother's deep sigh of disapproval was unmistakable to Anita.

"Good men don't like fat women," she said matter-of-factly as she doled out a larger serving for her daughter.

Just let it go, Anita, let it go, Anita counseled herself.

"Hey, if you didn't want me to eat so much, you shouldn't have made it so tasty," Anita said, in a vain attempt at humor to fend off the darkness growing within her. She raised her glass and waited for her mother to do the same, but she didn't.

"To Daddy," Anita said hopefully. But her mother said nothing; she had bowed her in head in a silent grace. Anita took a long drink and then bowed her own head. *Help me get through this,* she prayed to nothing and no one in particular.

***

Anita managed to get out of the cab without incident, but she stumbled as she climbed the steps to her front door. Fumbling for her keys, she tried to focus. *Yeah, that last glass was one too many...*when after several failed attempts she finally unlocked the door, she continued to herself, *or two or three or four too many.*

The house was dark, and strangely silent. "Mitsy?" she called out. No answer. "MITSY?" Her fear was rising. Where could her little companion be? She began a frantic search, turning on lights, nearly falling more than once as she moved in panic through the house towards the kitchen where she prayed she would find Mitsy sound asleep in her bed. Instead, she found her lying in the middle of the room, still. Anita fell to her knees and scooped up the lifeless Mitsy, holding her tightly against her chest as she rocked back and forth, sobbing uncontrollably. Pieces of a plastic bag, remnants of a deadly feast, lay scattered on the floor.

It was nearly three a.m. when Anita awakened from a fitful sleep. Her head was pounding and her entire body ached from lying on the kitchen floor, Mitsy at her side. Self-loathing and unbearable sorrow filled her awareness as she struggled to get herself up. Lifting Mitsy, she gently placed her on her doggie bed, tears once again streaming from her eyes. She groped her way into the downstairs bathroom, took four Excedrin and lay down on the floor again, next to Mitsy, blaming herself and hating herself without mercy as she drifted back into an agonized slumber.

She awoke again at six a.m. with the first dim light of dawn. The pain was only worse in her body, the self-recrimination louder in her head. In the shadow of love, hopelessness clawed at her heart.

Mitsy is gone.
Like Ronny.
Like Daddy.
Like me.

The Homecoming

Grace had never cared much for him as a teenager, but because he was important to Anita now, she tried to make an effort to like him. Still, he was just another lost sheep in her eyes—he was then when he used to visit her Ronny, he was now as he stood before her.

"Grace, I need to speak to you. Could I come in?" he was saying, but he was already inside before she could respond. "It's Anita..." Jake's face was a sickly grey color, and he seemed to be trembling...

***

An uneasy feeling had been growing in Victor ever since he had stepped off the plane. By the time he walked through the doorway into his apartment, he knew something of significance was happening, but he didn't know what. Dropping his backpack and bags in the hall, he went into his studio and flopped down onto the large upholstered chair near the piano. What was wrong? Something had changed. Closing his eyes, he slowed his breathing and relinquished control of his thoughts, allowing them to surface of their own volition—watching them like scenes in a movie...

He was back in India, standing with his bags in the little garden at Krita Baba's compound.

"I am leaving now," he was saying to his guru. "The car has come to take me to Mumbai."

Krita Baba moved closer to him and took his hand. "Little brother, you are not leaving here," he said softly, "you are living here. Your Father's house is so big you cannot leave it; you merely go from one room to another."

The scene dissolved and Victor found himself back in his chair. The studio was so quiet. *Anne has some connection with this*, he thought and picked up the phone from the table beside his chair.

"Hello?" He could hear the strain in her voice.

"It's Victor."

"Oh Victor…" There was a pause. "It is so good to hear your voice." She paused again. "I just received a call from Jake… Anita committed suicide." Victor said nothing, but Anne could hear him breathing.

"I'm glad you're back," she said.

"I knew something was going on as soon as I got off the plane. Do you feel like talking?" Now the silence was on Anne's side. "Are you okay?" he asked.

"No… I'm not." Victor had never known her to be so emotional. "I had no sense of it—nothing! How the hell could I have missed the signs? I can't believe I didn't…"

"You feel guilty?" he said softly.

"Yes, damn it! Yes… I do." Victor closed his eyes as he recalled what Krita Baba often said to His followers when they were in distress: "There are no victims; nobody is to blame."

"Victor, are you there?"

"Yes, dear, I'm just trying to take this all in."

"When did you get back?" she asked.

"I just walked into my house a few minutes ago."

"My God, you must be exhausted. I'm sorry to have laid all this on you so soon."

"I am tired, Anne, but it doesn't matter. I am terribly sorry to hear about this but I cannot say I'm totally surprised. It has been my experience that there are no accidents regarding the circumstances or the time of one's death."

Anne felt herself squirm. Apparently not much had changed for her in the year he had been away.

"I find your comment disturbing, Victor," she said softly. "First, I find no comfort in it, and second, it seems to imply that Anita's suicide and the pain and suffering that led to it were somehow pre-ordained. This I just cannot accept."

"I know, Anne, I understand. We all change; we all stay the same. There is so much I want to tell you about my journey to the East and also to hear what has been going on with you. But now is not the time. I'm sorry to have disturbed you."

"You're right, Victor, now is not the time to talk about your journey, but I have missed you and I'm glad you're back."

"Have any arrangements been made?"

"Jake is helping Anita's mother with the funeral arrangements. As soon as I find out more, I'll be in touch. But let's get together soon."

"I look forward to it."

When they got off the phone, Anne and Victor both slumped back in their chairs and both closed their eyes. The relationship was ambivalent for each of them—in different ways. For Anne, she was well aware she was attracted to Victor. She enjoyed being in his physical presence and liked the sound and almost dreamy cadence of his voice. She absolutely loved when he played the piano. During his absence, this was perhaps the thing she missed the most. And she did find his ideas interesting—sometimes more interesting than she wanted to admit. His mind made sense to her, and though she found some of his ideas kind of crazy, she found him always to be quite sane. But there was also something about Victor that was alien to her—like a cold wind that made her shiver and want to hug herself for warmth.

Always the analyst, always the seeker, Anne had taken the opportunity afforded by his trip to India to assess their relationship—especially with regard to what she felt at times was an over-reaction to his opinions. There was a quiet authority behind his remarks, yet he seemed lacking in any of the obvious signs of arrogance or aloofness. In any case, it wasn't the authority she reacted to—in her life she had met some truly remarkable individuals whose authority she found neither intimidating nor disturbing. In fact, she had found them interesting and even inspiring, sometimes in spite of their assumed self-importance. But with Victor it was different. There was something in the way he spoke about the world and its legacy of unbroken suffering that got under her skin—something she could feel deep in the foundation of her individuality… like a cracking… a crumbling—that shook her to the very core. She found her reaction to him to be profound and complex; both the therapist and the spiritual wayfarer were challenged and inspired, but the woman, the mother, the human being, was dismayed and disturbed. Now, after their brief conversation about Anita's death, she realized with painful clarity that after all her introspection, both the relationship and the man remained enigmas to her.

For Victor too, the conversation with Anne had aroused the feelings of ambivalence he experienced around their relationship—feelings that reflected the conflict within himself between his own humanity, which unrelentingly drew him into relationship with the world, and his deepest intuition, which just as insistently reminded him the world and all its experiences were mere illusion. How often had Krita Baba reminded his followers of this with a quote by Hafiz, "A thousand times I have ascertained and found it to be true, that the universe and all the affairs of the universe are truly nothing into nothing."

Much deeper than any idea or mere belief, and having nothing at all to do with faith, Victor's intuition still lacked experience—the direct experience needed to transform this intuition into living Truth.

Consequently, he found himself in the uncomfortable position of being suspended between two chairs where despite his knowledge and his deepest longing, he remained attached to and affected by the world and all its experiences.

Being with Anne was like looking into a mirror that reflected the ambivalence of his situation back at him—and Anne, owing to all the work she had done on herself, was a very accurate mirror, perhaps second only to Krita Baba in the precision and clarity of her reflection. It was not always comfortable for Victor, looking out at someone only to see things about himself he did not wish to see, but he was also wise enough to realize his ambivalence about Anne was not with *their* relationship specifically, but with relationship itself—relationship with the world—with the illusion of an *other*.

Krita Baba, being perfectly aware of Victor's state, had promised to help him. He had said, "I will help you to be in the world but not of it," and went on to explain to him that he was in the state of *Hawa*—the junction between consciousness of form and consciousness of energy. He said that at the appropriate time he would give Victor an internal push and the world he experienced would cease to exist, to be replaced by sights and sounds and powers he now could not even imagine. Then, Krita Baba explained, Victor would be free of his present conflict. But, he added, higher consciousness with all its powers and enchantments were still illusion into illusion and would in no way assuage Victor's deeper longing for reality.

"You said you would teach me to live in the world, but not of it," Victor had asked. "How is that possible?"

"With love," his guru had replied.

Victor was startled when the phone rang. It was Jake.

"I was trying to call you before, but your line was busy. I'm so glad you're back—I have something to tell you about Anita."

"I know," Victor replied, "I was just on the phone with Anne. She told me about Anita."

"God, Victor, I have so many questions about everything, but right now I'm so busy, I can't even think."

"I'm glad you called, Jake. If there is anything at all I can do…"

"Yes, there is, that's why I called. Would you consider playing the piano at the funeral?"

"Yes, of course."

"And would you come with me when I go to Mrs. Burrows'

house tomorrow so she can talk to you about the music?"

"Yes."

"Good, I can pick you up and we can go there at noon."

"That would be fine, Jake. Would you like to come to my house an hour early for tea?"

"I would love that. I really want to talk to you. Should I come around eleven?"

"Perfect, Jake, see you then..."

∗∗∗

Anne reached for the phone. She held her breath as it rang, fearful Margot might not pick up; almost as fearful she would.

"Yes?" came the familiar voice. Anne breathed a sigh of relief. Margot had been her mentor and something of a supervisor for more years than she could count. They had a monthly ritual that was mutually rewarding—it was a lifeline, and it kept them both honest. It was her counsel Anne needed now.

"Margot..."

"That you, Anne?" Anne could feel the warmth in her voice.

"Yes."

"What's wrong? What's happened?"

"I've just learned that one of my patients, the young lawyer, Anita Burrows, committed suicide."

"What? Anita Burrows? I'm stunned!"

Her shock was comforting to Anne; it was a reaction that made sense to her and restored a measure of faith in her own reaction to the news.

"Talk to me, Anne—what happened?"

"Oh, Margot, I don't really know. Her friend Jake, you remember?"

"Yes, yes, go on..."

"He rang this evening and told me. I gather she took a bottle of Valium and washed them down with vodka. Jake had been away for a few days—he shares the house with her—he found her."

"Anne, listen to me carefully. You know as well as I do, if a person is determined to die, they will make it happen."

"Yes, but... but I never had any sense of her being suicidal."

"Again, listen to me. You also know people are incredibly adept at hiding—from themselves and from others, and sometimes especially from their analysts. You know how many years it can take, my dear Anne, to uncover the truth! Are you listening?"

"Yes." Margot had the voice of unerring authority, earned through decades of experience as an analyst who worked with some of the most profoundly ill patients Anne had ever heard about or known. She possessed an uncanny ability to get inside her patients and locate a kernel of wellness and nurture its growth.

"Anne, I know how painful it is when this happens—I *know*. We do our best, we try our hardest, but we are not God, nor are we meant to be. Anita's journey is her own. You were privileged to walk with her for a while and," she added, "I'm not just saying this to fluff your skirts, you did make a difference."

"But she committed suicide."

"Yes, Anne, I understand. I certainly don't have all the answers but what I do know is that you *listened* and Anita knew she was heard and she was seen. And that makes a difference—maybe we don't have the sensitivity or understanding to measure what it is or how it manifests, but I tell you, it makes a difference." These were the words Anne needed to hear to calm the maelstrom within her.

"Look, I have some time tomorrow morning, shall we grab a coffee, say, at ten—my place?"

"I'd love to, Margot. Thank you..."

***

Suffering from jet lag, Victor was wide-awake and sitting on the side of his bed at four in the morning. He had been dreaming about Krita Baba when he awoke. A melody—a sacred melody—that was often sung in his guru's presence by his Hindu followers lingered in his mind. Victor got out of bed and wandered through the darkness to his studio, sitting down at the grand piano. With his left hand, he played two sounds a perfect fourth apart, while his right hand found the simple melody of the chant. He played slowly and respectfully as he recalled the Sanskrit words the music accompanied. Over and over he repeated the chant singing softly:

Guru Brahma,
Guru Vishnu,
Guru Devo Maheswarah,
Guru Saakshat Para-Brahma,
Tasmai Shri Guruve Namah.

Dawn was breaking when he emerged from his reverie. He stopped playing, leaving his hands still resting on the keys. Picturing his guru in his mind, he repeated Krita Baba's English translation of the chant:

The Guru is God as Creator of Illusion,
The Guru is God as Preserver of Illusion,
The Guru is God as the Destroyer of Illusion.
I acknowledge the Guru
— the man who has become God
— as the Supreme God.

Victor walked into the kitchen to make tea. He felt strange; for the first time in a year, he was alone.

***

Anne loved the quiet elegance of Margot's old apartment building with its marble foyer, elaborate chandeliers, and uniformed doorman. Within its granite walls she felt transported back to another world, a more genteel and graceful world, remote from the cares and concerns of contemporary life's complex and frenetic existence.

Stepping from the elevator into the little corridor outside the apartment, she was greeted by her mentor and the smell of strong French roast coffee.

"Come in, come in. Make yourself comfortable there in the front room. The coffee is ready. I'll be right with you." Anne settled into one of the two large overstuffed chairs by the window overlooking the park and watched as Margot turned and disappeared down the long hallway with its staggering collection of ornate, antique mirrors, hung and propped everywhere along the way. Anne found the mirrors fascinating—how they would present an array of various and diverse reflections to someone as they walked through the hallway. She had never asked, but felt quite certain the arrangement of the mirrors was designed with that intention—to show a person a procession of passing perspectives and glimpses of themselves as they moved along.

Anne loved everything about her mentor's apartment with her remarkable facility for decoration. Her home had the look of exquisitely organized chaos—unusual artifacts gathered from all over the world, together with tapestries, sculpture, and paintings were everywhere on display. Anne smiled to herself, recalling the day she noticed a tiny troll doll in amongst the vast array of books tumbling over themselves on her shelves. Perfect, she had thought. And then there were always the striking arrangements of fresh-cut, exotic flowers tucked away on a corner table, or on the floor—wherever you might least expect them—simply waiting to be discovered. But this morning, Anne was drawn towards the window and the clouds drifting past in the pale blue sky.

"You seem a million miles away Anne, and tired," Margot said while offering her a cup of coffee from the gleaming silver tray she carried into the room.

"Thank you, Margot," Anne said, reaching for the white bone china cup and saucer. "Hmm, yes... both true."

"Tell me," Margot said softly, as she positioned herself attentively on the chair next to Anne.

"I was just noticing the clouds—that's what I am feeling this morning—like a cloud, drifting, weightless."

"And do you consider that a bad thing?"

"I don't know, but it is disconcerting."

"Do you know why you're identifying with a cloud today?"

"Of course, it's related to Anita's suicide…" Margot noticed Anne momentarily look down at the floor as she attempted to gain insight into her state. "I tossed and turned all night, recriminations flooding my brain. Then this morning, I had this dream…"

"Yes?" said Margot encouragingly.

"I was alone, looking into a courtyard of some kind—on a stone path underneath gothic archways—when I think of it now, it reminds me of the Abbey at Mont St. Michel."

"Yes."

"I was trying to get to the end of the path—I knew that something wonderful was waiting for me there—but with each step I took, the path became steeper, the light at the end more dim. I was tired. I saw a stone bench and lay down upon it. Then the scene shifted and I was in what was once a stone church. It was entirely empty, no windows, nothing—just me lying on a stone slab—like a table, or altar of some kind.

In the far corner of the nave, a door opened, and a shapeless black presence entered, moving towards me. Then I saw my son, but he didn't seem to understand what was happening. I tried to warn him, the presence was moving in his direction, but he didn't turn or acknowledge me in any way, just walked out a different door. Now I was alone and I knew the presence was aware of me. It came at me fast and menacingly—I knew it wanted to take me. Then I woke up."

After a few moments, Margot prompted, "So, what do you think?"

"Well, it's interesting to me that it has left me in this state."

"I agree…"

"It seems so clear I am working through the sense of loss, disconnection, I feel about Anita, who like my son, I was unable to save from death…"

"But you did save your son in your dream… I mean you, the dream writer/director/set designer and actor, had him walk out the door."

"True. I hadn't thought of that. And actually, when he left it was simply that he was moving on, continuing on his way, as it were… much like Anita. Each time she walked out my door, she was returning to her life—her journey—leaving me to mine."

"Exactly how it is. What about the courtyard?"

"Yes, I find that interesting as well… Do you remember me telling you about Xavier?"

"The exotic Portuguese man you met at the Louvre when you were living in Paris?" Margot said with a smile.

"Yes Xavier, the egotistical *child!* Even at twenty-two, still reeling from the sheer romance of it all, I knew it. It was the same old story—what attracts you in the first place can be the undoing later on."

Margot nodded her head and took a sip of coffee. "Sometimes knowing is not enough."

"Yes, quite true—that certainly was the case with me. But I digress, my reason for bringing it up in the first place was that Xavier and I visited Mont St. Michael very early in our relationship…"

"Ahhhh."

"We were on one of our famous 'let's just do it' trips. While casually thumbing through a guidebook, I came across a picture of the cathedral spire rising from the mist; the Archangel Michael was perched on top, high above the world. When I mentioned how beautiful and mysterious it seemed we took off to see it on impulse.

And so there we were at the Abbey of Mont St. Michel, and Xavier and I were lagging behind the tour group because of course Xavier kept wanting to sneak off to investigate the places the tour guide was not showing us. Seeing a little iron gate between two buildings with a sign, 'défense d'entrer, s'il vous plaît,' he took my hand and pulled me away from the group. After jiggling the handle and finding it unlocked, he pushed it open and pulled me inside.

We found ourselves in the courtyard where the monks were allowed out into the world—only the walls surrounding it were so high, the only part of the world they could take in was the sky—'To keep one's thoughts always on heaven.' Xavier had charged ahead, but I was transfixed, overcome by an extraordinary feeling of tranquility. I can still see myself so clearly, feeling everything I felt at the time as if it were right now, wishing never to have to leave that place."

"Those are special memories, Anne, when you are present within them."

"Yes, they are few and far between, but somehow they all connect in a timeless way."

"And how do you connect the memories of the Abbey to your dream?"

"In my dream, I was remembering the longing I felt in the Abbey, the longing for the light and tranquility that seemed so close—so possible to achieve. But in the dream it was difficult, the goal faded away and I got tired and simply lay down—just 'gave up.'"

"And how do the Abbey and the dream connect to your life now and Anita's suicide?"

"This is what I'm trying to put together. I know they all do connect—I feel they do—and I'm thinking perhaps the path I have chosen, my professional path with whatever dreams and visions I have about its ultimate worth, simply feels too hard. I guess I'm telling myself I'd like to stop, give it up."

"Well, that certainly makes sense," Margot said thoughtfully. "Would you like to know what popped into my head while you've been talking?"

Anne nodded her head slowly and a gentle smile formed on her lips. "Always."

Margot brought her hands together, her index fingers lightly touching her bottom lip. She was no longer looking at Anne but appeared to gaze at the Persian prayer rug that hung on the wall behind her chair.

"I'm struck first by the prominence of the church and its symbolism in your associations and in your dream," she said and lowered her eyes to meet those of her protégé. "It feels so—so cold," she continued, "the stone walls, the emptiness, the fact that you are alone. There is no warmth, no comfort, to be found there," she extended an upturned palm, "and yet that longing is still so strong in you." Anne nodded in agreement. "I also wonder what the connection is between Xavier and Victor. I am drawn to ask how you are feeling about Victor these days."

"Victor? Well, I hadn't made that connection, but okay; he was gone an entire year and returned only last night. He called me and, after our conversation, I called you. Anita was one of his students."

"Right, right. You and Victor met at her recital. And he called you when he returned. Had he heard about Anita?"

"No, I told him. He called because he felt something had happened and I was somehow involved."

"And do you find that at all interesting?"

"No, well yes; it is an interesting coincidence."

"Coincidence... well yes I see," she turned her head slightly to the side. "Let me ask you this Anne. Does Victor remind you of Xavier? I ask because I am wondering if he represents to you a kind of conduit between your present and your longings of the past, and speaking to him in the midst of your shock over Anita's suicide precipitated your dream. I am thinking your dream may be more about you feeling you are losing touch with your spiritual search rather than your professional aspirations when the wonderful light at the end of the path is becoming dim. Could it be you are telling yourself that to give up is to invite a premature death? That scene in the church made me think of a body in a sepulcher."

Anne gently shook her head from side to side. "It so amazes me, the connections you make, Margot. Your analysis rings true to me and I find it intriguing that you called Victor a conduit. There are things that are similar about him and Xavier, but I'm thinking the greater significance is how I connect Victor to the light—to my spiritual path—perhaps more than I care to admit."

"There is something more we can explore if you're willing," Margot said after a brief pause in their conversation.

"Yes, go on."

"I'm wondering whether your identification with Anita goes deeper than what we have discussed in these quasi supervision sessions before. Could it be, metaphorically speaking, that Anita's suicide is Anne's 'suicide' as well? Think about it: Anita had given up on her spiritual search and was putting all her energy into a professional career. Did you need her to succeed and find joy in her choice in order to indirectly affirm your own faith in the path you have chosen for yourself?"

"Transference? Margot, next you'll be telling me she's my daughter and her death represents the death of my son, again."

"If the shoe fits…" and they both laughed.

"Actually, it all boils down to the Greeks, Margot—if Oedipus had never been born, think what a wonderful world it would be! Right?"

"It's good to see that smile, Anne. Laughter is always good—I hope we never lose this capacity to laugh at ourselves. Now I know this has been a rather lengthy conversation, but there is one more thing I would like to add. I too feel I have failed—failed you as a supervisor. I should have been more alert to the possibility Anita was hiding her deepest pain, and that perhaps you were unconsciously colluding with her. That is *my* role. When I was thinking about this last night, it hit me hard that Anita was, so to speak, half a twin.

"Identical twins are one thing, fraternal twins another. Of course, we are told the risk of suicide increases when a family member or friend has committed suicide. I've seen some research to suggest that the risk doubles when a person's identical twin has committed suicide, but it also goes up when a non-identical twin has committed suicide. Frankly, the genetics of this does not interest me. It is the relationship of twins that does.

"From what you've told me, Anita and her brother were very close—almost to the point where the two combined represented one complete balanced being. Her brother's suicide left Anita partial—there was a gaping hole in her psyche. Her father had acted as a stabilizer, but then he died as well. Anita was impulsive and rather reckless when it came to alcohol. All in all, she represented a huge challenge to 'wholeness' despite the gains she had made. And remember, her nightmares had never stopped—she held a tremendous darkness within her soul. Perhaps we failed to give it sufficient respect—I don't know—I just don't know..." Margot's voice trailed off, leaving both her comment and their conversation without the benefit of a final punctuation.

Conversations

At exactly eleven a.m., Jake, dressed in a grey suit and tie, was standing teary-eyed at Victor's door listening to the sounds of the piano coming from inside. Not until the final chord was struck did he presume to knock.

He all but fell into Victor's embrace when Victor opened the door, and the two remained like statues for almost a minute. "I'm sorry, Victor; I didn't mean to be so emotional," he said when embarrassment finally took ascendancy over his grief.

"There's never a need to apologize for honesty," Victor said as he escorted his charge into the living room, where the tea was already brewed and cups set out on the coffee table in front of the couch.

"The tea smells great," said Jake.

"It's Indian style. The spices, milk, and sugar are all brewed together. I hope you like it. Let me pour you some."

"So…" Victor said slowly after a few sips.

"I'm really glad you're back, Victor. The last few days have been very stressful for me. I have so many questions to ask you."

"I understand, Jake, but first, tell me how you have been sleeping."

"Sleeping? Not very well at all—lots of dreams of Anita mixed with weird memories of the past and her brother, Ronny. I keep waking up in the middle of the night sweating, my mind going a million miles an hour." Jake put his cup down on the table and leaned towards his friend and teacher. "Victor, you seem to know so much, do you know why she did it?"

Victor sighed and took a sip of tea. "Is knowing why important?"

"I think I feel guilty. I keep thinking I could have done something. I guess that's why I want to know."

Victor put his cup on the table, "Jake, there was nothing you could have done—nothing anyone could have done. Nobody is to blame—not even Anita. The whole affair is an *unnecessary necessity.*"

"What do you mean?"

Victor turned his palm up and cocked his head to the side. "Jake," he said softly but with conviction, "sometimes we need to get off the train in order to learn that we should have stayed on board in the first place." Jake looked down at the table, his brow deeply knit.

"But," he said quietly and looked up, "Anita's dead—the train is gone." Victor smiled. Was that a hint of amusement Jake saw on his face?

"There is always another train, my friend."

"I don't know, Victor, but at least she's finally free."

Now it was Victor's turn to look down at the table.

"If only that were true," he said.

"Victor, Grace keeps saying suicide is a sin, and she's deeply worried Anita will go to hell."

Victor looked earnestly at Jake. "Jake, I am not speaking from a religious or moral perspective here. You said you want to understand. I am telling you now what Krita Baba has told me. What are generally called heaven and hell are in fact states the consciousness of the soul associates with after the physical body is dropped. There, in the states of heaven and hell, impressions from the previous life are balanced to a degree that allows the consciousness of the soul to take another physical body."

"Impressions?"

"Every action, be it physical or mental—even thoughts and feelings—create impressions on the mind. You can think of the mind as being like very soft clay—very easily impressed by anything that touches it. Everyone gathers innumerable and diverse impressions throughout the course of a lifetime. In order to move forward—to reincarnate—these diverse impressions must be reconciled. It is in the heaven and hell states that they are brought into an approximate balance."

"Approximate balance?"

"Yes, if they were perfectly balanced, then the soul would achieve the real freedom you hoped Anita would achieve. That real freedom is what some call Union with God, the Kingdom of Heaven, Self-Realization—there are many words people use to describe it. Whatever they call it however, it is the goal and ultimate destiny of all souls. But unfortunately, in the heaven and hell states, the balance is only approximate; it is always slightly tipped to one side or another."

"How come they don't they get it right?"

Victor could not repress a wry smile.

"*They?* There is no *they*, dear boy. The process is quite mechanical. But to answer your question; the balance is not achieved because there still remains a tremendous momentum of the force of life impelling the process further. That momentum has to be dissipated through millions of lifetimes."

"Like slowing down a car before it stops?"

"Correct."

"And all this happens mechanically? No one is driving the car?"

"It is quite mechanical, Jake, though the process is guided at certain critical points. This is the work of the real masters."

"Like Krita Baba?"

"Yes."

"And suicide—how does Anita's suicide fit into all of this?"

"Suicide terminates a life before all the impressions needed to be experienced in that life are experienced. As a result, the consciousness of the soul gets stuck, so to speak, in a state of limbo between its former life and its next. Consciousness is like a bubble rising from the bottom of the ocean; its nature is to rise, but it gets stuck under some overhanging rocks. The unexperienced impressions are like the rocks."

"That sounds terrible, Victor. What can we do?"

"Early this morning I called Krita Baba. He said he would help."

"But what can he do? He doesn't even know Anita."

"Krita Baba is no ordinary man, Jake. He has attained Supreme Reality. He is God Realized—God in human form. If he says he will help, it is neither a platitude nor an empty promise. He can do what we cannot. A little more tea?"

"Yes, thank you, it's very good. Victor, I don't understand this God in human form business. Are you saying that Krita Baba is Jesus?"

"That is a good question, Jake. No, Krita Baba is not Jesus, but he does enjoy the same state of consciousness as did Jesus. Krita Baba has lived many lifetimes—many millions of lifetimes—and has arrived at the goal—Supreme Reality. He experiences himself as that Reality and experiences everyone and everything as himself—as God. This state is the goal of all life—it is your goal too Jake… it is your destiny, and he can help you."

"How can he help me?"

"His ways are infinite, Jake, and each soul's journey is unique. I am not privy to that knowledge, but what I can say is that one way or another, he helps you to realize the Jake you now believe to be so real is merely a dream—an illusion—of your own true reality— the reality which appears to you now he helps you to realize is no more than a dream. You said, 'at least Anita is finally free,' in truth she *is* free, Jake. She always was, is, and will be free—she is eternal, infinite, beyond birth and death, beyond all suffering and is one with Infinite Bliss. This is the Anita Krita Baba sees, but the Anita we see, the Anita she sees, is an illusion within an illusion, and in this illusion she is not free. Krita Baba sees Anita this way as well. He sees her reality and he sees her illusion. He will help her to negotiate the path of illusion and achieve consciousness of her reality."

"And why would he help her, Victor?"

"Because he sees her as himself. Because he loves her."

Jake put down his cup and let out a low moan. His lower jaw began to tremble; then he took a deep breath and steadied himself.

"What does he look like, Victor?"

Victor stood up and walked over to the bookshelves. He picked up a small framed photograph, walked back and handed it to Jake. Jake stared at it intently. Victor could see his jaw begin to tremble again, and then the tears came and the heavy sobs. Victor placed his hand gently on Jake's shoulder.

"He is the man in my dream last night," Jake said slowly while still staring at the shirtless image of a grizzled old man sitting cross-legged on the ground. "I remember the eyes, just like this, they seemed to look into my very soul. He told me not to worry and then he disappeared."

Victor returned to his seat. He nodded his head and smiled. Jake looked at the picture for a long time then gently put it down on the coffee table.

"There is a lot I don't understand, Victor."

"That is the beginning," Victor replied…

***

"Mrs. Burrows, you remember my friend and piano teacher, Victor Linton?"

"Thank you for coming," the ashen-faced, grey-haired woman said, her voice flat and drained of all emotion. *She looks bad*, thought Jake, as he remembered the woman he formerly knew— the powerful, intimidating woman who was the mother of his best friend. Victor reached out to take her frail hand.

"I'm very sorry for your loss," he said and looked into her tired, dull eyes.

"Please," she said, gesturing into the house.

Jake had never seen the place look so disheveled. She led them into the kitchen. Victor watched her as she grabbed a dirty cup and small plate off the table and dropped them on the pile of unwashed dishes in the sink. It seemed to him that everything was out of place. Cans and open boxes were scattered on the counter, the floor looked like it needed to be washed; it seemed the only things in their proper place were two clean dishtowels folded and neatly stacked on the counter near the sink. Victor regarded them with more than a passing interest.

"Pull up a chair, Victor," said Jake as he took a seat at the kitchen table.

"Mrs. Burrows," he said, motioning to the chair at the head of the table where he remembered she used to sit, like a judge at her bench, back when he and Ronny were teenagers. Through the dull silence that followed, Jake could hear the ticking of the old clock on the wall—the relentless, unchanging tempo reminding him of seconds that seemed to pass like hours as they had sat like prey in the presence of her cold critical eye. *How many millions of seconds have passed between then and now?*

Victor looked over at the prematurely old woman. He felt he could almost read her thoughts; could her purgatory be any worse than that which she envisioned for her daughter? He looked at the wooden cross behind her, hanging on the wall over the sink. *How extraordinary,* he thought. *This symbol that has come to represent Christ's suffering for the creation has such a dark and loveless energy about it.*

"Are you a Christian, Victor?" she asked, breaking the silence.

Victor looked into her eyes—as dark and loveless as the old cross.

"I believe Jesus Christ was God in human form," he said softly.

"Do you love Him?"

"Really, Mrs. Burrows, with regard to love, I am not even a beggar at that table let alone a guest."

Jake, obviously uncomfortable with the way the conversation was going, leaned his head against his fist and looked down at the table.

"I see," she said coldly. "You know my Anita was a Christian, but she strayed in doubt and was weak in belief, and now she did this *thing*, and I am so worried she will be cast into hell."

Victor looked over at Jake and then back to her.

"God is merciful," he said slowly.

"So I asked Victor to play at the funeral—you know Victor was still Anita's piano teacher," Jake said, trying to change the subject.

"She was very promising when she was a child. Then she got distracted…" her voice trailed off. "What do you intend to play?"

"I once played a song for Anita in her lesson," Victor replied. "She had heard it before and she was very moved by it. She asked me for the music and began to learn it herself. I would like to play that song."

"A song—what was the song?"

"The song was 'Begin the Beguine' by Cole Porter."

The old lady closed her eyes and said nothing for a minute.

"I remember that song," she said slowly, and then in a voice like a whisper from light years away, said softly:

"Oh yes, let them begin the Beguine, make them play
'Til the stars that were there before return above you . . .
'Til you whisper to me once more, 'Darling, I love you!'
And we suddenly know, what heaven we're in,
when they begin the Beguine…"

She closed her eyes again. Jake and Victor both watched as deep sobs rocked her body. She covered her face with her hands when the tears came—a swollen river finally bursting its banks, surging through the decaying levees of pious hate carefully constructed to repress a lifetime of guilt and hypocrisy—surging, sweeping them to the ground, releasing her life and her spirit from her self-created bondage.

"Darling, I love you," Victor whispered softly to himself…

***

On the train ride out from the city, fragments of Anne's conversation with Margot replayed themselves in her mind. *"What about Victor?"* she heard Margot say. *Indeed, what about Victor?* she thought now.

It was mid-afternoon by the time Anne walked through her front door. Glad to be back in the nurturing refuge of her home, she brewed herself a pot of tea and then retired to the sanctuary of the deck overlooking the ravine. Comfortable in her favorite chair, her thoughts drifting slowly like the clouds overhead, she found herself transported in time to a day nearly five years before...

She was standing in Margot's hallway regarding, with a mixture of amusement and aversion, the oddly angled reflections of herself—a wild array of disconnected feet and legs, face and torso. She had laughed out loud at the impression it made.

"This is definitely an accurate representation of me today, Margot."

"Oh? Are you feeling discombobulated?"

"Broken first, then discombobulated," she answered lightly.

"Well, it's always good when we can laugh at ourselves," Margot said as she gestured toward the front room.

"So Anne, tell me what's going on," she continued after they had settled themselves into their usual places near the window.

"Well, Margot, we've talked before how sometimes there seems to be a common theme among my patients..."

"Yes."

"...and how I've wondered whether this is something I've unconsciously imposed upon them." Margot nodded as she reached for the glasses that hung from the string of colored beads around her neck.

"Well, this past month, I swear, the theme has been 'shatter the analyst.'"

Margot adjusted the glasses on her nose. "How intriguing; Tell me more," she replied.

Anne sighed. "It's a bit difficult to explain, since confusion reigns..."

"Never mind, just jump in anywhere."

"Okay, I'll start with Bill. Do you remember the advertising executive whose emotional life is a vast wasteland?"

"The one who believes the world owes him a debt of gratitude?"

"Yes, that's Bill. He started the session with a summation of our work together, how he had been reflecting on it for some time and had come to the conclusion it was doing him a world of good. He especially appreciated how I had permitted him to re-adjust our sessions to come just once a week. He said it was working really well for him."

"But what he meant was…?"

"Yes exactly; what he meant was I didn't care enough about him, or appreciate the magnitude of his suffering sufficiently."

"And what makes you say that?"

"Because he didn't even make it to the end of the session before he 'fired' me."

"Yes," Margot replied with studied impartiality. "And what else?"

"Then there's Betty…"

"The woman caught in such tremendous guilt over her conflict with her ailing mother?"

"The same. All month she's been treading water in a sea of ambivalence about whether she should allow her mother to move in with her or to ignore her complaints as attention seeking and put her into an assisted-living situation. She would go back and forth with me on this, convinced at some level she was using our sessions to come to a rational adult decision…"

"But?"

"But really all she *so* wanted was for me to tell her what to do."

"Well, that would make it much easier for her of course. Then, if it turns out to be the wrong decision, you become the bearer of the blame and she remains the martyr—that's one of her themes, as I recall."

"Exactly. So, she came to me with a dream about being in a lifeboat. It was very small and the seas were rough and swollen. She could see something approaching, swimming towards her, and she became frightened. And then she realized it was me, and right behind me was her mother. She knew the boat would sink if she attempted to get the two of us on board."

"So she saved her mother."

"No surprise there, but how she interpreted the meaning of the dream certainly was a surprise—or at least, it was quite a different spin than my own."

"How so?"

"Well, my initial sense of the dream was that the 'lifeboat' represented a feeling of accomplishment—a result of our work together—and that she was now potentially capable of taking care of her mother."

"That sounds quite reasonable to me, but perhaps you were guilty of wishful thinking and a bit of projection in this, yes?"

"Oh, I'd say so! Hector the Projector strikes again! Betty said her dream made her realize she had placed herself in the position of needing to rescue *me*, and very nearly at the expense of her own mother. She said she saw now, quite clearly, that *our* relationship had superseded her relationship with her mother, who desperately needed her help. She was positively elated at this revelation, said it was a great awakening, and with that, summarily ended our work together."

Margot sighed. "Yes, I can see how that might shake you up. However, it was a positive move on her part, don't you think?"

"I know, one must take responsibility, and I agree it was a decisive moment, but it blindsided me."

"And I suspect you are left feeling that this is exactly the point at which some really important work could have begun—a genuine healing of her troubled relationship with her mother."

"Absolutely, I'm still convinced my interpretation of her dream was valid. After all, it was she who placed herself in high seas, and in a small boat, thereby creating a position where forces beyond her control could overwhelm her. She was setting herself up to not have to face personal failure but to become, once again, a martyr."

"And continuing to work with you would make it difficult to

continue her charade?"

"That's what I'm thinking, yes."

"Of course, that is possible," Margot said as she slowly turned the beads on the string that hung from her glasses. "But it is her choice, Anne, and she didn't exactly leave you much room for negotiation."

"No, I guess not. I did not question her decision; she showed such uncharacteristic resolve, I felt it was best to leave it alone, wish her well, and leave the door open."

"Perhaps that was as much as anyone could do. As I recall, Betty had very strong dependency needs, so for her to take such decisive action in severing a relationship does suggest to me there was tremendous power in her dream. Ah, the magnificent mystery of the unconscious!"

"Yes, the magnificent mystery of the unconscious. You couldn't have put it better."

"So these attacks on the analyst you mentioned to start with—are there more? Because I am beginning to wonder now who's doing the attacking? You brought up the unconscious influence we can have on our patients, in terms of calling forth 'themes.' Could you say more about that?"

Anne let out a deep sigh.

"I hadn't consciously made the connection until just this moment, but now I'm wondering about the effect a new man in my life is having on me."

"A new man?"

"This is going to take some explaining," Anne said tentatively.

"We have time, Anne, take it."

"Just over a month ago, Anita—you remember Anita?"

"The law student, right?"

"Right. Well, Anita invited me to her first piano recital. Actually it was I who suggested she begin taking the lessons after learning in one of our sessions she had taken lessons when she was a little girl."

"And she stopped after her brother's suicide?"

"Exactly. So, she began taking lessons with a man named Victor Linton, an absolutely extraordinary teacher, by her own account, and an altogether remarkable human being. By the time of her first recital, I'd already had the opportunity to process any number of reactions I'd had to comments she'd reported to me—comments touching on life and meaning, universal laws, and the like."

"From a piano teacher?"

"Yes, well apparently Victor Linton was no ordinary piano teacher and the things Anita had told me he said triggered all manner of unpleasant reactions in me."

"Really? That could cause some difficulties."

"Of course I did manage to keep my reactions from Anita, but, to myself, I readily admitted to feelings of jealousy, annoyance, and defensiveness."

"So you looked at that?"

"I had to. It was obvious I felt some of his ideas threatened the basis of Anita's and my work. But in the end, after working through it, I was mostly intrigued."

"Did you still feel threatened?"

"Yes, a bit threatened, I'd have to say—yet intrigued."

"A testimony, I would say, to the strength of your own work on yourself. Please go on, Anne."

"Well, I had reached the point where I wished I could meet him for myself; so I was quite pleased to receive her invitation and have an opportunity to experience the master in action, so to speak." Margot shifted in her chair, crossing one arm in front of herself and resting the elbow of the other on it. She propped her head on her palm in a posture of thoughtful reflection.

"The recital was in Victor's home, his studio being a large room at the back of one of those old walk-up apartments in the Sheffield neighborhood—quite serene. I don't know what I expected him to look like, but it was not what greeted me when he opened the door. Anita had said he was sixty, but standing in front of me was a man whose face looked ten years younger, with eyes infinitely older. I don't know how to explain that. But he's quite distinguished looking, with a full head of silvery hair. I'd say he's about six feet two—a well-built, but slender man, with sculpted features—square chin, straight nose. I suspect he was athletic in his youth, and he still carries himself easily. But it's his eyes—his eyes are blue and have an innocent sparkle despite the age that's also reflected there. I have to admit that I'm more than a little fascinated by them. In his eyes I sense a lucidity and intelligence laced with a wicked sense of play and good humor."

"You saw all that when he met you at the door?" Margot sounded incredulous.

Anne laughed. "Well perhaps I'm getting a little ahead of myself. I was interested in him right from the beginning—rather jazzed actually—and observed him closely throughout the recital."

"And the recital itself; what did you think about that? I've been to more than a few student recitals myself. They are often fertile ground for revealing all manner of interesting psychological disorders."

"I know what you mean, Margot. This recital was really very nice—small, only about a dozen people including the students. All the students played well and seemed to be quite poised. Anita impressed me most—it was almost as if she fell into a trance as she played. I saw none of the tortured Anita I'm so used to meeting in our sessions. And that I attribute to the influence of Victor Linton. It was a quality that came through in all his students—in their presence and in their playing. Usually with recitals I can't wait for them to be over—to release all concerned from the stress and suffering—but I must admit this time I really hated for it to end. My only disappointment was that Victor didn't play, which I mentioned to him later when Anita introduced us. He was very gracious and invited me to come by any time he would be happy to play for me. And that's how it all started."

"How lovely, Anne—very fairytale like," Margot said with a hint of a wry smile. "So what is it that Victor has set in motion in you?"

"Well, to put it simply: Victor is having a profound influence on me. And our conversation now is making me think that it is his way of being, and his ideas, which I haven't even begun to describe to you, that have caused me to doubt my efficacy."

"Shatter the analyst, I see. You're carrying that within you and are particularly sensitive to picking up the theme, as you referred to it, among some of your patients."

***

Anne took the tea cozy off the teapot and poured another cup. "*What about Victor?*" she could still hear her mentor's voice.

"Yes, what about Victor?" she repeated aloud to the clouds that drifted silently in the sky beyond the treetops.

The Dream of Being Us

Anne and Victor sat next to each other, each with their own thoughts, in a pew near the rear of the chapel. The late afternoon sunlight was filtering through the stained-glass windows; the scent of lilies was strong in the still air, and the solemn beauty and grandeur of the old church seemed to evoke a feeling of a benevolent and comforting eternity beyond the moment.

Jake had done a truly remarkable job helping Mrs. Burrows with all the details of a traditional church service—despite the fact that neither he nor Anita had ever found any real comfort or support in the rites and rituals of the Catholic Church. But he selflessly carried out Mrs. Burrows' wishes, and his sincerity, coupled with Anita's tragic story, had opened doors for him at one of Chicago's Coalition of Welcoming Churches. There, in the presence of a kindly and helpful Episcopal reverend, Jake had wept with gratitude and longing.

Anne watched the remaining guests arrive and take seats. It was like watching a dream—she felt disconnected from the moment, still caught in her own painful ruminations over Anita's suicide and the tremendous burden of culpability she continued to experience. Anita must have known this would be everyone's reaction, she mused. Why else the note: It is not your fault—addressed to no one in particular? Now, in the confluence of Anita's suicide and Victor's return, Anne's questions about suffering and what meaning could be found within its pain, surged like wildfire, burning away the undergrowth of tentative and hypothetical explanations that had distracted, but never quite convinced her.

Why is suffering intrinsically woven into the fabric of life? From some of the things Victor had said, things some part of her dared not even consider, the question arose, "Might suffering actually be totally irrelevant?" If that were so, what about her cherished belief that suffering played an important role in the arena of personal growth? Was that simply further evidence of her ignorance of the Truth—her own self-deceptive fantasy constructed from decades of misinterpreting the spiritual writings and practices she had researched and even engaged in? Perhaps she really had lost her way, and perhaps that was what her dream was really about?

She looked over at Victor. He seemed his usual calm, attentive, and detached self. How can he be attentive *and* detached she wondered, but her musing was interrupted when Grace Burrows entered the chapel with Jake at her side.

Anne had only met her once, a few years ago at Anita's recital—not that long ago really—but the woman entering the chapel was a different woman. Her dark auburn hair had gone almost completely grey, and there was nothing imperious about her now. Standing at Jake's side she seemed remarkably small and frail. What of the suffering she must be going through: her beloved husband lost to cancer, and now *both* her children dead from suicide? Anne gave an involuntary shudder at the thought, as tears spilled from her eyes and ran down her cheeks. She dabbed at her face and leaned closer to Victor. He seemed so peaceful—almost serene—like the photograph he had sent her of the statue of the Emerald Buddha ensconced in a niche high above the hustle and bustle of an ancient Thai temple.

"Victor," she whispered to him. Victor leaned closer.

"Yes…"

"Victor, do you remember the little poem you sent me about the Emerald Buddha?" Victor turned his head and saw the tracks of her tears down her cheeks. Then he closed his eyes.

"I think so," he said.

"Tell me," she said and leaned even closer to him as he whispered:

"Birth and breath,
Life and death,
The sacred and the mundane,

Joys and sorrows,
Good and bad,
Curses and prayers,
Pass beneath you —

I look up, gazing at you in your heavenly tower and
I wonder: When you see only everything,
Does this everything include nothing?

I close my eyes and watch my thoughts,
Does any of it really matter?

Your presence beyond reminds me
My world is dust crumbling into dust —
I contemplate,
What is seeing everything without seeing nothing?"

"Does God even know our suffering, Victor?"

Victor smiled and took her hand. "That God in the temple, when He is asleep, does not experience suffering. That same God, when He is awake, also does not experience suffering. But that God, when He is dreaming the dream of being us experiences suffering. Dreaming is the stage that precedes God's awaking to His real state of Infinite Bliss."

"So suffering does have a purpose?"

"Yes, dear, suffering is part of the illusion that sustains reality."

They both turned when the priest entered the chapel and made her way to the altar. They watched her make a simple bow before turning to face the mourners. A delicate smile showed briefly on her face; then she closed her eyes and whispered something—a prayer, Anne guessed.

"Let me welcome you all, for all are welcome here," she said with a quiet strength and warmth that revealed no trace of condescension or pomposity.

"I never met Anita, but I wish I had. Still, over the past few days, having had the privilege of meeting and speaking with some of you about Anita, I feel I have been honored to learn a little about this sweet soul—who she was and what she brought into your lives. In this way, through you, I feel I have come to know her too." Again, the slightest hint of a smile played upon her face.

"Anita suffered tremendous losses in her brief life and was overwhelmed by the vision of only more loss on the horizon; yet she was thinking about all of you until the very end. That is the meaning and the motivation I find behind her wish for all who knew and loved her: 'It is not your fault.' These are her words." She paused briefly.

"It is not your fault." She paused again, longer this time.

"It is not your fault."

In the fading light of early evening, the chapel bathed in the warmth of candlelight, the priest prayed over Anita's casket. Anne could not hear her words, nor did she need to. After making the sign of the cross over the casket, the priest raised her outstretched arms towards the heavens, and said with an extraordinary depth of feeling, "Lord, have mercy on us all," after which she bowed her head and crossed her arms over her chest, clutching a small crucifix to her breast. Anne felt the power of the image and the simple prayer the priest intoned. At length, the priest dropped her arms and once more surveyed the assembly.

"I have a favorite poem by the German poet Rainer Maria Rilke. It comes from his *Book of Hours*. I would like to share it with you.

"God, give us each our own death,
the dying that proceeds
from each of our lives:

the way we loved,
the meanings we made,
our need."

Anne closed her eyes. "The way we loved, the meanings we made...," she repeated softly to herself as the priest retired to a seat near the wall of the chancel. So absorbed by the poem that had so perfectly captured her feelings, Anne did not notice Victor sliding quietly out of the pew and walking slowly to the piano in front of the pulpit. After seating himself, he closed his eyes.

The funeral itself had meant little to him. He found it uncomfortably naïve and sentimental and so he had tried to find his place in the gathering by tuning in to Anita's presence. *My dear sweet angel,* he spoke silently in his heart, *do not worry or fear. Your Beloved loves you and will help you. All that you and we experience is just an illusion. Death does not even exist. I play this song for you—this song that touched you so—the song that reminds you that in the end we will be with Him again under the stars.*

Victor began by playing a long slow arpeggio across both hands. The rhythm slowed as it reached its highest note and hung suspended in the room like a star in a musical firmament. Waiting for the perfect moment, when every sound had all but died away, he began the unaccompanied melody—very slowly, very quietly— playing freely with only his right hand—his left resting gently on his thigh. A murmur ran through the congregation as many recognized the familiar old tune.

Beginning the second verse, he brought his left hand back to the keys to add just the right touch of harmony to the melody. The chords entered without fanfare—sparingly and with respect— hinting at, rather than articulating, a gentle Latin rhythm. Then, when the song moved into the second section with the variation of the melody on the silent words, "So, don't let them begin the Beguine..." the chords fell suddenly quiet and only the melody could be heard again. The tune continued, narrating without words the story of the lover's separation from the beloved, her doomed attempt to forget him, and how in the end she recalls the tune of the Beguine that had been playing when they were last together. With that the crumbling walls she had built to shelter the all too poignant memories fall into dust and she cries out, "Oh yes, let them begin the Beguine, make them play…" and the lover and the Beloved, united again, sing and dance—together and forever—lost in a divine embrace.

***

Descending the steps from the chapel, Victor at her side, Anne never felt so light, so alive. Something she could not explain or even describe had touched her—as if a veil had been lifted for a moment, freeing her. Life, death, life again… she could see the cycle, feel the unbroken continuity, and the touch of the merciful compassionate hand that guided it all.

Stepping out onto the sidewalk, she took Victor's hand. "If love's hand can be so beautiful, then what must love's face be like?" she whispered to Victor.

Victor, paying her compliment the highest respect, said nothing.

The Lesson

"I'm glad you called about our lesson tomorrow; I was thinking about calling you. What with the funeral only a week ago and you being away for so long before that... You know, I haven't been practicing very much, and I was thinking maybe I should cancel our lesson and take another week to get back on track."

"Come."

"Come?" Jake repeated.

"Yes, Jake, I think it might be the best thing. There is always work to do, and we will start from wherever you are."

"That sounds right, Victor. It's probably just what I need—and besides, if we have time, I really want to hear more about India and your guru, Krita Baba."

"If you can come at seven you will be my last student of the evening and we can talk after your lesson."

"Can do. Thanks, Victor, I'll see you then."

***

"Yes, go ahead and sight-read the little *Sinfonia in G Minor* by Bach," Victor said after looking in the black book he kept with comments on each student's lessons. Jake squirmed a little on the bench at the piano. He had sensed from the moment he walked in the door that Victor was all business. And it was true, whatever personal relationship he had with a student, no matter how close they were, when Victor was teaching, all personal history was set aside and he was only about the work at hand.

"I haven't looked at it for over a week and, to tell you the truth, I never got very far with it while you were away," Jake said meekly. "It's really beautiful and I guess I'm kind of intimidated…"

"That's okay," Victor stopped him, "just read it now without any preconceptions of where you think you should be or would like to be."

"I guess it wouldn't hurt to give it a go." Victor smiled and watched as Jake fished the music out of his briefcase and set it on the piano. Without the slightest hesitation, he began to play. He played, faltered, began to play again and faltered again. Victor, sitting on the little chair at the side of the piano bench, raised his hand.

"Jake, you're going too fast and you are rushing," he said gently. "Remember what we've always talked about. You are not reading to play it or perform it; you are reading to learn it. Go slow; pay attention to everything you are reading—your mission is to learn."

Jake nodded his head as he remembered some of the things Victor had been saying from the very beginning. "People are in the habit of making unnecessary mistakes. They play things over and over with some tacit and totally unsubstantiated idea that the next time will be better. They get into the habit of making mistakes and then trying to correct them—not to mention the mistakes they make of which they are never even aware. Go slow," he would say calmly and patiently. "Your mind is the teacher; your fingers are the student; don't let your fingers get ahead of your thinking—you must teach them to do exactly what you want them to do.

"Get all you can from the first thoughtful reading and then continue to stay in control of your work until the music is finally realized."

"Can I try again?" Jake asked. Victor nodded and Jake began to play.

"Stop!" Victor raised his hand again. "Remember to start from stillness. Both times today, when you began, you just slid into reading without acknowledging the beginning of your effort.

Silence is the source of sound; always respect the source; begin from silence."

Jake took a deep breath to gather himself. Then, more slowly and very thoughtfully, he began to read the *Sinfonia*. He read straight through the piece, without stopping or being stopped, allowing himself the freedom to suspend the tempo if he needed the time to think through a chord or a rhythm or a fingering.

"Yes," Victor said softly after the last sounds had died away...

***

"I'm so glad I came in for a lesson today," Jake was saying as they walked to the Little Tokyo Restaurant on Halsted Street. "It was a great lesson—great to be back—I'm even relaxed now, probably for the first time since... since Anita..."

Victor nodded and picked up the pace. Soon they were seated at a small table in the lounge sharing a bottle of cold sake.

"You know, Victor, so much has happened lately, I don't know where to begin, but I'm glad you're back and we can finally talk. I really enjoyed getting your letters and hearing about the places you visited and about Krita Baba—even though I still don't actually get this whole spiritual thing." Victor smiled and took another sip of sake.

"So this is what you want to talk about?"

"Yes."

"What?"

"Yes."

Victor smiled again. "I mean, Jake, this whole spiritual thing, as you called it, is a big subject. Do you know specifically what it is you want us to talk about?"

Jake pursed his lips and closed his eyes. "I guess that's it... it's such a big subject, I don't even know where to start and then when we do start talking I always start to feel like I'm going around in circles—especially when you talk about Krita Baba. Not only do I not know who, or even what, he is, I don't have any idea at all about... um... why he is. Does that make sense?"

"Actually, Jake, it makes perfect sense. We need a starting point. Let me see if I can help. So, a man looks at a stone and knows he is not a stone. He looks at a plant and knows he is not a plant. He looks at a worm and a fish and a bird; he looks at an animal, and he knows he is not them either. He says, 'I am a man,' because that is how he experiences himself. If he were content with this—if he were fully convinced that he was a man—then that would be the end of it, there would be no need for anything more—no masters, no gurus, no teachings, no religions. But it doesn't end there, does it, Jake? Because when a man looks at himself he realizes, somewhere deep down in the very core of his being, there is something more—that he is something more. And so he looks around for something else—for something more to identify with—but cannot find any forms—any beings—beyond him. Still he feels—he knows—there is—there must be—something more, and so he tries to invent words to describe what he cannot see.

"He begins to talk about Self, or God, or Realization—whatever works for him—and he searches for a way, a path, a teaching, a religion... something he can follow, something he can do, in order to reach this Self, God, or Realization."

Jake had been sitting with his head propped against his hand, his elbow resting on the table.

"Are you following me, Jake?"

"Yes, I can follow it all; I remember talking about it before your trip. It's like life leaves us incomplete and we sense that and we begin to search. I get that, but what I don't understand is where these Perfect Masters like Krita Baba fit in."

"Right Jake, I was about to come to that. A Perfect Master is someone who has achieved it all—God, Self, Realization. For them, their Godhood is not grounded in faith, or conviction, or intuition; it is a matter of direct experience. For a Perfect Master to say, 'I am God' is as natural—actually more natural—as for you to say you are a man."

"And how does this God Realization happen? Is it something

like the Resurrection—death brings God Realization and then the person comes back to life?"

"Not at all, Jake. God Realization always occurs in a human body—in life and not in death. But what follows is different for each individual depending on their destiny. Some *drop the body* almost immediately after Realization, while others retain the body for some time. The difference is not in their state, Jake, they are all equally 'Realized,' but the difference is in the degree of responsibility each has in regard to the creation. A God Realized individual who retains the body, has responsibility to the creation, and also regains consciousness of creation, is called a Perfect Master—a Man God. Krita Baba is such a one."

"But how do you know? Can you tell just by looking at him?"

"This is an interesting question, Jake, and the answer is both no and yes. On the surface, a Perfect Master may not look like anyone special but—and this is very important—when you are in the presence of a Perfect Master and he is not purposely veiling his true state from you, then you feel—you know unequivocally—you are in the presence of God. You know this because *you* become changed. You don't think normally; you become charged with divine love so intense that all your desires, concerns, and opinions become temporarily suspended. It is nothing you do; it is not up to you at all; in fact, you couldn't resist it if you tried." Victor paused and poured another glass of sake. "To love and serve such a Perfect Master is absolutely the most expedient way to reach the goal. To be in the presence of a real Perfect Master achieves more in a moment than an individual can accomplish in thousands of lifetimes of efforts, practices, sacrifices, penances, meditations and good deeds."

"Victor, this is rather a lot to take in, let alone accept, all at once."

"I know it is, Jake, I know. What do you think of having a little sushi?"

"Sounds good. I'm beginning to feel hungry and the sake is giving me a bit of a buzz." Jake reached for the a la carte order card and a pencil and began to check off various items. When he was finished, he handed it over to Victor.

"You *are* hungry, aren't you?" he kidded and added a few more items to the order before handing it back to Jake. "What do you think?" he said.

"Good," Jake replied and motioned to the waitress when she passed near the table.

"You would like to order some sushi?" she said with a smile.

"Yes," Jake smiled back and handed her the order. "How did you know?"

"I saw you checking things off," she replied. Neither the gesture of reaching behind his head to rub his own neck, nor the slight blush that appeared on Jake's cheeks went unnoticed by Victor.

"Pretty girl, don't you think?" Victor said when she left the table.

"Uh yeah," Jake mumbled as he reached for the card advertising Japanese beer stuck between the soy sauce and the little vase with the fake orchid.

"Really pretty," Victor prodded. "Did you notice her breasts when she bent over the table to take the order?"

"Not really."

"Come on, you must have. The smooth ivory color of her skin over the black tank top?"

"Really, Victor, I wasn't looking."

"Then why were you blushing?" Victor teased. "Why don't you ask her out? I could go to the bathroom and you could call her over to the table..."

"Victor, I can't believe you're talking like this. I mean we were just having this spiritual conversation. It makes me feel uncomfortable."

"And what kind of spirituality would it be if it denied the power of beauty? What kind of spirituality would it be if it segregated itself against sex and lust?"

"So that's it, you said all those things about her to make a point?"

"Actually, I said what was on my mind. I had noticed her from the moment we first walked into the bar. You have to admit how beautiful her long black hair is—and the way she moves—just look at her over there. Admit it; you would love to take her out."

"Victor, even if I did… I mean, Anita just died!"

"I'm aware of that, Jake, but what about it, are you being sentimental or concerned with appearances?"

"No, it's out of respect."

"I see, respect. Do you mean respect for Anita? Do you think she even knows, let alone cares, if you go out with another woman?"

Jake all but jumped out of his chair when the waitress suddenly appeared at the table with the sushi, the beer ad dropping out of his hand onto the floor. Victor grinned in delight.

"It's right over there by her foot," he said, pointing at the floor. Jake looked down automatically at the card and the waitress's legs and short miniskirt.

"I'll get it later."

"Oh, I'll get it," the waitress said as she bent down close to Jake, who slid away from her to the other side of his chair. Victor could not contain his amusement and laughed with glee.

"Will there be anything else?" she asked after retrieving the card and arranging the sushi on the table. Victor deferred the question to Jake with a thrust of his chin in his direction.

"No, thank you, this is just fine," Jake mumbled without looking at her. An awkward silence enfolded them after she walked away; the gulf between their moods was too great to span. Victor picked up a piece of salmon and put the whole thing into his mouth. He gestured an upturned palm at the wooden platter. Jake picked up a piece of tuna without looking directly at his friend.

"Why did you do that?" Jake finally asked.

"You rubbed your neck," Victor replied.

"What do you mean?" the irritation was evident in his voice. "Don't play with me, Victor."

"It was a gesture of denial, Jake. You couldn't admit your

attraction to her, and then when I said something, you couldn't admit it to me. You said you wanted to speak about spirituality. Frankly, I don't like the word at all, but if we must use it, I would say that real spirituality is not a game for the weak or fainthearted; when it becomes tinged by any kind of hypocrisy or repression, one's progress and real efforts end right there."

"Well, you could have just told me that; you didn't need to be so cruel."

"Yes, we all want spirituality, but only on our own terms. Talk is easy—and cheap. Imagine if our piano lessons consisted only in talking about playing the piano—how successful do you think they would be?"

"Not very," Jake admitted. "But in this case, I was only asking you about things; I just wanted to talk."

"You wanted to learn?"

"Yes."

"Are you learning?"

"Yes."

Victor raised an upturned palm and smiled. Jake took a deep breath. "For the serious seeker, it does not get any easier, Jake. Progress on the spiritual path is determined not so much by what you acquire as what you lose. I have heard it said that in the spiritual game, the loser rejoices and the winner feels ashamed."

"Because loss is gain?"

"Yes. When I was in India, I heard an old follower of Krita Baba, Amrit, talking to a man named Abdul. Abdul had asked Amrit a question about what he had learned after all the years he had spent with his guru. The old follower answered in this way: 'Abdul, what is the difference between you and me?' he asked.

"'I don't know,' was the reply.

"'The difference is this,' said Amrit. 'You one hundred percent believe that you are Abdul, while there is one little part of me that knows I am not Amrit.'"

Jake looked perplexed.

"So, is it a matter of letting go? Like giving up some idea of who or what I am?"

"Well sort of, Jake, but I have heard people talk about 'letting go,' and generally it is not understood that what needs to be let go of is the person who is trying to let go."

"Are you saying I'm supposed to let go of myself?"

"Yes. Can you do it?"

"No."

"That is why I don't talk about letting go."

"And what about suffering Victor? Where does that fit in?"

"A lot is made of suffering on the spiritual path. I maintain that none of it is necessary, while at the same time, it is inevitable. Jake, suffering is not the means by which progress is made, suffering is the result of attachment—attachment to our bodies, our thoughts and feelings—attachment to everything we think we are. We need to lose ourselves to find ourselves. What you experienced tonight is just a glimpse of the process. Spirituality is not at all what you think it is."

"More sake?" the waitress asked when she returned to the table.

"More sake?" Victor repeated to Jake, who was still trying not to look at the waitress.

"I think I'm fine," Jake said softly.

"I think we're fine," Victor repeated to the waitress. "The sake was very good and the sushi was excellent as usual."

The waitress gave a slight bow. "Thank you, sir. Then will there be anything else?" Victor cut his eyes over to Jake and then back to the waitress.

"May I ask you your name?"

"My name is Miyu," she said with a delicate smile.

"Miyu," Victor repeated. "What does it mean?"

"Japanese names often have many meanings. Miyu means 'beautiful,' but it also means 'tie' or 'bind.'"

Victor noticed the soft blush of color appear on her cheeks.

"That is so interesting. Thank you, Miyu, you have been an excellent server."

"Thank you, sir, I'll just leave the check until you are ready."

"I still think you should ask her out," he said to Jake after she left the table.

Jake smiled. "Give me another week or so," he said, trying to avoid the subject, then he added, "I'm very glad we came here tonight, and I'm sorry to have reacted like I did. I really do want to know about these things; I know they are important—I already feel like I'm not the person I thought I was a month ago. And I've had more dreams of the man I now know is Krita Baba. My interest is not superficial."

"I know, Jake, I know," said Victor as they rose from the table.

Friendship

"This place is so incredible, Victor; I feel like we've gone back in time to the late fifties."

"Worth getting up so early?"

"Yes, this was such a good idea—it's exactly what I need."

"Me too—us too. We really haven't had any time together since I returned—what with Anita's suicide and the funeral…" Victor's voice trailed off as he squeezed Anne's hand. "Look down Main Street. There's the famous Friendship Mound."

"Impressive," Anne joked. "Race you to the top?"

"Let's not, and say we did, it's higher than you think."

"Ah, Grasshopper, a wise choice to bow out of the race," she kidded. "I think some breakfast is in order before we go riding. What do you think?"

"Okay, but let me think," Victor said, casting his eyes up and down the street. "We could go to the *diner* across the street, or we could go to… the diner across the *street*."

Anne paused as if deep in thought. "Well, actually, I'd prefer going to the diner *across* the street."

"All right, all right. I don't want to argue. The diner *across* the street it is, but watch out for all the traffic," he joked as he zigzagged back and forth, steering them across the empty street. Anne loved how they could play together; she hadn't realized how much she missed it—how much tension had come between them since Victor's return.

"How did you ever find this place?" Anne asked, admiring the pristine condition of the old leather upholstered booth and its grey Formica table trimmed with gleaming chrome.

"I've been coming to this area since I was little boy. My mother had a cousin, Lily, who moved out here with her husband and their son some fifty years ago to escape the grind of city life. Her husband died a while back, and their son is long since married and living in New York City, but Aunt Lily continues to live in Friendship. Her farm is just a few miles out of town—that's where we're going to get the horses for our ride."

"Some coffee for you and your lady friend, Victor?" said the elderly lady with snow-white curly hair, and a pink flowered apron.

"Hello, Nora, how are things?" Victor said warmly.

"'Bout the same as always I believe—keeping things going here at the diner, getting over to the church functions when I can."

"But you look great, Nora, as always—keeping well?"

"Thank God and a healthy constitution," she winked as she nodded at Victor.

"Amen to that, Nora. I'd like you to meet my friend Anne."

"Hello, dear. Any friend of Victor's is a friend of mine."

"Thank you, Nora; it's a pleasure to meet you. It seems like you've known Victor for a while."

"Yes, dear, I've known him since he was just a little nipper."

Anne looked at Victor and smiled broadly. "A little nipper, I can see it. A tall skinny little nipper at that," she kidded. Victor raised one eyebrow in response.

"So what brings you all to Friendship today? You here to see your Aunt Lily?"

"Yes, I thought we could go horseback riding and hang out with the greyhounds as well."

"I know she'll be pleased to see you. I'll be right back with your coffee. Coffee for you too, dear?"

"Yes, thank you."

"Are you still making your fabulous blueberry pancakes?" Victor called after her.

"Of course," Nora said without looking back.

"Anne, Nora makes the best pancakes in the world. Are you interested?"

"Absolutely."

"I heard," Nora called over her shoulder. "I'll bring you back the coffee and then get started on the cakes."

"She's so alert, and spry," Anne observed as Nora made her way behind the counter to the coffee machine.

"Always has been—she has twice the energy of a person half her age."

"So, greyhounds?" Anne said with a smile as she sipped her coffee.

"Yes, greyhounds. Aunt Lily is truly one of a kind. She has always taken, as they say, a road less traveled. Anyway, before greyhound rescue became fashionable, Lily would drive her old van to the racetracks up north and down south and beg the greyhound owners for the hounds they were going to retire. In those days, 'retire' was simply a euphemism for a rather grizzly fate. So Lily would offer to pay to take them off the owner's hands. She was not always successful."

"It wasn't that the owners were that attached to their dogs?"

"Hardly, but a racing greyhound is a very expensive animal. The owners didn't want other people to use them for breeding. So Lily would pay a local vet to have them spayed or neutered, show the proof to the owners, and then bring the hounds back to the farm where she would house, feed, exercise, and love them. There were times she had as many as twenty hounds on the farm."

"And there are still greyhounds on the farm?"

"Oh yes, you'll see." Victor turned and sniffed the air when Nora arrived with the pancakes.

"Smells so good!" he said as Nora placed them on the table, "takes me back to when I was a kid."

Nora smiled and laid her hand on his shoulder.

"Isn't he the sweetest thing?" she said to Anne, who had to admit that this side of Victor was indeed the sweetest.

"And charming too," Anne added.

"You seem pretty sweet as well, dear. I'm very pleased Victor has found himself such a lovely lady. How did you two meet?"

"It's a bit of a long story, Nora," Victor said.

"Are you a musician too, Annie?"

"A music lover, I would say. However, I'm a doctor by profession—a psychoanalyst."

"I see; beauty and brains."

"Thank you, Nora," Anne said modestly.

"You're an astute judge of character, Nora," Victor added.

"Of course I am, dear. Well, I'll be back in a little while to see if you need anything."

Anne could feel her enchantment with Victor growing all over again. When Victor was in such a warm and expansive mood, life itself took on an entirely different color and vibrancy. Being with him then was more than easy—it was as natural as if they had known each other their entire lives—and yet it was as fresh and interesting as the day they first met. Anne held her coffee in both hands warming them as she gazed over the cup at this mysterious man in front of her. Unexpectedly, her eyes began to well up.

"What is it, dear?" Victor asked tenderly.

Without shifting her gaze, Anne allowed a tear to spill down her cheek. "I'm just so… happy," she said, smiling.

"You think so now. Just wait 'til you taste your pancakes! Whatever you do, don't let them get cold." He smiled back and then suddenly reached out his hand to touch Anne's. "I am very happy too," he said softly.

Looking into his eyes, Anne could glimpse the depth of this man, the one the world seldom saw, because Victor could be a subtle master of disguise when he needed to be. But now he was open to her and allowed her to see. There was pain—deep and sorrowful—but the joy was real as well. And that 'something else' she had seen before that sent shivers up her spine—that left her feeling completely alone in his presence and made her lose her bearings, as if she were peering into the deep void of the universe—that was hidden now as she looked into his eyes. This morning, this Victor was reaching out toward her, inviting her in.

"Apparently my skills have not declined," Nora said while feigning to inspect the empty dishes.

"You probably don't even need to wash them—just put them right back on the shelves," Victor joked.

"They were definitely the best pancakes I've ever had," Anne chimed in.

"Thank you. Will there be anything else, kids—some more coffee?"

"I think we should get going, Nora. We have a long day ahead of us," said Victor.

"Just pay me up at the register when you're ready," Nora said as she placed the check next to Victor's cup.

***

"Victor, these dogs are so beautiful!" Anne marveled when they were greeted at the car by five wagging hounds. Getting down on one knee, she was at eye level with a shiny black female who approached her and stopped inches from her face.

"Just look at those eyes. They're incredible. Victor, I've never been this close to a greyhound before—and just at look you, aren't you the handsome one," she said to a large brindle male who appeared with Victor as he emerged from the other side of the car.

"One of the few dogs I can touch standing up," he said, resting his hand on the hound's back.

Victor started off in the direction of the farmhouse. "Come on, Anne. Let's go find Lily."

About halfway to the house he stopped and turned to Anne.

"I just want to give you a heads up. Dear Aunt Lily is not quite what she first appears to be," and although Victor was smiling as he spoke, Anne could see a hint of seriousness in his eyes.

"Uh, okay. Thanks," Anne replied, more curious than concerned.

Arriving at the house followed by four hounds, the large brindle stuck as if with Velcro at Victor's side, they saw a magnificent honey and white female greyhound resting on the verandah by the front door. Posed regally on her elbow on a bed of woolen blankets, she watched intently as Victor, Anne, and their wagging mob approached.

"If it isn't the Grand Dame," Victor said, crouching down to pet her; she in turn greeted him with a matronly kiss on his cheek.

"Didn't expect to see you still looking so beautiful at your age."

"And why wouldn't I still be beautiful, even at my age?" came a voice from the doorway.

Anne turned to see a little old lady in faded work jeans, moccasins, and a suede Native American vest over a long-sleeved white shirt. A broad smile lit her face.

"Aunt Lily!" Victor rose to his feet and embraced her. Anne smiled as she watched Aunt Lily all but disappear from view—only her tiny thin hands were visible on his lower back as she hugged him affectionately.

"This is my friend Anne. Anne, Aunt Lily," Victor said.

"I'm happy to meet you, dear," Aunt Lily said warmly.

"It is my pleasure," responded Anne as she gazed at the wrinkled, aged face. Thin, with an aquiline nose and large, clear brown eyes, she resembled the hounds who shared her life.

"Well do come in, you two, so we can visit a little before your ride," Aunt Lily said, turning quickly into the house.

"She moves like a young girl," Anne wondered aloud.

Stepping inside the front door, Anne was surprised to see a single large room subtly divided into different areas. Immaculately clean and uncluttered, numerous tribal rugs of various sizes and designs were scattered over a dark, stained-pine floor. Three more resting greyhounds acknowledged the visitors with a slight movement of their eyes.

Aunt Lily led them to the center of the room where there was a cozy sitting area with what looked like two single beds covered in more Native American rugs. Large potted plants were carefully placed to create a sense of intimacy. With a lithe move, the old woman parked herself on one of the beds, folding her legs beneath her; Anne, feeling a little dazed, followed Victor to the bed across from her.

Aunt Lily closed her eyes and became very still. After what seemed like an unusually long time, Anne began to wonder if she had possibly fallen asleep. She turned to Victor, who just smiled warmly, but her growing uneasiness was becoming more and more palpable. She recalled a similar feeling from those days long past when she had briefly experimented with hallucinogenic drugs. *Must have been the pancakes*, she joked to herself.

"What kind of doctor are you, dear?" the old woman asked when she opened her eyes. Her voice was soft and gentle; still, Anne could detect an unmistakable edge just below the surface and found something unsettling in the way she looked at her. *How did she know I was a doctor?* she thought, but assumed either Victor had told her or Nora had maybe given her a call when they left the restaurant. Anne looked around the room but could see no phone. Turning toward Victor with an inquiring look, he indicated with a bird-like cock of his head to the side that he didn't know either.

"I'm a psychoanalyst," Anne replied.

"And what do you do?" the old lady persisted.

That's not such an easy question, thought Anne. Most people assumed they knew what she did simply upon hearing her title. It was a difficult thing to try to explain. Anne decided to be simple; she knew she couldn't read the old woman and had no idea what she might be after.

"People come to me with psychological and emotional problems and I try to help them," she said.

"They are suffering?"

"Yes."

"And do you know why they are suffering?"

Anne grimaced at the question. Either by accident or design, Aunt Lily had given voice to the most vexing question of her life.

"Finding that out is an important part of what we do," Anne replied, trying to distance herself from the question.

"And do you?"

"Do I what, Aunt Lily?" her agitation becoming more obvious in her voice.

"Do you find out why they are suffering?"

"Sometimes, yes."

"And so what *is* the cause of their suffering?" Aunt Lily persevered.

"Well, the cause is different in each case."

"So different causes create different effects and the effects are experienced as suffering?"

"Yes," Anne said, impressed in spite of herself by the old woman's lucidity, but hoping that her answer would be the end of it.

"But you see, dear, what I'm asking is if you know *why* suffering is the effect. What does suffering have to do with it at all? Is it even necessary?"

By this time, Anne was beginning to wonder if the woman was clairvoyant for these were the very questions that had for years been Anne's constant companions. Never far from her awareness, they lurked behind her every thought and action, never allowing her to rest for long. Now, in the wake of Anita's suicide, they had only become more insistent.

"You are asking me the questions I ask myself," Anne conceded. "I admit I have no definitive answers," she said sincerely, "but what makes you ask?"

"Your patients' suffering hangs on you like ornaments on a Christmas tree."

"Excuse me?" Anne said with surprise.

"It attaches itself to you, dear. When you try to rid them of their suffering, that suffering has to go somewhere. Really, what you do is not at all helpful."

Quite knocked off balance by the old woman's remark, Anne struggled to make sense of what was going on. Part of her was angered and felt she had been attacked, but she was also frightened; the image of her patients' suffering hanging all over her was more than a little disquieting. She tried to comfort herself with the thought that perhaps Aunt Lily was unbalanced. Victor had said she was not what she seemed to be… but no, this was not really about balance or imbalance, it was about truth, and Anne could not ignore the undeniable authority of Aunt Lily's ancient presence.

"Aunt Lily, I'm not sure why you are telling me all this, but I am interested in what you have to say. The whole question of suffering and its meaning and purpose plagues me. It is perhaps the central question of my life, so if you have more to say, I would like to hear it."

The old woman smiled and slowly nodded her noble head.

"You are an intelligent and well-educated woman; I am just an old woman who lives out here with my dogs. But I do see things that others may not. Sometimes I'm inspired to talk; sometimes I'm inspired to keep quiet. I'm talking to you now because I see you're ready." The old woman's smile seemed to deepen; her eyes twinkled with the light of the sun that slanted into the room.

Anne involuntarily released a deep sob. She felt like the breath was being squeezed out of her body. Things were letting go inside of her—layers peeling away. She knew the old woman was right, she was ready—more than ready, she was desperate.

"What did you mean when you said that what I do is not at all helpful?"

The old woman glanced at Victor sitting quietly at Anne's side. There was something probing, questioning, in her gaze. She turned back to Anne and said, "There is a saying: 'The saint is bound by a golden chain, the sinner by a spiked one, but the goal is to be rid of all chains.'

"This means that every word, every thought, every deed creates a binding—our chains. The quality of these bindings depends on the quality of the actions that produce them. Some bindings bring pain; some bring pleasure. But it's the experience of that pleasure or pain which frees our consciousness from the bindings. So I ask you, can you remove the chain or merely attempt to mitigate the consequent pleasure or pain they create?"

Anne closed her eyes. She was trying to take in so much so quickly that her normal thought processes were becoming overwhelmed.

"Chains? I don't know about chains or bindings—and I don't know if there even is a *single source* underlying all suffering—but in answer to your question, I would say I cannot remove the underlying *sources* of my patients' suffering in that I cannot undo what has already been done.

"But you also said you could see the suffering of my patients hanging on me. I find this distressing, still, I have to ask, if they are on me, then am I not taking them away from my patients?"

"That is correct," the old woman said as she touched the tip of her thumb with her index finger and held it up in Anne's direction. "But the effect is only temporary, and the suffering eventually leaves you and goes back to them. Remember, the experience of pleasure and pain is the natural way in which the effects of the actions committed are alleviated. It takes a very long time—many, many, lifetimes—but the end for every soul in existence is assured. This is why I say to you, if you cannot remove the cause, don't remove the suffering."

Anne had been hearing the old woman's words in a state of high excitation, yet she was also extremely lucid. Not so much out of defensiveness as much as dismay she asked, "So, what am I to do? Are you suggesting I should give up my work?"

"*Do?*" the old woman slowly shook her head. "Who can really do?

"Anne, we are talking about suffering. Suffering is the byproduct of the pursuit of consciousness—consciousness that will enable the soul to know itself. Think of consciousness as a mirror the soul looks into to see itself. If the mirror is covered with dust, the image is distorted. Only when the mirror is wiped clean is it able to accurately reflect the soul's Perfection."

Anne felt suspended in the old woman's gaze. Time seemed to stop.

"Anne," the old woman said gently, "you asked what you

should do. My advice is to continue doing exactly what you are doing, but with this one difference. Try to remember that what you are doing has no greater or lesser importance than the work of the janitor who sweeps your office or the postman who delivers your mail. Remember too, you are equally a slave to illusion and its suffering as your patients are. Guard against pride and self-importance which bonds the dust to the mirror and makes it difficult to remove... do you understand, my dear?"

"I understand that I only see a very small part of the picture. You imply that I live and work in ignorance—I am more than willing to admit that. The more I seem to know, the less I feel I understand. Yet somehow, I must continue. You said before I was 'ready' and that is why you were telling me these things. I too feel I'm ready, that I have been ready," she hesitated, trying to find the right words, "to move on..."

The old woman stopped her with a wave of her hand. "Who are you, Anne?" she asked.

"I've begun to ask myself that very question," she replied with an ironic smile.

Returning her smile, the old woman replied, "When you begin to feel you are not Anne, that Anne is merely the clothes you are wearing for the time being, you are on the way. It may be uncomfortable, like sitting between two chairs, but this is the way. In this game, loss is gain."

The old woman turned to Victor. "Dear, please go see if Tom has brought the horses around."

Anne felt dizzy, lightheaded, yet strangely calm. She was aware of Victor's departure as if watching from a great distance. She glanced back at the old woman sitting across from her and became intensely aware of her own body and the energy flowing within it—as if she were expanding beyond the ordinary physical limits of size and shape by which she usually defined herself. As the awareness grew stronger, the physical appearance of the old woman seemed to change, diminishing before Anne's eyes—being effaced—and in her place an intense, white light—a shimmering egg-shaped field of luminosity—remained.

***

Victor immediately became aware of the deep peaceful silence when he returned. Both Anne and Aunt Lily were sitting perfectly still; their eyes were closed.

"The horses are waiting," he said softly.

Anne opened her eyes, gracefully accepting Victor's extended hand.

"Thank you, Aunt Lily," she said, turning back to the old woman. "What you said was not easy for me to hear, but I feel better for hearing it. I'm very grateful."

"Enjoy your ride, dear," she said softly and closed her eyes again.

The Cabin

Tom, the elderly Menominee man who helped tend the hounds and the horses, was waiting outside the house holding the reins of three magnificent steeds.

"Anne, this is Tom. I have known him for what seems like forever," said Victor.

"Hello, Tom. I'm happy to meet you."

"And me you," he replied, handing her the reins of a statuesque chestnut mare with a white blaze on her forehead. Anne looked into her steed's eyes and stroked her soft warm muzzle.

"May I assist the lady?" Victor asked nobly as he turned the mare's stirrup and offered Anne his arm.

"I would be honored, kind sir," she answered with a smile and stepped into the stirrup. After adjusting the length of her stirrups, Victor mounted the tall black stallion and settled himself into the worn black saddle inlaid with silver studs.

"Ready, folks?" asked Tom.

"Yes quite," said Anne then watched in awe as Tom took hold of the luxurious flowing mane of his large black pinto and in one swift move swung himself onto the bare back of his horse.

"Impressive," she said aloud.

"That's nothing," Victor responded. "Tom has always been quite the horseman. Can you still ride a galloping horse standing bareback?"

"Not today," smiled Tom.

"That would be something to see," Anne replied.

Tom turned and called over his shoulder. "Hey, Adi, Cloud, Jasper: come!" and three greyhounds, one white with brindle spots, one black, and one a dark brindle appeared from behind the house to join them.

Tom took the lead, followed by Anne and then Victor, with the hounds trotting easily alongside. Soon falling into rhythm with her horse's gait, Anne's body began to relax, her mind strangely calmed by the gentle sound of their guide's voice softly chanting a Menominee song. He led them to the entrance of a large rolling pasture, stopping the horses just inside.

"Wait!" he commanded, turning back to the hounds and making a gesture with his palm in their direction. The greyhounds stood perfectly still, fully attentive, with their ears perked straight up. Tom urged his horse on into the pasture; Anne and Victor followed. They rode about a hundred yards and stopped.

"I'm going to run the dogs for you. Keep a good hold of your horses when I do. Don't let them follow."

Anne took Victor's lead and tightened her grip on the reins of her mare. Tom rode ahead and stopped after doubling the distance between them and the hounds. Then he turned back and made a loud shrill sound.

"Yahee!" he yelled, and simultaneously both the hounds and his horse were off at full speed. Anne and Victor could feel their own horses straining to follow, but they held a tight rein and managed to keep them in their place. Within seconds, the hounds, led by the white one with brindle spots, flew past them in hot pursuit of the racing steed. Even with the horse at a full gallop, the hounds closed quickly and caught him within another hundred yards. Tom stopped his horse and quickly dismounted to inspect the dogs. Anne and Victor trotted up to meet them.

"Fantastic, fantastic; that was so incredible!" Anne was saying as she dismounted. The dogs all approached her as she kneeled down, stopping with their heads just inches from her face. "And congratulations to the winner," she said to the white one with brindle spots, who stared at her with his nose less than an inch from her face.

"His name is Adi," Tom said.

"You are so beautiful, Adi. I wish I could take you home with me."

"That could be arranged," Victor prodded.

Tom looked up at the sky. "Let's get you to the head of the trail," he said. Once mounted, he handed his saddlebags over to Victor saying, "Here are some sandwiches Lily packed for you, and there's bottled water at the cabin. You've got about an hour's ride to get there, and remember not to leave any food around when you go. Don't want to attract the coons."

"Agreed," responded Victor. Tom turned toward Ann and jutted his jaw in her direction.

"Very nice to meet you, ma'am," he said and flashed a warm smile.

"Likewise," responded Anne.

Tom turned to Victor, repeating the same gesture.

"You've got about four more hours of daylight," he said.

"I understand. Thanks, Tom."

Tom turned and led them the short distance across the pasture to the head of the trail and then, without further comment, turned his horse back across the field, the hounds trotting happily behind.

Victor took the lead along the narrow trail, his stallion setting a leisurely pace. Few words were exchanged along the way. It was an easy trail, at times running along a little stream, at times through small gullies and over gentle hills. The trees had begun their autumn turnings; through their branches, the cloudless sky appeared a soft powder blue. The setting was idyllic. Anne and Victor rode in comfortable silence toward the old log cabin on the hill.

"We'll leave the horses here and walk the rest of the way to the cabin," Victor said as he dismounted, Anne following suit. After slinging the saddlebags over his shoulder, he led their horses to a clearing by a small creek and tied their reins loosely to an old birch tree.

The ancient majesty of the woods was overpowering. Birds

twittered in the distance; a crow cawed from afar. Victor indicated a few small stone steps, partially hidden in the undergrowth, and started towards them, Anne following behind. Seemingly meandering in an aimless fashion, the stones formed an irregular path up the side of the small hill. Anne found it difficult to match her stride to the arrangement of the steps, whose placement seemed to have been carefully calculated to afford an opportunity to experience oneself in a different way.

"Don't watch your feet," Victor suggested.

When they reached the cabin, Anne let out an involuntary gasp at the vista that appeared before her. In the distance was a bluff, the rock face weathered with cracks and crevices. She turned to Victor with a questioning look.

"It's a special place, Anne. The Menominee have lived in these lands for 10,000 years—maybe more, some say. The rock bluffs were spared by the glaciers that cut out the surrounding plains during the last ice age. Many who have come here considered these bluffs to mark a portal into the spirit world—a place of power—a most suitable place to begin what Native Americans call a vision quest. Hungry?"

"Yes, not to mention thirsty and tired as well," Anne replied, though at some other unspoken level she was experiencing awe and excitement at this mysterious land and its compelling energy.

The cabin was a small, one room affair with an untreated pine floor—a miniature and very much more austere version of Aunt Lily's house. A simple wooden table and three chairs stood in the center of the room, a rustic kitchen area with a wood-burning stove filled an entire side, and a small bed covered with a colorful Native American rug ran lengthwise against one wall. Victor tossed the saddlebags on the table and found the cabinet with the bottled water. Anne made her way to the bed, sat down with a heavy sigh and untied her boots. Making herself at home, she pulled her feet up close to her body and wrapped her arms around her knees. Victor opened two bottles and held one up in Anne's direction.

"Yes please," she said and extended her hand. Propping herself up against the wall, she sipped water while Victor unwrapped the sandwiches then, picking up a small glass vase from the table, carried it to the sink and turned on the faucet. The old pipes squeaked and gurgled as he filled the vessel. After returning it to the table, he disappeared out the front door only to reappear almost immediately holding three delicate leafless stalks supporting little orange flowers.

"Very nice touch," said Anne as he arranged them in the glass.

"Thou waitest late, and comest alone
When woods are bare and birds have flown.
The frosts and shorter days portend
The aged year is near its end," he intoned.

"Ready to eat?"

"Almost," Anne replied. "Come here first; I want to ask you something."

"About Aunt Lily?"

"How did you guess?" she said with a smile.

"And what, pray tell, do you want to know about the old dear?" he asked as he sat down on the edge of the bed.

"Anything! You said she was unique—that was an understatement. What's her story?"

"Fact or fiction?" Victor smiled.

"Stop it, Victor," she said, and gave him a light jab with her elbow.

"Okay, okay. I'll tell you a little of what I know of her story. Aunt Lily was born when my mother was five. My mother always said Lily was an unusual child. She was apparently quite precocious physically, and remarkably alert to all and everything around her, but for a long time she never spoke, never even uttered a sound."

"She apparently got over that one," Anne kidded. Victor smiled.

"My great aunt is said to have worried herself sick over the fear her only child might be some sort of wild, untamed creature, but my grandmother did not share her feelings. She had a special affinity for Lily and seemed to have no trouble communicating with her. My grandmother would repeatedly, and in a very matter-of-fact way, tell her sister not to worry, that Lily would speak when she had something to say."

"She seems to have plenty to say these days," Anne mused aloud.

"True. Anyway, it was the occasion of my mother's ninth birthday and there was a family gathering at my grandmother's home—the family homestead as it were—in Missouri. In honor of my mother, also an only child, there was of course all the usual hubbub and fanfare with much ado about what a big girl she had become and people saying things like who could believe she was already nine years old.

"Well, at some point, everyone gathered around the table for the ritual blowing out of candles; of course, Aunt Lily was included. As the story goes, just as my mother took a deep breath to blow out the candles, out of the silence of anticipation there came a strong young voice declaring, 'Nine is not very old.'"

"Are you serious, Victor?"

"My mother swore to it—and usually followed up by adding that Aunt Lily always spoke the truth, and never lost her sense of timing."

They both laughed, but then Anne continued, more subdued, "But how is it… where does it come from, this vision she has—this ability to understand, to see? I don't even know how to describe it."

"That's more difficult to answer because Aunt Lily doesn't speak about her personal spiritual journey, and seldom entertains questions about it, she just lives it. What I can tell you is that she traveled extensively in the East as a young woman—a rather outrageous thing to do for a woman of her era. And I also know she developed a close relationship with Tom's great-grandfather when she moved out here. He was a highly revered medicine man and must have been nearly a hundred when Aunt Lily met him. I have my own thoughts about his influence on her but little in the way of details."

"Did you know she was going to speak to me like that? You

could have given me more warning."

"I really didn't. Aunt Lily acts quite ordinary around most people most of the time. She said she saw things; she must have seen something in you. She said you were ready."

"Actually, Victor, I swear she did something more than speak. I truly believe she somehow altered my state. When she was talking, I *felt* her words as much as heard them. It was as if she were talking inside me."

"Yes, I felt that too. She can have that effect. How would you describe it?"

Anne sighed and looked into Victor's eyes. "It's difficult to put into words. The only way I can think to describe my state would be to say it was a condition of hyper-lucidity, as if all filters had been removed—the gate keeper was asleep so everything came in without questioning. Now though, I have questions—and lots of them."

"I bet you do," said Victor and smiled. "How about over sandwiches?"

"Excellent idea."

Victor rose quickly, and with a slight bow and gallant sweep of his hand, announced grandly, "Your table is ready, madam…"

***

"I knew I was hungry, but that bordered on embarrassing," said Anne after devouring her sandwich.

"I'm impressed! But note: I've drawn my sword to protect my plate from your ravaging," Victor joked, holding aloft a plastic knife. Anne smiled, but then her eyes narrowed and she drew back the corners of her mouth.

"Aunt Lily talked at length about bindings. What was it she said about the sinner and the saint?"

"The saint is bound by a golden chain, the sinner by a spiked one."

"But the goal is to be free of all chains."

"Yes."

"And she linked it all up with actions as the cause of bindings."

"Yes, impressions. Impressions are both the cause and the result of actions."

"Yes, I thought of that word when Aunt Lily was speaking. I don't think she used it, but I know you have. The problem I have is that I think you use the term in a different way than I understand it, yet I think its meaning may hold a key to my deeper understanding of suffering."

"So, how do you use the term?"

"Well, in my world, the world of cognitive neuroscience, impressions are irrevocably linked to stimulation—neuronal firing. No impressions would mean no neurons firing—death. My question is, if this is true, then how does one rid oneself of impressions and remain alive?" Victor closed his eyes and folded his hands in his lap under the table. Anne watched the rise and fall of his chest with the rhythm of his breath. She involuntarily released a gentle sigh as her body responded to his. Victor opened his eyes and looked at Anne. His look was soft, *loving,* she thought.

"What I think would only be another opinion. All of this we are talking about is for me, as they say, not settled law. But I can share some things I have heard from Krita Baba and Amrit, his oldest and closest follower. Your question is right to the point because at one level, without impressions, there would be no life—no universe—because impressions, in the way Krita Baba uses the term, actually *create* the universe and all the experiences in the universe, including the experience of oneself. If all the impressions were wiped out, the universe and the false-self would disappear."

"False-self?"

"Yes, remember I said 'at one level.' That level speaks about life and the universe as real. In Krita Baba's consciousness, however, it is all an illusion. The self we identify with until we are perfected is a false-self."

"So all this stuff about actions and impressions and suffering is talking about the illusion and not the reality?"

"Yes."

"It's difficult for me to imagine, let alone accept."

"I understand. It is equally difficult for me; Kabir used to say, 'Until you experience it, it is not true.'"

Anne smiled, remembering the first time she heard Victor mention that quote.

"Around and around and around they trot till they can't sit down on their tender spot."

"It's a little sore right now," Victor said as they shared the welcome relief of a laugh.

"And so for the sake of our conversation, let's say I accept it as fact that all of this," she made a sweeping gesture with her hand, "and even the experience of myself, is illusion. I still have to live and work in this illusion—it is after all the only 'reality' I know. Let me ask you this, would it be accurate to say that these impressions that create and preserve the illusion are like the grooves in a vinyl record?"

"Exactly."

"And these impressions must go and yet consciousness must still remain—like smoothing out the vinyl?"

"Yes."

"And so that leads us back to my question. How can this be accomplished?"

"The tender spot?"

"Yes."

"Krita Baba says that from ancient times, various methods have been known and employed—yoga in all its different forms would be one example—but he also says that the most expedient way is by associating with a God-realized master. A God-realized, or Perfect Master, alone really knows and can do. Remember when Aunt Lily made a point of asking who can really do? A Perfect Master works in illusion but remains always merged in reality. Amrit once told me this story: A mass murderer went to a Perfect Master for help. He realized his soul was in grave jeopardy because of all the people he had killed. So he joined a group who had gathered in the presence of a Perfect Master. He was an old and grizzled looking man who wore nothing but a piece of burlap cut from an old gunnysack. Seeing the stranger in their midst, he nonchalantly inquired why he was there.

"The man spoke quite openly and honestly. 'I am a bad man,' he said. 'I have killed many people and I am terrified for my soul. I have heard about you and come begging for your help.' Of course, all in the group had turned to see the man who was confessing to being a murderer.

"'Let me get this straight,' said the Perfect Master, feigning the tone of a scholar or a philosopher. 'You are a murderer?'

"'Yes.'

"'And you have come to me for help for your soul?'

"'Yes.'

"'I see. Now tell me, how many people have you killed?'

"'Ninety-nine,' the man replied, and all of the people gave a collective gasp.

"'I see,' said the Perfect Master. 'You have killed ninety-nine people, and you want my help for your soul?' his voice sounding thoughtful and inquiring.

"'Yes, that is the truth.'

"'I see. You have killed ninety-nine people. You are sure it is ninety-nine?'

"'Yes, I am sure,' said the murderer, who was beginning to wonder at the Perfect Master's questions.

"'Ninety-nine and not one hundred,' the Perfect Master persevered while the murderer grew more impatient.

"'Yes, I have killed ninety-nine and not one hundred.'

"'And you are coming to me for my help?' The man jumped to his feet. He felt the so-called Perfect Master was either crazy or teasing him.

"'Where are you going?' asked the Perfect Master in mock surprise.

"'I feel I have made a mistake in coming here. I don't believe you are taking me seriously. I am leaving.'

"'On the contrary,' replied the Perfect Master, 'please sit down. I promise I will help you.' The man sat down again.

"'Now let me get this straight,' said the Perfect Master. 'You are a murderer and you have killed ninety-nine people and you are coming to me for help for your soul?'

"'Yes.'

"'And you are sure you have killed ninety-nine people?'

"'Yes.'

"'And not one hundred?' Again the man jumped to his feet.

"'What are you doing?' asked the Perfect Master with all the innocence of a child.

"'I am leaving.'

"'Please sit down. I promised I would definitely help you,' said the Perfect Master. The man again sat down.

"'Now listen carefully to what I tell you. Will you do as I request?'

"'Yes.'

"'Very well. Do you see that tree by the road over there?'

"'Yes.'

"'This is what I want you to do. I want you to go and sit beneath that tree. You are to stay there; I will see to all your needs. You will have food and protection from the elements. You are just to stay there, but when people pass by on the road, you are to go to them and bless them.'

"'Bless them?'

"'Yes bless them; you can say may God's blessing be upon you—anything like that you wish. Can you do it?'

"'Yes,' replied the murderer, who was happy to be given a penance for his sins.

"And so the man began to stay under the tree and bless people when they went by. He stayed there for years—after a while, people even began to think he was some kind of great saint.

"It so happened that one day a messenger on horseback came galloping down the road at top speed. The murderer was out in the road, busy doing his blessings, when the man rode by. Not seeing him coming, the murderer stepped in front of the charging horse, the horse reared up and the rider was thrown into the air. Picking himself off the ground, the rider was absolutely furious.

"'What the hell are you doing, man?' he shouted at the murderer. 'Are you crazy? You fool! I am delivering an important message from the king. See what you've done, you piece of shit?' and he went on like that, railing against the murderer, who himself was getting more and more angry.

"Finally, the murderer could stand the abuse no longer and picked up a large stone and crushed the messenger's head. Just then, at that very moment, the Perfect Master arrived, said simply 'One hundred,' and bestowed upon the murderer the highest state of liberation. The Perfect Master gave him the state of God Realization."

"Victor, I have absolutely no idea what this story means," Anne said after a long pause.

"You see, Anne, the messenger was carrying orders from the king for the execution of one hundred innocent people. By killing the messenger—his one hundredth murder—he saved one hundred people. The Perfect Master knew this in the beginning, knew exactly what was necessary to balance the murderer's actions and liberate him from their consequences."

But Anne's dismay and irritation were in no way relieved by the explanation. "I get it," Anne said, "but I don't think I like it. It disturbs me on many different levels."

"As it did me when Amrit first told it to me. Do you remember when Aunt Lily was telling you about the mirror?"

"Yes. I like that story," Anne replied with a smile.

"Well, applying the metaphor to this story, the Perfect Master could *see* the dust that distorted the murderer's consciousness and also knew how to wipe it clean. He created the perfect circumstances for the murderer to save one hundred lives. He knew all along what would happen, but, of course, neither the murderer nor anyone else had any idea what the Perfect Master was actually doing. All along, the murderer was thinking he was doing a penance of some sort because he had been so bad. But the Perfect Master didn't care one iota about the morality of the man's life. High and low, good and bad, intelligent and stupid, black and white, Hindu and Muslim, strong and weak, beauty and ugliness have no effect on Him. He is beyond all dualities—beyond life and death itself—seeing every state of consciousness, every experience, as different states of God—different states of His own dream. The sole function of a Perfect Master is to liberate reality from illusion—to liberate Himself in others."

"Okay, I'm full now. I don't think I can take in another word."

Anne took a deep breath and got up from the table; putting her hands on her hips, she bent backwards to stretch. "Ah that feels good," she said and then proceeded to walk slowly around the table. Victor following suit, stood up and began to follow her around the table. Anne looked back at him and smiled, then walked around the table three more times, increasing the pace as she went, before turning back to face him. Victor stopped abruptly, feigning a rear-end collision.

"So, what can we do—is there anything we can do, Victor?"

"We can call the police and then our insurance companies. We can file a claim," he joked.

"Seriously, Victor, if all this is true, what is there for us to do?"

"I thought you said you were full?"

"I am, but…"

"The one thing I hold on to is this," Victor said. "Krita Baba was always reminding us whenever this same question came up that just a moment's contact with a Perfect Master is more beneficial than literally thousands of lifetimes doing work, penances, austerities, meditations and the like." Victor took a deep breath, walked to the bed and sat down. Anne followed and sat down beside him.

"It still leaves me with a feeling of hopelessness," she said. "I mean you just said thousands of lifetimes. That is a long time to be piddling around waiting for a Perfect Master to appear and do whatever it is he does."

Victor smiled. "Well put," he said, adding a quote by Hafiz, "'When his time has come, the prey finds the hunter.' But helplessness and hopelessness are really not bad things—if they remind us of our real situation. I think that was the point Aunt Lily was making when she questioned your motivation for your work with patients. As soon as you think you are doing something, especially something valuable or important, the more you are identifying with those impressions."

"Thereby making the grooves in the record deeper, so to speak?"

"Yes, but on the other hand, if one gets identified with hopelessness and helplessness and adopts the attitude of, 'Oh, woe is me, I can do nothing, it is all so hopeless...' then one has become identified with those impressions of futility."

"Damned if you do and damned if you don't. So why not just continue to revel in illusion knowing that one day it will all sort itself out?"

"One of Krita Baba's older followers put it this way, 'We're all on a train, but we are not driving it. The train will get to its destination, so why not occupy yourself along the way with things that make you happy?'"

Anne drew back the corners of her mouth and slowly nodded her head. Her eyes were cast down to the floor at her feet. Then she became very still. Victor sensed the sudden change of energy. He knew the conversation was over. He turned on the bed, crossed his long legs underneath him, closed his eyes and began to watch his breath. He sensed the repeating rhythm—in and out— the expansion and contraction of his stomach muscles. *I,* he repeated mentally to himself with the inhalation, *am,* he said with the exhalation over and over again—like the tide, day and night, birth and death.

Anne turned to face him—copying his position on the bed. She began a centering exercise she frequently used in which she brought her attention to the sensations of her body, centering her attention in the area of her lower abdomen. After a few minutes, they simultaneously opened their eyes. They both saw immediately the total openness in each other. There were no barriers; no thoughts arose to separate them. Victor reached out both of his hands to hers, guiding her closer. Spontaneously she responded, lightly mounting his crossed legs, her legs and thighs embracing his torso. Their eyes were lost in each other's—no distinction existed. Instinctively, their breathing responded. As she exhaled, he inhaled; as he exhaled she inhaled. They had become like one sea without a shore.

There was no disruption in their union when they separated to undress—no moment of distinction when she mounted him again and he entered her. Their faces very close now, they continued to gaze deep into each other's eyes. What did they see? What do two perfectly clear mirrors see when they are placed before each other? Time slowed. Time stopped. Time disappeared. This was not about orgasm, it was not about pleasure; it was about consciousness of oneness, not with each other—each other no longer existed—it was about the union of the drop with the ocean—the soul with the Oversoul. It was not about pleasure; it was about bliss…

***

They drove back from Friendship in the happiest of moods: all smiles, little talk. But as they got closer to the city, Anne noticed Victor becoming agitated and his driving more hurried. "Are you okay, Victor?"

"Something is happening, Anne; I don't know what, but I feel I need to get home immediately." Anne knew Victor well enough to let it go and keep her concern to herself.

After dropping Anne at her house, Victor sped back to his apartment and within minutes, the phone rang. It was Amrit saying Krita Baba wanted him to come back to India immediately. "Why, what is it? Is something wrong?" Victor asked in alarm.

"Neither right nor wrong," came the reply, "but very important. Come now."

"Yes," said Victor.

"And Krita Baba wants you to bring the woman with you."

"Anne? He wants me to bring Anne? Why?"

Victor heard Amrit laugh loudly.

"Befitting the fortunate slave, carry out every command of the Master without any question of why or what," he said, quoting the Persian poet Hafiz.

"Me? He wants to see me? That's crazy, Victor!" Anne said when he told her. But she agreed to go.

It took almost twenty-four hours for them to receive the expedited visas, another twenty-four hours for the international flight and the taxi ride to the ashram. As soon as they arrived, they were escorted to a little room where Krita Baba was waiting. Victor rushed in with palms joined and prostrated himself at his guru's feet. Anne stood nervously at the door until Krita Baba motioned her in. Not comfortable with the gesture, but not knowing exactly what to do, she placed her palms together and made an awkward little bow to Krita Baba, who directed them to sit on the two chairs facing him.

"Don't worry," he said to Anne, "I want you to be comfortable. Is there anything you need?"

"Some water please, I am very thirsty."

Krita Baba told Victor to fetch a glass of filtered water. Victor all but jumped to his feet in response and quickly left the room. Suddenly alone in his presence, Anne found the atmosphere surrounding Krita Baba to be most extraordinary. *So this is love*, she said to herself and began to weep.

"I want you to know it is no accident that you are here," he told her. "I am very pleased you came."

Victor returned to the room and handed Anne the glass of water. He looked concerned and worried as he took a seat beside Anne.

"The two of you had sex," he said. "That is why I have called you."

"I am sorry, Baba!" Victor said and began to weep.

Krita Baba chuckled softly and told him he was not displeased at all and went on to explain the significance of the event. "Two moths fly to each other. Why are they attracted so? It is the flame of love, unseen, unknown, and misunderstood, around which their heart's wings long to circle and dance. In the flame of each other's hearts, two moths shed the illusion of separation. Oh heart, inspired by images of beauty and the reflection of love, you create your beloved and dream the dream of union's bliss. Oh flame, to know yourself, you dream yourself the moth to awaken as fire. Oh moth, you are the dream of your own flame, as is the beloved you seek. In truth, both you and your beloved are one. Dream and dreamer, moth and flame, awaken in union—wings of separation consumed in the flame of love. Do you understand?" he asked, but their tears were their only answer. "Anne and Victor are the two moths, I am the flame. Through ages and lifetimes, you two have been together seeking me in each other. You have been lovers, friends, siblings and parents to each other. You have circled me, the flame, from the beginning. Your union in Friendship marked the end of the beginning and the beginning of the end. This is why you are here now." He chuckled again and raised his finger with authority, gesturing in mock sternness, "But now, no more sex. Do you understand?"

"Yes," they answered simultaneously. "Good. I am very pleased with you both." He turned to Anne. "My dear, you know that Victor will be joining me shortly—to live out his remaining days with me?"

Anne nodded her head.

"You will not be back here again to see me," he said gently, "but I will always be with you, and you will always find me in your heart. Anne, I love you and am very pleased with you. I will help you. Will you remember me?"

"Of course! Of course! I love you!" she said through her tears. "But the thought of never seeing you again is unbearable."

"My dear," Krita Baba responded lovingly, "we have always been and always will be together. Separation only exists in the dream of the moth. Remember, I am always with you; I always love you, and you and Victor will come to me one day soon. Don't worry, be happy!"

SuperVisions

Startled into consciousness by the unrelenting buzzing, Victor had no idea whether he was still in India, or on the plane, or in a taxi somewhere, but somehow managed to pull himself to his feet and stagger to the intercom. Their return from India had been the journey from hell, with flight delays in both the Frankfurt and London airports and crowded accommodations on all legs of the journey. Always surrounded by restless, coughing Indian children, even Anne felt cramped, her knees pressed against the back of the seat in front of her in the center aisle of the plane where they invariably found their seats. At least she managed to doze a little, but Victor, all six feet plus of him, sat contorted like an Indian fakir, unable to move or rest for the nearly twenty hours of their journey. When he finally got back to his apartment, he fell face down on the couch in his living room and was out like a light.

"Yes?" he groaned into the intercom.

"It's Jake, Victor. I'm here for my lesson."

"Lesson?" came the groggy reply as Victor slouched against the wall and, fighting to keep himself from falling back to sleep, tried to figure out what was going on. "You didn't get my message?" he finally said.

"What message? Victor, are you okay?"

"Yes, I'm okay. I left you a phone message before I left; you didn't get it?"

"My machine's busted; do you want me to come back later?"

"No, Jake, come on up," Victor replied and buzzed him in.

"My God, man, what the hell happened to you?" Jake said with obvious alarm upon seeing his teacher leaning against the door, hair tousled, a four-day growth on his face, and his clothes wrinkled and disheveled.

***

"He what?" Jake said with astonishment after they were settled in the living room, Victor sprawled on the couch with his feet up, Jake in the big stuffed chair across from him.

"With Anne? You went with Anne?" Jake's eyes were as wide as saucers as he listened to Victor's story of being called to India by Krita Baba. "You were there only a few hours?" Jake repeated, and then slumped back into his chair, eyes closed, trying to absorb Victor's incredible story.

It took at least ten minutes before Jake opened his eyes and said with unusual conviction, "Supervisions."

"Supervisions?" Victor repeated and cocked his head slightly to the side. Another minute passed.

"Yes, everyone, all the time, supervises and is being supervised by someone else."

"That is fair to say," Victor replied.

"Children are supervised by their parents, who in turn are supervised by their parents. Teachers supervise students, and are likewise supervised by the headmaster, patients by their doctors, doctors by their mentors and superiors…" Jake's voice trailed off as he followed his own train of thought to the inevitable question, "So where does it all end, Victor? Who has the last say? Where does the buck stop—does the buck ever stop at all?"

Victor swung his body slowly around into a sitting position. He was more awake now, stimulated by Jake's question.

"Yes, Jake, it does. I recall a time in India with Krita Baba. It was after morning tea on the second day of my first trip to be with him. I was in my room organizing the few things I had brought with me when Amrit came to my door saying Krita Baba had sent for me. Of course, I dropped everything and followed Amrit to a massive Pipal tree in the center of the compound. On the ground beneath the tree was a large mat where Krita Baba sat surrounded by a small group of Indian men. He motioned me to a spot at the front of the group, indicating to Amrit that he should sit next to me, and then inquired as to my health and if I had slept well.

"The feeling of the gathering was intimate, casual, yet respectful. The Indian men, I learned, had arrived early that morning from Hyderabad—a distance of more than seven hundred kilometers— traveling by bus over some very crowded and dangerous roads to be with Krita Baba for only a few hours before returning home.

"Everyone, including Krita Baba, was smiling. Joy shined on the faces of the men; the atmosphere was charged with love. There was a young man in the group who had a question. He wanted to know if Krita Baba was the Avatar. Krita Baba turned to me and asked if I understood the question.

"I had heard the word before; it was used to designate an individual who embodied a particular quality of God. Thus one may be said to be an avatar of Brahma, the Creator; Vishnu, the Preserver; or Shiva, the Destroyer. The term was usually applied to an advanced soul, a guru, or a saint. It could even be applied to a Perfect Master.

"'Is he asking if you are an avatar of God?' I replied.

"'He is asking me if I am *the* Avatar, Victor; I will explain. Here in India, the term avatar is generally used in the way you suggest. It is applied to an individual who personifies an aspect of God. But Raj is asking me something else; he is asking me if I am *the* Avatar.'

"'You see, Victor, every seven hundred to fourteen hundred years, God takes a human birth and comes into creation. This *direct* descent of God into human form is called *the* Avatar—the Christ—the Ancient One.'

"'The Avatar is not a Perfect Master, though his presence in creation is precipitated by the five Perfect Masters of the age who *bring him down* and awaken him to his responsibility to his creation. Zoroaster, Gautama, Krishna, Jesus, and Mohammed were all incarnations of the Avatar, I am not. When I drop the body, I will have nothing more to do with creation. I will eternally enjoy the *I am God* state but will have no more consciousness of creation. Perfect Masters do not reincarnate. But the Avatar's responsibility to creation is eternal because his Divine Love for all souls who dream the dream of creation is eternal. He comes again and again.'

"So, Jake, based on what Krita Baba said, I conclude that it is with the Avatar where all authority begins and ends. To use your own words, it is the Avatar who supervises—the buck stops with Him."

"God in human form; I've always wondered about that—I mean, why does God, as you put it, come down? Look what happened to Christ."

"Remember, Jake, nothing happens to the Avatar that He does not will. But to answer your question, there is a story about a king who once asked his adviser the same question." Victor smiled fondly at his friend. "Of course, in these stories, the adviser always turns out to be a Perfect Master. The adviser said he would answer the king's question, 'but,' he said, 'it is such a beautiful day, let us first take a little cruise on the royal barge.' He also suggested they should bring food and drink and that even the king's young son should accompany them. The king agreed, arrangements were quickly made and within minutes, the king, his son, the adviser, and a huge royal retinue of servants and soldiers were sailing down the river on the barge.

"It was indeed a beautiful day and all were having a most enjoyable time when the king, remembering his question about why God takes a human incarnation, addressed his adviser, who in turn grabbed up the king's son and threw him into the river. Without a moment's hesitation, the king jumped into the river and saved him.

"The king was furious. 'Why did you do that?' he demanded after he and his son were back safely on the barge. Nonplussed by the king's rage, the adviser took a sip of tea and said simply:

"'You could have ordered any of your guards or retinue to

retrieve your son, but you jumped in yourself to save him. Why? Because you love him. You love him as your very self,' he said calmly.

"'I still don't understand,' said the king.

"'You asked me why God takes a human incarnation. God does not *need* to incarnate, He has His agents and masters who can do his work, but God *wants* to be among us because He loves us and knows that He and His creation are not two, but one.'

"Jake, I could use a cup of coffee—would you like one?"

"Yes, thanks, Victor," Jake said absently, his mind still absorbed by his teacher's story. "Can I help?" he asked.

"I've got it covered," Victor replied as he got up and made his way into the kitchen. "In the meantime, why don't you go play something on the piano."

"Sure..." Jake answered with a question in his voice.

"Well, you did come here today for a lesson—right?"

"Sure…" Jake repeated. "What do you want me to play?"

"Bartok," Victor called from the kitchen. "Did you bring the first volume of *Microcosmos*?"

"Where do you want me to start?" Jake called from the studio.

"Start with thirty-two—*In the Dorian Mode*.'"

Jake settled in and began to play.

"*Lento* Jake—slower—take your time—and more *legato*," Victor directed from the kitchen. Jake stopped and took a deep breath, then started again at almost half the speed. His playing became more thoughtful as the music began to weave its spell, evoking images simultaneously ancient and modern, pristine and serene. By the time he finished *Slow Dance* and was playing the beautiful counterpoint of *In the Phrygian Mode*, all of his self-consciousness had disappeared. Victor too had fallen under the music's charm and followed it with full attention as if he were playing it himself. It was not until Jake had finished playing the *Free Canon* ending the volume that he became aware of Victor standing at the door smiling.

"Nice, Jake, thank you," he said. "The coffee is ready."

"So Christ was the Avatar?" asked Jake after they had resettled themselves in the living room.

Victor corrected, "Christ *is* the Avatar—it is an eternal state; Jesus *was* the Avatar—he embodied that state for a period of time."

Jake looked puzzled. "What's the difference?"

"I'll try to explain," Victor said patiently, "because there is an important difference. The terms Christ and Buddha refer to the *state* of the Avatar. This state is always the same, but the embodiment of that state is different depending on the time and circumstances of the advent. So Jesus was the embodiment of the Christ state as was Krishna, Gautama, Mohammed and Zoroaster. You see, these terms can sometimes be a little tricky and people get confused. A good example is when Jesus *the Christ* said 'I am the way… there is no way to the Father but through me.' Some people take that to mean Jesus was the one and only incarnation of God in human form and all others who share that claim are false. But when Jesus the Christ made that assertion, he was speaking as the Christ and not as Jesus. Do you see what I mean?"

"Because the Christ comes again and again, but as Jesus, He came just once?"

"Yes. Jesus will not come back again, but God as the Christ will incarnate *again and again* at different times and in different places with an appearance that is appropriate for the circumstances."

"Unlike the Perfect Masters?"

"Correct, Jake. When Perfect Masters drop their bodies, they do not come back."

"But the Avatar comes back again and again?"

"Yes."

"Whew, Victor, that's heavy. You know, it sort of flies in the face of everything I was taught by the Church."

Victor smiled. "Ah, the Church and its teachings…" he said and closed his eyes. Jake watched the smile slip away from his teacher's face, to be replaced by an expression of sad resignation.

"…again and again…" Jake repeated to himself, remembering Victor's words, feeling suddenly very tired.

***

Jake was never really sure what happened next; but what he did remember—remember very clearly—was a vision of being in the presence of his Lord—enfolded in His love. He had experienced a deep joy; the tears that ran down his cheeks when he opened his eyes were testimony of that. But with the return of normal consciousness, the joy quickly faded and all his questions—so many questions—deep questions connected to the abuses he had experienced as a boy and the suicide of his friend—returned in full force.

"You seem miles away, my friend." Victor's voice cut through his reverie.

"I just had a vision or something; maybe it was just a dream."

Victor, sitting serenely across from him, saw the tears but said nothing.

"I experienced some kind of bliss, Victor, but when it was over, all my old shit just came back on me. It made me think of that story you once told me about a student who found his teacher scurrying around on the ground under a streetlamp looking for a key he'd lost somewhere else."

"In the dark."

"Yes, and then you said that the meaning of the story was that things that are lost in the dark are found in the light. It sounded totally ridiculous to me at the time; I never got it at all and when I told you as much, you nearly doubled over with laughter."

"And now, Jake, do you get it now?"

"Well, at least I'm beginning to see that maybe I don't need to go backward in order to go forward."

"That's a good start, Jake, but perhaps we have been doing enough thinking for today; do you feel like taking a walk along the lake?"

"Sure, that sounds great," Jake agreed, "and it will give me the opportunity to tell you some good news."

"Good news? For sure," said Victor as they rose to put on their jackets.

"I took your advice, Victor. I asked her out!" Jake said gleefully.

Victor stopped at the door, his jacket half on and half off. "The waitress at Little Tokyo?" he asked with a smile.

"Yes, Miyu. We've been out twice."

"Not all those who wander are lost..."

– JRR Tolkien

In the few weeks since her visit to Friendship, the world of the ravine outside Anne's windows had changed remarkably. Bright yellows and reds had replaced the deep green of late summer, and the sky was reappearing where trees had begun to shed their leaves. The day was still young; Anne's appointment book lay open on the desk, neglected since early morning when she had wandered to the window to catch a glimpse of the sun's first rays and listen to a mixed chorus of twittering birds heralding its arrival from their hidden aviary in the trees high above. Anne stood silently in a new and unfamiliar repose she had discovered since her meeting with Krita Baba. In an inexplicable and unpredictable way, she would find herself in moments simply taking in the world around her without comment, without needing to know or understand. It was freeing, liberating, and yet at other times, she felt uneasy, as if something fundamental inside her had shifted and changed her center of gravity.

Returning to her desk, she picked up her appointment book and began to thumb through the pages.

"Noon: Bob. One o'clock: Terri. Two o'clock: Elaine. Three: Carlos. Four-thirty: James... Jacinta, Vicky, Mary, Helen, Stephen, Greg..." she closed the book and sat down heavily at her desk, holding her head in her hands, her elbows propped on the desktop.

"How?" she asked aloud. "How am I supposed to keep doing this?" The conflict of emotions she had of late begun to experience regarding her life and her work was intensely profound. The spontaneity that accompanies conviction was now gone, replaced by questions and doubts that inhibited her thoughts and words and deeds. Even her patients, perhaps most especially her patients, had noticed the change.

"What's wrong with you, Anne? You don't seem yourself today." Greg was the first to have said something about it, but then Elaine, Vicky, and even James had all made similar comments during their recent sessions. And they were right; their analyst had changed—and this without warning, without asking or receiving their permission. It was understandable they felt abandoned.

"Margot?"

"Is that you, Anne? I almost didn't recognize your voice."

"*I* hardly recognize my voice these days," Anne laughed, but the uncommon resonance of uncertainty was obvious to them both.

"Look, I was wondering if you had any free time in the next day or so. I know we have a meeting scheduled for next week, but I'd really like to talk sooner if possible."

"Of course. How about tomorrow at three? At my office if that's okay for you."

"Perfect. See you then," Anne paused. "And thank you, Margot. It's important."

"I know, dear. You would never call otherwise. See you at three."

***

How right it felt to be meeting Margot at her office and not her home—she needed the structure, the impersonality, the authority of her mentor now. The dream she'd had that morning seemed to embody the conflicts that had brought her life as of late to a state of almost total gridlock.

Anne walked purposefully through the damp cold streets to the train station—the early morning's promise of a clear day now broken by a veil of thick grey clouds that blocked the sun. *How appropriate*, she mused to herself at the dreary, rainy afternoon that so perfectly mirrored the mist enshrouding her heart.

Anne was looking forward to this conversation but feared it as well. Something within her knew she stood on a precipice between past and future, known and unknown—possibly chains and freedom—and this conversation with Margot was another step inching her closer to the inevitable leap awaiting her.

Approaching the office building and seeing she was nearly half an hour early, Anne detoured into a nearby coffee shop. Over coffee and a croissant, she passed the time gazing distractedly at the busy urban scene outside the window. A man standing across the street, seemingly looking directly at her, caught her attention.

Just my imagination, she thought and she took a sip of coffee.

Can't be, was her startled response, when his face opened into a broad smile. *My angel, Victor would probably say*, crossed her mind when a bus passed between them and he was gone as suddenly as he had appeared.

This is madness; now I am creating my own deus ex machina *to save me!* But Anne could not deny the feeling of joy that had fixed her face in an ear-to-ear grin.

"I am always with you... Don't worry; be happy." She could almost hear Krita Baba's voice as she stared down into her coffee.

"We are poor indeed if we are only sane," she chuckled to herself and shook her head, *Winnicott most definitely had that right...*

***

Though a more austere seriousness had faded her mood by the time the elevator arrived at Margot's floor, Anne still felt the unusual impulse to hug her long-time supervisor when she saw her enter the waiting room to greet her. Dismissing it more as a symptom of neediness than any actual affection, she simply smiled in response to her mentor's friendly greeting and followed her into the office.

"So tell me, what is it that brings you here ahead of our scheduled meeting time?" Margot was her usual warm and welcoming self.

"Whew, Margot… there is so much to tell."

"Begin anywhere."

Anne sat up a little straighter in the large upholstered chair across from her mentor. "As you know from our most recent conversations, I've been struggling with…" she hesitated, "feeling I'm losing my center—the source of my motivation in my life and my work."

"Yes, I would say that is well put."

"And then this morning I had a dream I believe is very significant."

"Go on."

"It had to do with being involved in some kind of ritual. People had come from somewhere, bringing with them silks and robes and candles. It was a ritual of great beauty and joy, and although it was quite foreign to me, I felt very happy. The people made me feel most welcome and shared with me the beautiful gifts they had brought. The whole atmosphere was one of incredible bliss. There was singing and operatic chanting and I joined in, somehow knowing the words and tune—in fact, when I awakened, I could still hum the refrain—but it's gone now."

"Hmm," Margot urged her to continue.

"In the dream, I was sobbing with sheer joy, unable to contain it, and then I heard the woman standing next to me simply say, 'Oh, Anne.' Her tone wasn't at all harsh or judgmental; still it felt like an admonition for me to get a grip on myself. But the joy was so deep I couldn't have stopped myself if I tried. Only later, when I awoke, did I realize the woman was Peggy, a close friend from childhood.

"In any case, my bliss didn't last for long; things started to change and all those wonderful people suddenly began packing up all their gifts—the candles and veils—everything. I became confused and disappointed; I knew the items they had given me had to be returned. Then it became my duty, and I'm not at all clear why, to go through all the other participants' luggage and dig out the items they'd been given. I felt quite awkward doing this and was very clumsy, and at one point, I even spilled some oil from one of the candles.

"By any normal standards, it wasn't a big thing, but to me my offence seemed monumental. I felt embarrassed and apologetic, but that didn't stop me from taking the opportunity to get one more whiff of the oil." Anne smiled sheepishly as Margot responded with a slight nod of her head.

"Carefully lifting the vessel to my nose, I inhaled deeply, but the scent had vanished and there was nothing. I thought, 'They have made me give everything back—and they have taken my *mudra*.' Then I woke up."

"You said the dream felt significant," Margot took a deep breath. "I would say so!" and she tilted her head almost imperceptibly to the side. "Well, my dear," she persisted softly, "what is going on?"

"Yes indeed, what's going on?" Anne paused before continuing. "I'm thinking a bit of background would help," she said and began to recount the unlikely details of her excursion with Victor to Friendship; her encounter with Aunt Lily; the circumstances surrounding their summons to India; and the subsequent audience with Krita Baba. She spoke dispassionately, giving no weight to any specifics nor suggesting significance to any particular event, but the power of her narrative spoke for itself. Margot's eyes grew increasingly large in wonder, and when Anne concluded by saying she had told Krita Baba she loved him, she slowly shook her head in a manner that could only be interpreted as disbelief.

"Well, your narrative certainly seems to shed light on your dream. What a series of exceptional experiences! I myself had a myriad of responses, even reactions, to your story. But returning to your dream for a moment, I was struck by your use of the word *mudra* when you were describing having to give back the gifts and specifically relating to the fact the oil had lost its scent. I'm not certain of the precise definition of that word, but it conveys to me the impression that they had taken away your personal power—the energy that animates the actions of your life. Am I on the right track here, Anne?"

"Yes, I think you may be on to something, Margot. Since it isn't a word I would usually choose, and yet was so clear in my dream, I felt it was important."

"But what does the word mean to *you*, Anne? What is a *mudra*?"

"I really didn't know what it meant either, it just came to me in the dream, but because the feeling was perfect when I said it in my dream, I looked it up. Loosely speaking, in Hindu ritual and classical dance, it's a symbolic gesture believed to have the ability to convey a precise meaning or state. Certain Buddhist traditions also recognize the power and significance of these highly stylized gestures and use them to guide and direct the flow of energy for healing, meditation, teaching, protection, confidence… I was amazed when I read that. I can't think of a more perfect symbol to capture how I have been feeling—how I have been functioning— since that fateful trip just over three weeks ago. It definitely feels like my *mudra* has been taken from me."

"It gives me shivers," was all Margot could say, and then she added, "the unconscious is an astonishing teacher…"

"To get right to the point, Margot, I'm feeling lost, and in my mind I keep coming back to my conversation with Aunt Lily as the source of this—as if Aunt Lily stole something very valuable from me."

Margot sat a little more upright and, resting her wrist on the arm of her chair, lightly touched her index finger to her thumb. "Aunt Lily does appear to be an extraordinary woman, but it seems to me you are conceding too much of your personal power to her. I'd like to return to your dream. I am particularly struck by the image of you having to go through everyone else's luggage to return the gifts that had been given. It makes me think you feel obliged to take back all that was good in what you have done for others. Luggage is such a potent image—the baggage we carry. So you have to go through their baggage and take back all the gifts. It doesn't stop there—there is not even a scent of what had been—all the beauty and joy... gone."

"Quite true."

"And I'm also really interested in the woman at your side—the one who suggested you 'get a grip' when you were in the throes of bliss."

"Well, when I woke up, it occurred to me that back in high school Peggy had urged me to participate in a community chorus performance of the Messiah."

"Uh huh."

"I found it wonderfully exhilarating and inspiring, but she didn't share my level of enthusiasm, describing the performance as lackluster and the chorus as rag-tag."

"So she had encouraged you in the first place and then sabotaged the enthusiasm you felt from it?"

"Yes, and it made me feel a bit foolish."

"Okay, and Peggy is a nickname for?"

"Margaret."

"And could Peggy, therefore be dream shorthand for Margot?"

Anne gasped when she realized the figure of admonition in her dream was possibly Margot and not her girlhood friend. Perhaps this was the source of her discomfort and sense of foreboding before their meeting?

"Though I don't consciously think of you this way, there it is—something in me cast you in my dream as my *internal saboteur*... the devil inside, always lurking in the shadows, waiting to destroy what feels good."

Margot smiled. "Fairbairn's image of the *internal saboteur* is such a brilliant metaphor. The concept really captures the flavor of the feeling there is always 'something' in us waiting to inhibit our growth, like a perverse alchemist who turns positive into negative. I do think your reference to it is appropriate here, which of course raises some interesting questions about your unconscious putting me in that role. Still, is it not true that what we see and how we see others is only the tip of the iceberg—merely the surface of what is really there?"

"I agree—and personally I think most of the time, it's really for our own good and the good of human interaction."

"Ah, but your psyche let the cat out of the bag, so you will have to work with it."

"And I will, but perhaps for now we should return to my dream?"

Margot smiled and nodded in agreement.

"I've also been thinking about the veils in my dream. Veils are something used to create an illusion, like the oil candles without scent, without substance. And even the ritual itself, with all of its paraphernalia, was only there for a moment and then packed up and gone like a traveling circus or magic show: all smoke and mirrors, nothing real. It makes me think maybe the whole business with Aunt Lily and Krita Baba was merely my projection."

"We all project, Anne; you know that what we *see* is the product of our associations, but I think it is important to be clear here, do you really think the 'whole business with Aunt Lily and Krita Baba' is, as you say, *merely* your projection? Or perhaps you thought I would see it that way and, in fact characterizing it as a projection could be a kind of defense?"

"To be frank, I thought you might—but in actual fact, I believe there is something in me that is rejecting the possibility of all this being real. I woke up this morning feeling out of sorts. I realized it was because I was dreading this meeting and now I think it has to do with that part of me that does not want to look foolish in front of you… or rather, me." Anne released a deep sigh.

Margot rested her elbows on the arms of her chair and laced her fingers together under her chin. "Well, for what it's worth, my sense of all this is that you have indeed experienced something quite profound. And while I agree with you about 'illusions' created by veils, what about the fact that veils can also be used to hide reality? When they are removed, the truth may stand revealed."

"'Open the folds of your veil and you shall see God.'"

"Quite well put."

"Actually, Margot, it's a quote from a Sufi poet, Hafiz, I heard from Victor."

"There you go," Margot agreed, as she leaned forward in her chair. "East meets West. You are aware, I am sure, of all the current interest in spiritual teachings within the field of psychoanalysis. I find this trend to be very interesting and potentially very useful, and dismiss Freud's assessment of religion as being merely an 'obsessional neurosis on the scale of the collective.'

"This is not to say that religious belief and practice cannot be, at times, a manifestation of neurotic, or even psychotic, illnesses, but many of us no longer feel compelled to atheism in order to claim our right to the title of psychoanalyst. Personally, I find the writings about the similarity of some of the tenets and practices of Buddhism, Zen in particular, and our practice of 'presence' with a patient quite interesting and relevant. And I know you will agree one can accept the marvelous research being done on brain plasticity without agreeing to a reductionist view of human beings as mere flesh activated by neuronal firing.

"The point is, are we not trained to tolerate ambiguity and accept the mystery of the unknown? What about the unconscious after all? From Freud to everyone who has followed him, the unconscious is always regarded and even respected as a force that can neither be denied nor ignored—no matter how mysterious or contradictory it appears to be."

"This is indeed a helpful reminder."

"Psychoanalytic theory these days," Margot continued, "does not pretend to cosmology, but think about it—at the core of Winnicott's object-relations theory is the hypothesis that what we see as manifest in one another—personality, for want of a better term—is primarily a 'false' self, developed to protect our true self or nature, which thus protected, remains untouched by the world. From this perspective, we could say that the goal of analysis is to facilitate the emergence of the true self, and perhaps in the process neutralize some 'impressions' belonging to the false self along the way. You have to admit, this sounds similar to what Aunt Lily and Victor and Krita Baba are saying."

Anne cocked her head to the side and nodded.

Margot went on, "I recently read something I found very interesting: a quote from a patient who was giving testimony to the power of her therapy. The gist of it was she felt that what she gained from her psychotherapy was essentially within her from the outset, but had been lost because it was out of reach—words which could easily come from a spiritual teacher speaking of God being within us all. I'm really just thinking out loud, Anne, and we've taken the focus of our conversation off you. So let me ask *you* a question similar to one posited by Aunt Lily, how do you see your life and work at this time—why do you do what you do?"

"I have to be honest—I do what I do because I enjoy it and because people tell me I'm good at it. I've often thought of myself as having a gift—like someone else might have a gift for music, or athletics, or cooking. I've also felt a certain responsibility to try to develop this gift because other people seemed to benefit from it, at least in a life way. I can accept that I need to be vigilant about insidious egotism, and that what I do is no more important than what another person does, but I am really struggling here—it's hard to accept that it doesn't help at all. And strange things seem to be happening in sessions."

"Strange things?"

"Well, for example. You remember Carlos?"

"The gay man who left his emotionally distant partner of ten years?"

"That's Carlos. He had started dating and was finding his new life as a single man far more interesting and validating than his old life had become. He felt creative once again and had gone back to sculpting with renewed vigor."

"Right…"

"So last week, he began his session saying he was really troubled because Wayne, his former partner, had started calling him and they had been speaking fairly regularly over the past several weeks."

"And the problem was?"

"The problem was, in his words, that he hadn't told me. Now a month ago, I probably would have explored what lay behind his feeling that he was *obliged* to tell me; most likely it would have led to revelations regarding his mother/confessor transference towards me and possibly facilitated his further movement towards self-reliance. But that day I simply said, 'So, how has it been, talking to Wayne now?'

"His whole demeanor changed, and he became quite animated—all his troubles seemed forgotten. He said he found himself speaking to Wayne with confident self-assurance, and Wayne seemed to be responding very favorably..."

"Not terribly surprising, really."

"No, I suppose not. But then he asked me point-blank whether he should agree to go to coffee with him."

"And?"

"And I said I had no idea, but it seemed like he wanted to."

"Okay..."

"And then I said, 'and why not, if you want to? Life is an adventure.'"

"Ah, it's true, that's not your usual voice..." Margot paused for a moment. "But can you tell me, where did this new voice come from?"

"All I can say is that it just felt right."

"I'll venture something here, Anne, and I am not just saying this to make you feel better. I have long believed your intuitive sense is very strong. You have the ability to speak from a place that is genuine in you and very often strikes a responsive chord in your patients. It seems to me that your intuition is continuing to operate—even if what you say may surprise you as well as your patients. It could be very interesting to see where this new sense of things takes both you and them.

"No doubt, some may find it jarring, I suppose, but that is simply more material to be worked with. And of course, one must never forget the power of the idealized transference—so you, and I, and every other analyst or therapist, must always be vigilant—to be authentic, to question our motives, to continue to analyze, so that our patients do not fall under the spell of their own projection of our omniscience or omnipotence. But it seems to me what you were communicating to Carlos is that you believed he was strong enough to take life on. That, my dear, is a very powerful message."

Feeling somewhat reassured, Anne continued, "Okay. But let me tell you what happened with Helen."

"Remind me who Helen is."

"Helen is the forty-two-year-old woman who's had a series of unsuccessful relationships with men."

"Oh yes; wasn't she raped by her uncle when she was thirteen?" Anne nodded her head.

"Right. Well these past few sessions, I have found it nearly impossible to listen to her or to follow the details of what she's saying because I get distracted by the sounds and rhythm of her speech. In our session last week, she was talking and I was trying to follow what she was saying when it suddenly struck me, 'She is playing a tune, a lament—like a child with a favorite record who simply continues to play it repeatedly—boring everyone around her, driving them to distraction.'"

"Interesting, so what did you do?"

"I interrupted her and simply said, 'It's time to change the record.' She stopped mid-sentence and turned to look at me from where she was lying on the couch. The look on her face was pure astonishment. 'What did you say?'

"'I said it's time to change the record.'

"Now she was sitting up, facing me, with her mouth half open. I definitely had her attention, and then I said to her, 'You've never had a pet, have you? I want you to go to the pound and find yourself an animal to love and care for. You need to find out how to love…'"

"Unorthodox, but makes sense," mused Margot. "How did she take it?"

"Well, she missed her next session. But when she came yesterday, she was full of stories about her new retriever. It was an entirely new song. And then she told me she wanted to pay for him to go through obedience training, which was very expensive, and she really felt she needed more free time to spend with him…"

"So she chose to terminate with you?"

"Yes!"

"And the problem is you weren't prepared for her abrupt departure?"

"I suppose. But I couldn't help but wonder if I'd lost the plot and had simply become another person who abandoned her, like her mother in the aftermath of the rape, who refused to even talk about it, or the many men in her life who said they loved her but eventually left, and so she withdrew."

"Did you abandon her? Think carefully now—where did those statements about the record and learning how to love come from? Were you bored, annoyed, fed up? What were you experiencing?"

"Actually, I felt quite clear and open. It was only later I began to doubt myself."

Margot took a deep breath and looked over at the clock on the wall. Anne always marveled at her mentor's knack for knowing exactly when their time was up.

"At the risk of sounding redundant," Margot concluded, "I'll say it again—you do have a gift and I suggest you continue to hone it. See where it takes you and your patients. Be vigilant—as always and…" she paused and smiled gently, "do remember dear, 'not all those who wander are lost.'"

***

Anne walked briskly to the train, her coat held closely around her against the chilly air. The rain had stopped and patches of blue had appeared between the thinning clouds. *Not all those who wander are lost,* she repeated to herself. *I like that!* Then, smiling to herself, her thoughts traveled back to that day at Aunt Lily's farm and Adi, the beautiful greyhound with the amazing eyes. *I need a dog too,* she thought as she boarded the train to Highland Park. *He'd understand.*

Flame of Love

Oh world,
the heart aches with longing,
tears bear witness to its silent vigil
for the Beloved who waits beyond the shadow of all expectations.

But how the heart suffers when ensnared
by false lovers, its longing fallen to despair —
the true Beloved remains unseen.

Two moths fly to each other.
Why are they attracted so?

Eternity whispers,
It is the flame of love,
misheard and mis-seen
around which hearts' wings
long to circle and dance.

Oh heart,
inspired by images of beauty
and the reflection of love,
you create your beloved
and dream the dream of union's bliss.

Oh flame,
to know yourself
you dream yourself the moth
to awaken as fire.

Oh moth,
you are the dream of your own flame,
as is the beloved you seek,
in truth both lover and beloved are one.

Dream and dreamer,
moth and flame,
awake in union —
wings of separation burnt to ashes
in the flame of love.

Jake sighed, placed his friend's poem on the little table and closed his eyes. It was now nearly five years since Victor had been called to live with Krita Baba, and three years since Jake and Miyu had visited him in India at the ashram with their two-year-old daughter Victoria.

The years since he first met Krita Baba seemed to have been touched by grace and prosperity. He had married Miyu and was deeply in love. Victoria had grown into a beautiful and intelligent child, and Miyu's interest in bonsai and ikebana had blossomed into a successful small business which left them free of material want and left Jake more time to actively pursue his love of the piano. He was happy—happy and grateful—yet he missed Victor profoundly, and his heart ached with intense longing whenever he thought of Krita Baba.

Jake withdrew a stick of sandalwood incense from a box on the table, lit it and placed it in the little brass holder he had carried back with him from India. The scent reminded him of India and especially Victor's room. He sighed again as the wispy white smoke carried the fragrance into his mind, unlocking the cherished memories of that last time he spent with his friend.

He remembered everything: the squeak of the metal bar as Victor unhinged the heavy carved wooden doors, the sound of his sandal on the stone floor when he stepped over the threshold into Victor's simple room. He pictured in his mind the shingled window, barred and unscreened, that looked out on the courtyard and the white plaster walls adorned only by a simply framed picture of Krita Baba with those deep sorrowful eyes and beaming smile. He recalled the one small closet, the single bed with mosquito netting, the chair and the desk with the two framed pictures Victor had requested—one of Anne and the other, Victoria, Miyu, and himself. He saw clearly the lamp, the lone candle and cup, and Victor's cherished six-volume set of the English translation of the talks of Krita Baba.

But what Jake remembered most—the memory he cherished most—was the image of his friend, even more thin than before, his luminous blue eyes even more knowing, more seeing, sitting cross-legged on his bed with the mosquito net pulled back around him like gossamer curtains—or wings.

Sitting on the chair across from Victor, the sounds of devotional music from the ancient village across the field drifting into the room through the window—shutters thrown open to catch the occasional night breeze—they talked softly long into the night about everything and nothing—sometimes laughing, sometimes sharing the cool tears of longing the soul reserves for its Beloved. Despite distance and the passage of time, he was once again there with Victor, his friend and teacher, his elder brother, as close as any two beings could ever be.

"Are you thinking about India?" Jake opened his eyes to see Miyu standing before him, her hair long and shining, hanging loosely to her pale shoulders, the light from the hall passing through her thin silk gown, illuming the soft beautiful secrets of her womanhood. She was smiling at him, her eyes black and lustrous, her lips full and sensual, delightfully turned up at the corners. God did he love her.

"Yes, you could tell?" his voice was soft and dreamy.

"I'm your wife; I can tell," she said softly. "May I dream with you?"

Miyu gently accepted Jake's extended hand and gracefully folded herself onto his lap. Jake closed his eyes again and became aware of the delicate fragrance of mogra in Miyu's hair. She had been wearing it that morning when he asked Krita Baba to help him get past the memories that still haunted him of the abuse he witnessed and experienced as a boy in the Church, and the guilt and confusion he felt and could not shake concerning his childhood friend and his suicide.

Krita Baba had raised his hand to stop him and then in an almost matter of fact way had said, "When the goal of life is attained, one achieves the reparation of all wrongs, the healing of all wounds, the righting of all failures, the sweetening of all sufferings, the relaxation of all strivings, the harmonizing of all strife, the unraveling of all enigmas, and the real and full meaning of all life—past, present and future. Yes, Jake, I will help you. I will help you to forgive in order to forget by realizing it is all a dream— a mere pouring of the empty into the void.

"I will help you to experience once and for all that in reality you are beyond birth and death, all pain and suffering—that you can neither hurt nor be hurt, kill nor be killed—that you are infinite and eternal—that you are God. This is my promise to you."

And Jake had seen it—had glimpsed the truth of himself and the authority from which Krita Baba spoke. These words were neither platitudes nor a visionary's idle or informed speculation. These words proceeded from truth, from absolute experience and so they were more than words, they were truth itself.

"I was thinking of that day with Krita Baba," Jake said as he stroked his wife's thigh. Even in the midst of his deepest spiritual revelations, his totally human love and passion for his wife was never diminished—nor did he ever feel even the slightest shade of conflict or contradiction. Life and God, the dream of illusion and the reality of awakening, were never at odds, were never adversaries, but were instead the lover and the Beloved bound by love, dancing the dance of union—the wedding dance.

"Ah *Koishii*, I know you were, as was I. I remember so clearly that day with Baba; it was the wedding day of our souls in Him. Do you remember what he said?" Jake leaned closer to his wife and felt the soft smoothness of her cheek against his. He moved his hand to her breast and held it gently. They both felt a warm current pulse through their bodies, uniting them in oneness.

Indeed he did remember—as clearly as if it were today: the two of them and Victoria alone with Krita Baba and Amrit, his closest disciple, in the intimate little meeting hall that had once been a local post office; Krita Baba wearing a white *sadra* sitting on a large stuffed chair; the sunlight through the window beside him illuminating the room with a soft golden glow; Miyu and himself on the floor sitting on large soft pillows.

Krita Baba held Victoria on his lap, smiling, playing with her—gently pinching her little cheek. Victoria was laughing and cooing with delight and, remarkably, within minutes fell asleep on Baba's lap. Amrit picked her up and laid her down on the blankets next to Miyu, as Krita Baba began to speak. "I am so happy you are here. I love you all so much, and I will help you to make your marriage a source of happiness for yourselves and your Beloved God.

"Hundreds of thousands of years ago life was not as it is today. It was a time, a moment in the eternal cycle of existence, when the light and not the shadow it cast pervaded. It was a time when all men and women were focused on God and though material prosperity was also at a zenith, people kept to a simple mode of life and did not desire for things beyond the sustenance and the preservation of a life necessary to pursue their one real desire—to attain union with God.

"These were not primitive times; in those olden days, people lived much longer and had abilities and powers modern man can only dream of. Of course, all actions create binding, so even the impressions formed from the minimal efforts to sustain their existence had to be removed and this is why Beloved God in the form of Infinite Intelligence created differences in the female and the male forms beyond what was necessary for the perpetuation of human life.

"You see, both the female and the male forms of the human being represent states of God—the male can be likened to the hands and the female to the water. The nature of the hands is to work and the nature of the water is to wash. When the hands work they get dirty—by this I mean they acquire impressions—and so need to be cleansed. Water is necessary for this cleansing, but to do a proper job, this water must be totally pure. In those days of which I speak, women were just like that—they were totally pure and unsullied—they were perfect—and consequently were capable of washing away any and all impressions that came their way.

"God instituted the holy relationship of marriage and wives were aware of their power, and husbands did not fear it as they have come to in modern times. On the contrary, husbands appreciated and worshipped their wives, and their wives, in turn, treated their husbands as God. Women and men worked together in perfect harmony, and by their simple and natural association with each other achieved God-hood. Masters and teachers were not necessary in those days, nor was religion with its endless and empty rituals, rites, and rules, nor education as it is now understood and practiced, which has become the very handmaiden of illusion.

"Please try to understand, however, that nobody was responsible for what has come to pass. Change is the very nature of existence, and the cycles of time of which I speak go on repeating endlessly. Those old days will come again and will pass again—the dark age of Kali we now endure will inevitably pass into the golden age of Krita only to return once again to Kali. These great cycles turn endlessly, but the aim of life is to be free of itself—this dream of the soul as being bound in transitory existence—birth and death, heaven and hell, pleasure and pain.

"The goal of life is not a better dream; the goal is to awaken. Think of the stone. Does it care if it is carved into the form of an idol and worshipped or if it is used instead to make a latrine? The rock does not care, and this is why I say, with consciousness, be like a stone. This is the meaning behind the great mantra, 'Be as it may.' 'Be as it may' is the highest state one can attain in relationship to illusion because it is in the very nature of illusion that by seeking pleasure, you will get pain; by seeking praise, you will get blame; whatever end of the stick you grab, the other end will inevitably find its way into your hand."

"But Baba," asked Miyu, "what are we to do? We have our whole lives ahead of us—and Victoria's. Pleasure does not seem to be the problem so much as avoiding pain—pain and suffering scare me to death. You say that it is illusion, but your *illusion* is my *reality*."

"How very true are your words. I am asking you to act as if your reality is illusion, yet as Kabir said, 'Until you experience it, it is not true.' So what can you do? First I say try not to worry. This is nearly impossible but still I say try. I will help you to awaken from this endless duality and realize oneness—realize God. To accomplish this, you need not live a life of privations or penance, nor do you need to practice yoga or pieties; you do not need to become saints nor do you need to understand everything and know everything. I ask of you neither your indifference to life nor your indulgence in it. Simply try to be honest with yourselves and each other and cheerfully take life as it comes to you, asking neither its why nor its wherefore, remembering always that it is merely a dream, a passing show, a movie constructed from your own impressions of illusion. Try to remember all this, but most important, remember me, hold on to me—with both hands."

Miyu reached down, picked up the poem from the table and read:

Oh world,
the heart aches with longing,
tears bear witness to its silent vigil for the Beloved
who waits beyond the shadow of all expectations.

"Oh Baba," she sighed, resting her head on her husband's chest. Soothed by the rhythm of his heart beating gently, she closed her eyes and fell asleep in his arms.

Reflections

She was usually a very good sleeper, but the last couple of nights she had tossed and turned, troubled by a recurring dream about having to get to a train station. When she arrived, she could see the train already leaving the station and felt disappointed...

Anne was out of bed and sipping coffee on the balcony before the sun was up, thinking about the dream of the night before that had haunted her sleep and left her feeling even more tired than when she climbed into bed at midnight. Was she supposed to be meeting someone at the train station, she wondered? It had felt like someone she knew was leaving, but she couldn't be sure and wondered who it could have been. Even the energy was ambiguous, was it male or female? Was it one of her patients? Was it Anita—could she have been dreaming about Anita after all this time? The feeling was close enough that she was drawn back inside the house to the file cabinet where she kept her therapy notes. Instinctively, she opened the third drawer and pulled out Anita's file, carrying it back to the overstuffed chair by the French doors. She hesitated before turning over the first page. It was the transcript of a dream:

> *I was in my bedroom... where I grew up. I was sitting on my bed. My mother was standing at the foot of the bed and she was saying the most startling things to me—startling because I had no idea she felt the way she did—it was very angry stuff I had never heard before. I tried to defend myself, but there was no way she would listen to me.*

There was a man lying on the bed by my side, and he started explaining everything she was saying, and it helped because I felt he was on my side—even though he was with her and what he said made me see things in a way I never had. He was a dark figure... I couldn't see his face... I didn't think I knew him. I only remember black clothes. And after I woke up, I couldn't remember anything specific he said, only that it made sense.

In my dream, there were so many lights on in the room—lights on the table next to the bed... lights on the dresser... lights in the ceiling of the closet, which was painted black—it was so bright it hurt my eyes. I began flipping switches... sometimes a light would turn off, sometimes another three or four would turn on. I could not find all the switches, but I knew they must be somewhere and I had to turn them off!

This was the last entry; it was dated two days before Anita killed herself. Scanning her notes, the session came back to her in lucid detail, everything from the clothes Anita was wearing—a dark maroon Gucci suit—and the tone of her voice—plaintive, while at the same time defiant—to the headache she was suffering with that day. She also well remembered what Anita had said about her dream:

"I'm not sure what the whole thing means, but one thing is pretty clear, my mother is really getting to me."

"How so?" Anne gently prodded.

"She's just so dismissive of Jake—which bugs me no end—and it's obvious she doesn't approve of us living together, even though we don't have sex. Of course, she never really comes out and says anything; she knows I'm not going to pay any attention to what she thinks anyway... I suppose she's given up on me."

Anne sat quietly and waited.

"And I'm guessing the guy on the bed is Jake. After all, there's nothing sexual going on between us on the bed; he's just there, and he understands me."

"And what about the lights?" Anne queried.

"The lights? I don't know—maybe I'm tired of everything being so exposed; as soon as I deal with one issue, another appears—it's so frustrating."

Anne remembered wondering which thread to pick up, there was so much material. Anita's assertion that the "dark figure" was Jake didn't quite ring true, but the fact that she did bring him up, twice alluding to the fact that they didn't have sex, seemed significant. Maybe Anita was struggling with the lack of sex in their relationship and this was her unconscious attempt to bring it into their sessions.

And then there was Anita's apparently offhand comment that her mother had probably given up on her, when in the dream it was actually Anita who had given up on her mother. Had she given up on herself? And the lights! What an evocative image. In the end, Anne had decided it was the dark figure that held the key.

"Would you like to hear some of my thoughts?" Anne said to her patient.

"Sure. Go ahead."

"I'm wondering about the dark figure lying on the bed—the man who was 'with' your mother, but who 'got' you. I couldn't help but think of your father…"

"I knew you'd say that."

"Oh?"

"It seemed really obvious to me too, when I first went over the dream myself."

"Yet today you told me you thought the dark figure was Jake." Anne's thoughts were rapidly forming around the longing and frustration Anita might be feeling regarding the lack of sexual intimacy in their relationship.

"Well," Anita paused and was silent for a moment. "It surprised me when I said it; it just came out."

"Would you like me to offer a suggestion and see if it fits?"

"Please… because I feel like there's something there I can't quite get my head around."

"Okay, here's what occurs to me. As I recall, early in your relationship, you had no sexual interest in Jake—you had mentioned feeling almost 'motherly' towards him. But over time this changed—you became ambivalent—and it's Jake who's taken on that 'parenting' aspect of your relationship by appearing sexually aloof from you."

"Yes that's true."

"So I'm wondering if Jake's apparent remoteness around this issue perhaps morphs into him being on your mother's side in your dream. Of course, his reasons for not engaging in sex would not be the same as hers, but still could leave you feeling as if they might as well be—in the sense that there is no way to challenge him or break through and it is this unwillingness on his part that is making you angry."

"I find that a little hard to accept." Anne noticed how Anita crossed her arms over her chest when she said that.

"It what way?" she responded.

"Not that what you say is implausible, but it's difficult to accept because it shows me as being… um… needy or weak…"

Anne nodded her head slowly and smiled sympathetically.

"It's true that in this work, as it progresses, one begins to feel that there are fewer and fewer places to hide."

"I can definitely attest to that—it causes me a lot of pain. But shattering my illusions *is* what I'm here for—right?"

"Yes, and yes to everything else you said. Shall I continue?" Anita uncrossed her arms and nodded her head.

"Yes."

"Anita, I'm thinking that perhaps the 'mother' in your dream is also you—an unconscious identification that, as you say, could be painful to admit."

"True. It is… painful to admit, that is."

"It would be natural then that you may be struggling, again unconsciously, to find a new way out of this. So, in your dream the dark figure gives you new insight yet still doesn't seem to change anything—this despite the fact that he 'gets' you—something you often say about Jake."

Anita nodded, "Yes, I can see that."

"Now another thing I find really interesting and significant is that you're trying to turn lights off—all the lights in the bedroom and finally in the closet."

"Yes, the whole thing about the lights is so vivid and seems so full of meaning, but all I get from it is a vague connection to something Victor said to me long ago in a lesson, about how truth is not found where it is lost but in the light."

Reading this comment from Anita caused Anne to look up from her notes feeling unable to take a breath. What had led her to the file cabinet and Anita's file when she was thinking about her own dream of the night before? Could the connection be more about Victor than Anita? Anne closed the file, placed it on her lap, and looked out into garden. Night had dreamed its dawn and awoken refreshed into a beautiful spring day.

Perhaps, she mused, *Anita's entire dream was really a message—in the form of a call to impartiality which she couldn't hear through the noise of her own impressions. The challenge wasn't to recognize that she had within her both the enemy, her mother, and the ally, the dimly perceived dark figure. The challenge was to not side with either—not the accuser, not the supporter—in order to dispel their influence. And then there was also the pointed metaphor about the utter futility of trying to turn off the light of life that keeps re-lighting as one moves through the various levels of sleep to the final awakening— represented by the light on the bedside table, the level of sleep, then the light on the dresser, the level of aspiration, to the lights in the closet where the ceiling is painted black like the infinite Void. And of course, what I totally missed at the time was Anita's absolute determination to turn off all the lights.*

Anne sighed. *Ah, the benefit of hindsight.* Still unable to free herself from the feelings stirred by her own dream and the tie to Anita's, her thoughts continued to bounce back and forth through time, from present to past, from Anita's dream to her own, and to the connection she now felt to Victor. *It's Anita's dream that holds the key; something about it forms the nexus between then and now.* Still, the link with her own dream eluded her; the idea that it was about having missed the train with Anita was not quite right—seemed to be missing some critical part…

Anne was startled out of her reverie when the phone rang. It was Amrit, calling from India. Victor had passed away.

Now it all made sense, the meaning of her dream was perfectly clear: *The train has left the station...*

Anita's file slipped unnoticed from her lap, scattering loose papers around her feet. "It started a few days ago..." the caller was reporting calmly. "It was his heart... everything was done for him medically that could have been done." Amrit went on to say that Krita Baba had told him earlier that morning to stay with Victor because it would be his last day. "Of course I informed him immediately when Victor passed, and in response, Baba told me and a few of the followers who were there at the time, 'Three weeks ago I honored my promise to Victor and pushed him beyond the state of *Hawa* onto the higher planes of consciousness. That is why he seemed suddenly withdrawn and disoriented to you. But Victor was not suffering; in this state, he was experiencing the sixth veil of the voice of God and the bliss of this experience made him forget the gross universe completely and forever.

"'Victor experienced real inspiration, the inspiration that flowed from his own subtle consciousness. That is why those of you who were with him in those last few days felt dazed in his presence.

"'Victor will take another body very soon—before I drop my body,' Baba said, 'and will be born again here in India near me. His consciousness will remain subtle, and in his next lifetime, I will push him on again, before I, myself, leave this body.'"

Amrit went on to say that Krita Baba wished him to convey his blessing to all of those who loved Victor and wanted them to know that his connection with them was assured and would remain unbroken. Victor had been their connection to Baba, but from the moment of their first meetings, no further intermediaries were needed. "Be sure to inform Jake and Miyu," was Amrit's final remark.

Anne gently placed the phone back on its base. A quiet murmur escaped her throat. Adi, who had come silently into the room during the phone call, was curled comfortably at her feet amidst the scattered papers. Raising his head at the sound of her voice, he looked straight into her eyes. She crouched down to him, their faces nearly touching, as soft warm tears traced shining paths down her cheeks. Adi brought his snout even closer and gently licked her tears. "He's moved on, Adi. He's moved on. God bless him," Anne said as she draped her arms over Adi's shoulders and rested her head against his forehead.

Closing her eyes, images of Victor began to play across her mind, like clips from a movie: Victor holding a glass of wine aloft in a toast, smiling, blue eyes twinkling; Victor riding on the black stallion along the forest path in Wisconsin, serene and confident; Victor reaching out a hand to assist her, always the gentleman; Victor seated at his piano, as if in another world altogether, weaving his magic in music.

Her heart, opened by the memories, overflowed with love's wine, flooding her whole being with profound joy. A deep conviction of the rightness of all things enveloped her—cradled her—as she thought about Victor and Anita, through whom he had come into her life.

She closed her eyes and saw Anita as vividly as if she were as close to her as Adi. No dark clouds surrounded her anymore, no regrets or remorse sighed in Anne's heart. Anita was haloed in light that beamed from the face of Krita Baba, who was smiling and caressing her cheeks saying softly over and over, "My child, my beloved child."

Anne trembled before the image—trembled with happiness so great she felt she could lose her own body. She opened her eyes.

"How is it, Adi," she said as she stared into his wondering eyes, "that one day a person walks up to you, a total stranger, and that meeting sets you on a path that changes your life forever?" Taking hold of the arm of the chair, she eased herself back onto her feet and walked slowly across the room to the baby grand piano standing mutely in the corner. She touched the deep mahogany lovingly, remembering the day Victor had come to tell her he was leaving for India and how he hoped she would accept his instrument as a gift.

"But I don't play," she protested weakly.

"One never knows the future," he said in response. "One never knows…"

And so the gift was accepted and had become a sort of memorial for all those she loved. Pictures of family and friends stood on the closed lid. She cast her eyes from one photo to another: Margot, looking obliquely over her glasses at her, a wry smile on her lips—gone three years now to breast cancer; Jake and Miyu on their wedding day, positively beaming with joy as they looked into each other's eyes; pictures of Adi as he romped through the field behind Aunt Lily's house the day she and Victor had gone to adopt him; Aunt Lily and Tom, ancient and peaceful, Tom looking off into the distance, Aunt Lily addressing the camera directly—both long gone now; the newborn Victoria in Miyu's arms, glowing innocence and vitality beneath her mother's loving gaze; and her own son, Nicholas, as an infant, toddler, teenager… Anne reached for one of his pictures, carried it to the window and looked at it in the light of day.

Nicholas was ten years old, sitting in the stern of a small sailboat clutching the rudder, all rapt attention directed up at the wind-filled sail. It was his maiden voyage—his first solo trip—yet she had always marveled at how masterful he looked at the helm. For a long while after his accident, she had not been able to look at the picture without feeling the bitter irony of his death. His brief life, lived passionately, so filled with promise and possibilities, swept away in a terrible moment of senseless tragedy.

She could never look at the picture for long, it gave her chills— maybe from the cold water that stole his life. She would always turn away and grasp on to whatever thought or feeling was handy—anything to divert her mind and dull the pain. But now as she looked at his picture feeling the rightness of it all, she smiled. Caressing the frame, she dared to touch the image of her son. *There are no accidents,* she thought, *no victims, no one nor anything to blame.* Calmly, even reticently, she returned the picture to its place on the piano, near the photo of Jake and Miyu.

I better call them now, she thought, and reached for the telephone. They spoke for just a few minutes. Anne repeated everything Amrit had told her. She could hear Jake breathing heavily on the other end, his voice sounding deep and withdrawn when they said goodbye.

Anne stood frozen in the moment like a marble statue, at a loss for what to do next, until some hidden prompting drew her back to her chair and the notes on the floor. After carefully re-ordering the papers, she returned them to the file cabinet, locked the drawer, and had taken but two steps before she abruptly turned back to the cabinet and unlocked the drawer. Just half-knowing why, yet fully aware of what she was doing, she removed all its contents and carried the stacks of files to the fireplace. Adi lay down on his rug near the hearth and watched attentively as his mistress methodically placed twigs and small logs onto the andirons.

"And how should we mark this auspicious occasion, Adi?" she said to her loyal friend. "Perhaps a glass of wine?" Adi tilted his head to the side. "Okay, then wine it is," she said. Adi followed her with one eye as she proceeded to select two crystal wine goblets from the china cabinet and a bottle of rare Argentinean Malbec from the wine rack, all of which she carried back to the hearth. She arranged them on the floor beside her companion and lit the fire. As the flames began to creep higher through the logs—like rivers of fire finding their way to the sea, she arranged some pillows for herself between Adi and the stack of files and sat down with a gentle sigh. She uncorked the wine and filled both glasses.

"To you, Victor," she said as she raised her goblet in front of the flames, "to dying, so we may truly live." She brought the goblet to her lips and took a long drink, then held the glass before the fire so that the wine glowed with its light. "There is a difference between the wine and the glass that holds it..." she whispered, recalling the sound of Victor's voice as he recited one of his favorite quotations, "...never mistake the one for the other," she said more loudly and then lovingly reached down and took his wine glass from the floor and spilled its contents over the flames.

Anne turned to Adi, and after caressing his ears and the back of his neck, reached over and lifted the first file, Anita's, from the stack beside her. "To dying, so we may truly live," she repeated softly as she crumpled the pages and gently placed them on the fire. "To dying, so we may truly live," she repeated while continuing the purge, and as the stack diminished, she began to feel lighter and clearer. She worked slowly and deliberately, losing all track of time, until the final scrap was consumed.

Adi dozed as Anne watched the flames turn to warm glowing embers, now no longer able to hold back the deepening shadows that filled the room. She poured the last of the wine into her glass and carried it to the stereo. The record was still on the turntable; she could hear the song playing before the platter began to spin.

Oh yes, let them begin the Beguine,
her own inner voice merged softly with young Ella's.
"Make them play
'Til the stars that were there before return above you . . .
'Til you whisper to me once more, 'Darling, I love you!'
And we suddenly know, what heaven we're in,
when they begin the Beguine..."

Afterword

Jake was sipping sake and watching Miyu fashioning thin copper wire along a branch of her prized Celastrus paniculatus bonsai, marveling at her ability to deftly avoid the tiny golden fruit that decorated the gnarled old branch, when they received the call from Anne. Miyu felt the change in Jake immediately.

She placed the wire on the table and turned toward her husband. Studying his face, she watched the procession of emotions like photographs in a slideshow—first shock followed by distress, then loss followed by sadness. At one point, she noticed a flicker of a smile play on his lips and flicker in his eyes—this when Anne conveyed how, in the end, Victor emanated bliss and light to all who were near him. The words he spoke when he put down the phone did not surprise her—she had had a feeling since awakening that morning.

"Victor has died," he said simply. "It's okay."

Miyu moved over to the couch next to him. She took his hand in hers and they sat in silence for a long time. Then, with a deep sigh, Jake reached down to the coffee table and picked up Victor's most recent letter and the long poem that accompanied it.

<u>Voice of the Stream</u>

My heart was so full that day as I walked in the garden, my body could not contain its swell.

Joy rose within me. My eyes filled with tears.

"Why do I love this garden so much?" I said aloud.

"Because, I made it for you."

I turned and saw him, arms held wide standing beside a tiny stream amidst a stand of white jasmine.

"I have known your father and your father's father and his father too, before the mighty tree of your lineage had yet become a tiny seed.

"I knew you then and I have loved you forever—before creation—before the time of time itself.

"Long ago, I revealed to your father seven times removed a hundred thousand shapes that clothe my mystery. In me he glimpsed the universes of form and energy and mind and all the worlds beyond the universe also. To him, I revealed my infinite colors, countless forms, and my attributes divine. Now see! The gift is yours."

"There is darkness. I see nothing."

"This darkness will fade. Can you see yourself?"

"I see a man, small and weak. His eyes are open yet do not see."

"That man you were has ceased to be. You are all life now, life from stone to tree, every creature, humanity."

"Yes! I am towering mountains and raging seas. I am mighty rivers and endless plains stretching past the reach of my eye and beyond the grasp of my mind."

"You have become the earth, its firmament and depths—and you are the source of its life also. But what is your source, and where is your home? Your journey has only just begun."

"I am light and fire bursting: planets encircle and adore me. Earth, dearest of all bows reverently at my feet."

"Now you have become the sun—the source of life to every planet whirling in your sight, but like the moon, you shine with borrowed light. Continue on, for all you are and all you see are merely shadows of Reality."

"That great and mighty sun I have ceased to be now appears a tiny sphere lost in the vastness of the firmament. Eighteen thousand blazing worlds I have now become. Nothing is beyond me!"

"Oh, arrogant one, you say that nothing is beyond you? I am beyond you. Your Self is beyond you. To become the universe is neither knowing you nor me—hidden still is Reality. Close your eyes to these worlds of form and time and enter the subtle sphere of dreams, where things are and are not what they appear to be."

"I am awake, yet still asleep, and in the distance I hear sounds of chiming bells and from some far away shadowy realm glimpse etheric cathedrals where echo harmonies of sweet melodies that sing, 'the essence of life is beautiful and free.'

"But now, what is happening? What is all this? The song has changed and waves of desperate cacophony overwhelm its sweet tune. My dream is now a nightmare. I cover my eyes but to no avail, for what I see I see within me, and I am terrified. Light submits to shadows. The sea is bound within the drop and happiness bows to sorrow in an endless chain of births and suffering and death."

"Be not frightened! This dream proceeds by my will. Souls inform themselves to know me, become drops to find the sea and don the cloak of darkness to realize the light."

"My Lord, your explanation eludes me and I remain sickened and confused, haunted by all the pain and suffering I see."

"Oh my dear one, listen closely to what I say. All suffer who know me not, for suffering is the remedy for forgetfulness. Suffering stirs the seed to awaken from its earthly cradle and don the tender form of shoot to thirst for light and glimpse the face of the sun. Nurtured in darkness, its destiny has always been the light. I am that glory, and I wait for you to see me and know me as I am. I wait beyond time for all life to come to me. In me all suffering is extinguished; in me the dream ends. See now what have you become."

"I have become energy itself and that sphere of dreams that once seemed so vast and terrifying appears to be no more than a single stitch on an endless tapestry of power. By your grace, dream and dreamer I have ceased to be. I am enfolded in unspeakable bliss. But who am I and what have I become? I no longer know my name."

"Your name is spirit and you have reached the pinnacle of angelic existence. The entire universe and the sphere of dreams that contain it are less than a speck of dust compared to you. Were I to give the order, you could take that speck upon your tongue, and in one swallow it would be gone. You are indeed great! Yet angelic existence with all its intoxicating power is merely a shadow of the infinite knowledge, power, and bliss of God. Go forth! You must now become mind."

"Oh, master, is there any respite in your gift? No sooner do I become one thing than you push me on again to another. First I was an atom on the sea of light and then became that sea. I saw life flicker in the light of the earthly sun and as that solar blaze I drowned in the effulgence of the starry universe that just as quickly disappeared within the sphere of dreams and passed like a shadow before me. I became the mighty domain of power. Now power bows powerless before me."

"My dear, there is no enduring rest upon this pathless path to truth. Only when the endless beginning and the beginningless end are both extinguished in eternity is eternal peace achieved."

"My lover, you have become the mind, the master of thought and feeling and arrived at the chamber of the heart. Remove your shoes and enter this holy abode."

"Oh, beloved, now I seem to be everywhere at once and can no longer discern what is me and what is not me. Inner and outer have no distinction; I am everything and dwell in my own ipseity of shifting feeling colors and ever-changing feeling forms. No constant exists for me—but you! You are everything and I am nothing and I do not even exist—except in you!"

"Hear me now! You have reached the abyss that stands between us. You must cross this abyss of non-existence."

"I cannot! I cannot even glimpse the other side. For all I have become, illusion I remain, while you dwell beyond and in Reality reign. You are the measure of my unendingness. In you alone I am contained. In your reflection I am revealed, my features defined. In the blinding effulgence of your divine light my own radiance quakes with fear of non-existence. How can I cross this abyss? My eye sees no way. My foot finds no holds."

"You say you see me everywhere, in everything, and you exist in me. Listen carefully when I say that in reality I too do not exist beyond you. Neither do I contain you, nor do you contain me, for in reality You and I are one—not we—come!"

"I cannot. I am terrified and fear for my life."

"Remember, my dear one, nothing real can ever be lost. When you awaken from sleep, only the dreams are gone. This final step of your journey is called Mahapralaya—where pure consciousness is retained after annihilation of the limited mind. Here you must trust me completely. Fear not for I will help you.

"Hear now my story:

"You are like a stream that flows through all of time, seeking union with the sea. Nearing journey's end, the stream flows into a vast desert and is trapped in the sands. Weakening more and more, it tries to struggle on, but finds its way to the sea blocked by a great mountain. Hopeless and helpless, its life ebbing away into the sands, the stream cries out, 'Oh help me, Lord!' and is answered by the voice of the wind.

'I am the wind; you must give yourself to me. In my arms, I will carry you over the mountain as a cloud and as rain you will merge with the sea.'

'But I will cease to be a stream. I will die!'

'You will not die,' whispered the wind. 'Only your dream of yourself as stream will end. Besides, where is your choice? A stream you can no longer be. Give yourself to me, or be lost forever in the sands.'

And so, totally helpless and without hope, exhausted beyond belief, the stream gave itself up into the arms of the wind and was carried as a cloud beyond the mountain's peaks. The cloud drifted over the sea where seeing itself reflected in the water below, began to weep.

'I await you. Come,' welcomed the sea.

And the cloud released itself as tears of joy and fell as rain into the sea.

'We are not we, but one,' spoke the golden sea and the stream, being no more, heard the voice and recognized it as its own."

Acknowledgments

To my wife Edna Kovitz. Her courage and trust in the innate goodness of all things have never ceased to inspire and amaze me.

To Ken Coleman and John Elmo for their thoughts and suggestions. To Cynthia Reimel for asking the question, "What is your book about?"

To our greyhound Adi for the joy of his constant companionship, and to *Greyhound Friends* of North Carolina for all the work they so lovingly do to assuage the plight of the racing greyhounds.

To Dorothy Mead, my co-author, for her openness and objectivity which contributed to a truly enjoyable writing adventure, and for her talents and skills that always perfectly complimented my own efforts in the process of creating our book.

To Lisa Wells for her energy and invaluable suggestions.

Finally and most specially, I wish to acknowledge Avatar Meher Baba, my spiritual Beloved, as the source of all the teachings regarding God-Realization, the spiritual path, and Perfect Masters discussed in this book. His is the real voice behind Krita Baba as well as many of the ideas espoused by Aunt Lily and Victor.

– Michael Kovitz

***

I am indebted to all the clients over the years who granted me entry into their private worlds, and to the teachers who helped me understand the meanings often buried behind their words and actions. Of the latter, I wish to acknowledge the key influence of David L. Downing, PsyD, who first opened the world of psychoanalysis to me through his dedication to the field, his articulate instruction and his dry wit. My gratitude also extends especially to Dr. Michael G. Mercury, clinical neuropsychologist and mentor, who demonstrated by his very being the most important aspect of any relationship is the respect that comes from humility.

I would also like to acknowledge the inspiration I have received from my psychoanalyst, Lynne Jansky, DPsA, whose influence can be felt weaving through the characters of Anne and Margot in their professional roles.

Appreciation and thanks to Chris Taw, Susan Johnston, and Glenn Bartz for their insightful and thought-provoking comments as the work progressed; and to Jeanne Troxel for her invaluable feedback and assistance throughout the publishing process.

And to Jeff McClendon, for his enthusiastic support and encouragement, words are inadequate to express my gratitude.

Last, but by no means least, my fellow writer, teacher, and friend, Michael—I bless the day he suggested this collaboration, thereby initiating an adventure of discovery and delight I could not have imagined. Underlying his intelligence and his poetic talents, his warmth, good humor, and uncomplicated devotion to Meher Baba have made the journey a real pleasure and a privilege.

– Dorothy Mead

www.ingramcontent.com/pod-product-compliance
Lightning Source LLC
Chambersburg PA
CBHW050503260626
47157CB00004B/1175